By Lisa Marie Rice

GHOST OPS NOVELS
Heart of Danger
I Dream of Danger

THE PROTECTORS TRILOGY
Into the Crossfire
Hotter Than Wildfire
Nightfire

THE DANGEROUS TRILOGY
Dangerous Lover
Dangerous Secrets
Dangerous Passion

NOVELLAS
Fatal Heat
Reckless Night
Hot Secrets

FATAL HEAT

AND TWO DANGEROUS NOVELLAS

HOT SECRETS and RECKLESS NIGHT

Lisa Marie Rice

AVON

This book is a work of fiction. The characters, incidents, and dialogue are drawn from the author's imagination and are not to be construed as real. Any resemblance to actual events or persons, living or dead, is entirely coincidental.

AVON RED
An Imprint of HarperCollins*Publishers*
10 East 53rd Street
New York, NY 10022-5299

FATAL HEAT. Copyright © 2011 by Lisa Marie Rice.
RECKLESS NIGHT. Copyright © 2011 by Lisa Marie Rice.
HOT SECRETS. Copyright © 2012 by Lisa Marie Rice.
Excerpt from *Dangerous Lover* copyright © 2007 by Lisa Marie Rice.
Excerpt from *Dangerous Secrets* copyright © 2008 by Lisa Marie Rice.
Excerpt from *Dangerous Passion* copyright © 2009 by Lisa Marie Rice.
Excerpt from *I Dream of Danger* copyright © 2013 by Lisa Marie Rice.
ISBN 978-0-06-227890-6
www.avonromance.com

First Avon Red mass market printing: May 2013

Avon Trademark Reg. U.S. Pat. Off. and in Other Countries, Marca Registrada, Hecho en U.S.A.
HarperCollins® is a registered trademark of HarperCollins Publishers.

10 9 8 7 6 5 4 3 2 1

*As always,
everything I do is dedicated
to my husband and son.*

Many thanks to my wonderful editor, May Chen, and to my fabulous agent, Ethan Ellenberg.

Contents

Fatal Heat
1

Reckless Night
177

Hot Secrets
237

Fatal Heat

A Navy SEAL Novella

Chapter One

April 2
San Sebastian, California

"That must have hurt like a bitch," a voice said out of the darkness. A female voice. A very sexy female voice. "Here, have a cookie."

Max Wright sat up painfully, shocked out of his funk. Someone lived next door?

Fuck.

He'd assumed he was going to put his broken body back together without anyone watching. His commander had simply handed him the keys to his vacation beach apartment and given him orders to get better. He hadn't said anything about neighbors. Not this early in the season.

Get better.

Those orders still had a bitter taste. Because with a lot of time and a lot of pain and a lot of rehab, he was walking—or, to be honest, limping—again, and he'd gotten back most of his upper-body strength.

But he was out of the navy and no longer a SEAL—permanently. So how was "better" in any way a possibility? Even in the same fucking ballpark of a possibility?

The voice was female. Soft, sympathetic, slightly amused.

He wasn't going to growl, *Yeah, it hurt like a bitch*, even though it had, because pain wasn't important. As every senior chief in the history of the universe screamed, *pain is weakness leaving the body*. Pain was nothing.

He wanted to snarl something but it would be to empty air, because there was a slight click, then a light *woof!* that had him raising his eyebrows, and he was alone.

With a plate of cookies on the tile divider between the two balconies.

Shit. No one to snarl at.

But . . . cookies.

Max had had no appetite since the attack, none. For the first month in ICU, they'd fed him through goddamned tubes bored into his belly, and when they took the tubes out, food tasted like cardboard dipped in shit.

4

The cookies smelled really good, though. *Really* good. The plate was within reaching distance, and a good thing, too, because getting up and walking at the end of another day in which he'd pushed the limits entailed a cane and a whole lot of pain.

As a matter of fact, the doctors had been adamant that he still needed to stay in the rehab unit for another month, maybe two. He'd had to check himself out, signing his name with a flourish and handing it to the nurse, who clicked her tongue in disapproval.

Tough shit.

Max wanted *out*. He wanted out of this place with all the sick people. He didn't need reminding he wasn't whole. He knew.

He'd been strong all his life. He knew what he was now.

Weak.

He wanted a place that didn't smell of Lysol and Formalin, a place where no one would harp that he was overdoing it, and a place where people didn't smile at him professionally when he was in a shitty mood. Goddamn it, snarl *back*.

It was a good thing they'd taken his guns away in rehab because he'd have ended up shooting someone.

Prison would arguably be worse than the rehab

5

clinic, so before he offed the next smiling sadist, he signed himself out. His XO, Commander Mel Dempsey, offered the use of his vacation beach house about half an hour north of Monterey, handing him the keys and telling him to get better.

It was off-season. Max wanted peace and quiet and solitude while he put himself back together again.

He didn't want next-door neighbors, female or otherwise. He liked women as much as the next man, maybe more, but not now. Not while he threw up if he moved too fast, not while one leg wouldn't bear his full weight, not while he was this pathetic . . . fucking . . . *cripple*.

Cookie Lady had a real sexy voice, and the very little he'd seen of her in the dim light—wow. But he wasn't coming out to play. Not for a long while.

He was going to eat what he could choke down, sleep as well as he could, pump iron, do the exercises the rehab doc had given him, and walk along the beach, making sure he didn't fall on his ass. All those good things. And keep his dick down.

Not hard to do.

His dick had disappeared after surgery. Oh, it was physically there, all right. Mainly as a tube to piss through. Not even a twinge of sex, not even with the nurses in the hospital. Not even with

Nurse Carrie, who'd looked really hot in white and had offered.

Max didn't want any. He didn't want anything at all except to get back on his feet and back in the Teams.

Not going to happen.

He didn't want pity or commiseration, he wanted to be left fucking *alone*.

Though, actually, the neighbor lady had left him alone. With cookies.

Goddamn it, who the fuck left cookies for a SEAL? SEALs ate rocks and shat nails. They didn't eat fucking cookies. They—

A stray gust of wind blew from the sea and he froze.

Damn, those cookies smelled good.

He had long arms. He didn't have to get up. He held a cookie up in the dim light and bit in.

Best cookies he'd ever had, bar none. White chocolate chip. Perfect cookie in a world of imperfection.

He sat and glowered at the dark sea and ate the plateful up.

In his dreams, it was always the same and always different.

He was in Helmand: the desolate dun-colored

peaks of the Hindu Kush rising sharp and jagged around him, the air so clear his binocs showed him the valley floor as clearly as if it were ten feet away instead of a thousand.

He saw everything with crystal clarity.

It was a mission to take out a real bad guy, Ahmed Sahar. A warlord who'd become Al Qaida's go-to guy and was funnelling arms to the Taliban. Also a world-class crazy. A fucking psychopath.

From his hilltop sniper's den, Max had watched two executions and the lashing of a young girl. He couldn't wait to have the fucker in his crosshairs. Sahar was a psychopath—but a crafty one—and stayed in his compound year-round. But they had intel that a major operation was in the works and Sahar would have to travel.

Max had been waiting for three days in his hideSTET under netting, pissing in a bottle, never sleeping, barely breathing. Because he really, *really* wanted to nail the fucker.

And—there he was! Coming out of the gates, looking around for his enemies. *Up here, fuckhead,* Max thought, finger loose on the trigger.

It was a convoy, but Sahar wanted to oversee something, and got out of his vehicle to shout at the lead driver. Max kept him in the sights: that gross, misshapen head he'd studied for hours while being briefed.

This was it. Sahar straightened and took one last look around as Max let out half a breath and gently squeezed the trigger. Sahar's head exploded. A swift clean head shot.

His work here was done.

Except when the bullet pulped Sahar's head, *another* crazy shouldered a long tube. Someone had told Max—who was really good with guns, who had shot maybe a million rounds in his life—that some Afghanis had a mystical relationship with arms. Max believed it, because though Second Psychopath couldn't have had a clue where the supersonic bullet came from—and it would take a team of forensic experts hours to ascertain the direction of the shot—Second Psychopath had no problems.

Second Psychopath's head swivelled and in one second he somehow nailed Max's position. Max watched as the tube foreshortened and Second Psychopath was rocked back on his sandals, something trailing a cloud of smoke spearing its way to him.

The world exploded in fire and pain . . .

Max bolted up, panting, twisted in sweat-soaked sheets, teeth clenched hard against any possible sound, the way he always woke up from his nightmares. The legacy of a childhood spent terrified of waking up his stepfather, who plunged into terrifying rages at the slightest provocation.

Nightmares without noise were his special gift, learned before he could talk.

But even without noise, they left him sweaty and drained and shaking. He hated it, hated them.

He slipped out of bed, lurched once on his bad leg, and caught himself.

Getting strong again would help. Being strong and staying strong had always been his touch-stone, was the reason he'd survived his child-hood. That was how he'd got his Budweiser. That and being too damned stubborn to quit.

Losing his strength after the RPG attack had been the hardest thing in a hard life.

Mel had a fully-equipped gym in the garage, but even if it weren't there, Max would have im-provised one. Plastic bags or empty milk bottles filled with sand, fingertip pull-ups from the door frame, a two-by-four as an ab bench—he'd done it all as a kid.

Time to sweat out the nightmare. When he walked into the gym with its gleaming equip-ment, the sky outside the window was slate gray. An hour later, wiping the sweat from his chest, it was pearl gray.

The ocean was forty feet away. Back in the day, forty feet was laughable, nothing. He could run it in a few seconds. He ran ten miles a day in boots, every day, and did a hundred push-ups at the end of the run. He didn't do it laughing, but he did it.

No running now. Maybe not ever. His doctors had originally said he'd never walk again and now look at him. Of course he didn't walk so much as lurch. Each step took a second and sent a wire of pain straight into his head.

But in the water . . . ah, in the water he was still a god. An injured god, slower than any of his Team mates, but still faster than most civilians.

Time to swim. He looked forward to his long daily swims where his mangled leg was merely a deadweight. Slipping into the water was a delight. He headed out into the still-dark ocean with strong, sure strokes, using his arms more than his legs, the sun sliding up into the sky at his back.

If he'd had the ocean a few steps away a year ago when he'd woken up from surgery, as soon as he could walk he'd have been tempted to swim as far as his strength could carry him—so far he could never make it back—and die a swimmer's death.

Better than the death that was staring him in the face: pissing into a bag, needing help to sip soup. If he'd had the means and the strength to end it those first few months, he would have. But they'd watched over him and nothing sharp was ever within reach.

And so he determined that he'd walk again and, by God, inch by trembling inch he'd done it. The physical therapist threatened to tie him down because he did too much, but he knew his own body. His body wanted to stand upright, wanted the challenge. Going slow was not an option.

He swam for an hour until his strength began to fail. He'd gone less than a mile. He hated that. During BUD/S he'd swim five miles, come out of the surf running, hit the grinder to pound out a hundred push-ups. Now he was exhausted as he trod water.

There was a small island three miles out. Some kind of research facility, his XO had told him. Santo Domingo Island. Goddamn it, he was going to get to the point where he could swim there and back, no matter what it took.

The swim back was slow, his muscles not pulling him smoothly and strongly through the water as they were supposed to. He started trembling.

Fuck this. It didn't matter that he wasn't even supposed to be upright. That the doctors had told him he might never walk again. He was a fucking SEAL. And SEALs didn't do weakness.

He dove under, swimming the last fifty yards under water, knowing he couldn't possibly do a hundred push-ups at the end.

Max strained toward shore, fighting the urge to breathe, at the very limit of his strength, when he suddenly heard his name called. A female voice, calling his name.

What the fuck? A mermaid? Some kind of underwater creature calling him down to his death?

He reared up from the water.

And something strong and hairy, moving fast, cannonballed into him, taking him back under before he had a chance to fill his lungs with air.

Oh no!

Paige Waring stepped back in dismay. A man had suddenly appeared out of the water, rising up like some mythic sea god. Max jumped him and he tumbled back under.

Her gorgeous, smart, totally undisciplined dog Max, who growled at some men and became instant best friends with others.

The man he'd jumped was so frightening-looking she couldn't understand Max's friendliness.

He looked like he'd eat you for breakfast and spit out the bones. And he was her new neighbor.

She'd known only that her new neighbor was a former naval officer recovering from wounds sustained in combat. Though Uncle Mel hadn't said it, she supposed her new neighbor was a SEAL, because that's what Uncle Mel was.

The man crested the surface, Max jumping and yapping happily around him.

He didn't look frightening—he looked terrifying. Last night she'd had the impression in the darkness of danger on a hair trigger.

A wounded officer next door. She was hardwired to try to do something for him. After all, he'd been wounded in the service of his country. So she'd baked cookies, meaning to go over and invite him to a glass of wine and cookies as a neighborly gesture.

Then she'd seen him, a huge figure in the semidarkness, face grim and frightening. One leg extended, thinner than the other one, which was thick with muscle. The damaged leg had looked so mangled and scarred, it hurt to look at it.

He'd turned to her, and even in the gloom his face was frightening, speaking of the terrible things he'd seen. The terrible things that had been done to him.

She'd murmured a few words, left the cookies on the balcony between them, and retreated to her apartment because the guy sitting out there in the dark didn't look like a nice neighbor. He looked like a killer.

Now he rose back up from the waves, water streaming off him. And up and up. He was tall and huge. Or had been huge. He was on the thin side, but he had the bones of a big man: broad-shouldered, long-legged, with enormous hands.

Crisscrossed with scars. Terrible scars. Life-threatening scars. On top of that mangled leg.

Paige stood and stared. He seemed like a creature from the mists of time, a ravaged warrior misplaced on their tame stretch of beach.

Max jumped him again and Paige broke out of the spell she'd been under. She had to save her dog. This man could hurt Max badly with one swipe of one of those enormous hands.

"Down, Max, down!" she cried, rushing forward into the surf, heart pounding. She was ready to face the man down to defend her dog, but heavens, he looked terrifying.

Max leaped again and she saw the man's weight shift to that mangled leg, and he faltered.

"Max!" Paige clapped her hands because a dog instructor—one of the many to whom she'd taken her loveable but absolutely incorrigible dog—had told her it was a signal for dogs to calm down.

Not Max—he was rollicking in the waves, jumping on the man.

The man made a gesture with his big hand, and to her astonishment, Max settled a little, dropping his front paws back into the sea.

The skin on his back rippled and Paige's eyes widened.

"No!" she shouted.

But it was too late. Max shook all over, drenching her and the man. He was wet all over anyway, but she'd have to shower again before heading to work.

Oh God. Max had knocked this man down and showered him with doggy-smelling seawater. Who knew how he would react?

And then the man looked at her and grinned. It was a mere flash, a movement of the edges of his mouth, a glimpse of white teeth, and then his face settled back into its usual grim lines.

"Cookie Lady," he said. "The cookies were great."

His voice was unusually deep and dark, completely out of place on this bright sunny morning. She shivered.

"Yes. Cookie Lady." She looked at him—at the height of him, the breadth of him, that face that was now totally unsmiling. It had to be done. She was in the wrong. Her dog had made a man with a crippled leg tumble into the ocean.

So she did the brave thing and offered her hand. Hoping he wouldn't notice that it trembled. Hoping he'd give it back unharmed.

Paige disliked shaking hands with macho men. She needed her hands to do delicate lab work. Often guys felt they had to prove their manhood with their grip. This one looked like he could crush her hand with no effort at all.

But . . . her dog *had* jumped him. And Uncle Mel was his commanding officer.

"I'm really, really sorry. I'd like to say that I don't know what got into my dog, but he's always like this. I seem to spend all my time apologizing for him. I'm Paige. Paige Waring."

His hand enveloped hers in a strong, gentle grip. His hand felt like warm steel. He might be wounded, but his grip was like touching a live wire, crackling with electricity. She was so surprised, she kept her hand in his as if the electricity had created some kind of chemical bond.

"Max."

At hearing his name, Max gave a happy bark and jumped both of them. Paige lost her footing in the surf and would have fallen if he hadn't immediately snaked a big arm around her, pulling her upright and against him in an unshakeable grasp.

His leg might be mangled and he might be overly

thin, but there was no mistaking the strength in the muscles she found herself plastered against.

It was intensely embarrassing and—whoa—incredibly exciting. The only other man who looked this strong was Uncle Mel, but she'd never been in a full frontal embrace with him.

She'd never felt a man this strong before.

Her father, bless his soul, had been thin and stoop-shouldered, and was undoubtedly right this minute leafing through ancient history texts in heaven. And the men she dated were mainly fellow scientists. Nice guys, but nerds mostly.

Nothing like this. Nothing at all.

Even though he'd been in the chilly Pacific, he radiated heat and a very male kind of electricity she'd never encountered before but recognized instantly, as if a hundred years of female empowerment and her PhD had been suddenly stripped away, leaving a breathless female reacting to an alpha male.

He was reacting, too, the merest hint of a stirring against her belly when Max barked and jumped them again.

Paige moved away, lifting Max's paws off them. "Down, boy," she chided. "*Down.*" Looking up, she caught a fleeting expression cross his face, his eyes flaring. It was over so quickly she wondered whether she'd imagined the whole thing. But in the meantime, her pulse quickened and her mouth went dry.

This was ridiculous and very unlike her.

He was a neighbor—a wounded soldier, formerly under the command of her godfather—and he'd been jumped by her dog. He deserved better than a hormone-stricken woman rendered breathless by beefcake.

She straightened, tilting her head back to look him straight in the eyes. Dark brown, very intense eyes. And highly intelligent ones, too. That shook her for a moment. She was totally unused to male intelligence as a subset of muscle.

Mostly, in her experience, male intelligence was linked to white lab coats. Definitely not huge expanses of tough, naked, tanned skin.

"I'm really sorry, Lieutenant—"

"Max," he said, and her dog woofed.

Why was he—oh! "Your name is Max, too?"

"Like your dog." He dipped his head, her hand still in his. "Maxwell Wright. Max for short."

"He's Maximilian. Max for short."

She tugged and he let go of her hand. It felt like she'd been unplugged from some arcane power source. "Lieutenant Wright." That had been the name Uncle Mel had said.

Another expression crossed his face. Not of heat and amusement, but of grief. Deep, painful grief. She'd just lost her father. She understood grief, understood it in her bones.

"Not lieutenant," he said. "Not anymore."

Involuntarily, Paige looked down at his leg. With that leg—much thinner than the other one, crisscrossed with scars—he wouldn't be an acting naval officer, no. One leg was brown and powerful, thickly muscled—the other pale, the muscles withered.

And all those other scars. Surgical scars, mostly, white lines with tiny tucks on each side, crisscrossing his chest. One round puckered scar in his shoulder, which even she could see was a gunshot wound, looked to be older than the others.

Her dog looked from one to the other while they were talking, brown eyes trained on his mistress and on his new best friend. He obviously decided all this talking was boring, and he hunched his shoulders, which is what he did before leaping.

Paige gasped. The other Max, the human one, was going to get jumped again, knocked down again. "Max, no! Bad boy!"

It was perfectly pointless because Max never obeyed. She stooped to grab ahold of his collar when human Max made another slight gesture with one big hand, and her Max relaxed.

Amazing.

Then she looked up again at the big man and realized just why Max had rethought his Jumping on Everyone is Fun philosophy. The man had "command" written all over him, just as Uncle Mel had. It was unthinkable that anyone, man or beast, would not obey him instantly.

It must be a great trait to have, one she sadly lacked.

Her Max whined, looking back and forth between them.

Human Max scratched Max's head, never averting his gaze from hers. It was unnerving, being watched so closely, particularly by a man who managed to project such a forceful personality even standing barefoot in the surf dressed only in swim trunks.

Maybe it was all those muscles.

She had to go. Though she felt almost mesmerized by the tall, silent, unsmiling man in front of her, she was going to be late for work if she stood around much longer, mooning over broad shoulders and an ability to hypnotize her notoriously unruly dog into a semblance of obedience.

"So. Um . . . " God. His eyes were so dark, so

compelling . . . she almost stuck her hand out simply to feel that electric connection again. But that would be crazy.

Paige wasn't crazy. She was a staid scientist, normally totally immune to hormonal urges like wanting to hold a man's strong hand after a few moments' acquaintance. Max lifted a paw to her thigh, wetting her sundress. Time to go. "I'm really sorry my dog jumped you, um, Lieutenant."

"Max," he said, his voice so deep she was surprised the water they were in didn't vibrate.

"Max," she repeated obediently. She tugged at her Max's leash. "I try to train him, but as you can see, I'm not very successful. He wasn't born with the obedience gene." She shot a wry glance down at the dog by her side. Alas, Max wasn't quelled at all to hear his faults described. His brown and tan tail wagged so fast it shot off drops of salt water.

"What is he? Looks like some border collie in there." The man's big hand was scratching behind Max's ears. Max knew they were talking about him, and his rump now moved together with his tail. He was in dog heaven.

She sighed. "He's a rescue and he's a mix. Some border collie, sure. The guy at the pound said there was also some Labrador and German shepherd, too. He all but *promised* me that Max was bred for decorum and obedience." With hindsight, Paige was astonished that a lightning bolt hadn't shot down out of the sky to strike dead that helpful college student at the pound.

Her dog grinned, tongue lolling out of his mouth, perfectly aware of the fact that neither decorum nor obedience was high on his list of doggy priorities.

"Come on, big guy." Paige nodded to her dog. "Walk's over. Time to go back home. I have to go to work. Some of us work for a living, you know."

Her dog was very smart and had learned quite a few words. Pity *stay*, *heel*, and *sit* weren't among them. But *work*, which meant she was leaving him locked up in her tiny backyard all day—well, he understood that word just fine.

Max had perfected the art of emotional blackmail. The instant he heard the word *work*, he cowered, whining. Big brown eyes looked up beseechingly.

Paige barely kept from rolling her eyes. She looked up at the tall dark man at her side. He wasn't smiling, not exactly. But his features had lightened.

"You're probably thinking that I regularly take the whip to him, the way he's reacting, when actually he's spoiled to death. If it were up to him, my main job would be taking him for endless walks and feeding him. 24/7. But the fact is," she switched her attention to her whining dog, raising her voice, "the fact is I've got a day job, which is what keeps *someone* in *treats*."

That was another word he recognized. He greeted it with a happy bark.

She turned back to the tall soldier. "So, I apologize again for my unruly dog, and now we'll get out of your hair." She tugged at the leash and Max did his usual cowering act, as if she were the Angel of Death come to smite him. "Come on, Max. Playtime's over." She tugged again, walking backwards. Sometimes she had to literally drag him away from the beach, his paws leaving tracks in the sand. She'd gotten quite a few dirty looks from that.

"He can stay with me." The voice was low but his words carried.

"I beg your pardon?"

"He clearly doesn't want to be locked up, not quite yet. And I—I have some free time. I'd be happy to take him for another walk. Keep him on the beach for a while longer."

She couldn't help herself. She looked down at that scarred leg. When she looked back up at him, she saw calm in those dark eyes.

"He won't make me fall. I have good balance. He caught me by surprise but it won't happen again."

"I don't know . . . he doesn't tire easily," she warned.

That earned her a small smile. "Neither do I."

Well, no. If he'd been a Navy SEAL he could probably outlast her rambunctious dog.

She looked at him carefully, not in any way hiding her scrutiny. He stood still for it, face remote and expressionless, and let her examine him.

Paige had no idea who he was, really. Though she complained often about Max's rambunctiousness and complete lack of obedience, he was a joy. On days when work was going badly, which was happening more and more often lately, coming home to Max was the one bright spot in her day.

She loved him fiercely.

Though Max was a friendly dog, he'd had several unexpectedly hostile reactions to men. One, a colleague, had turned out to be a wife beater; another, a drunk; and one notable evening, he'd growled at a perfectly normal banker who'd come to pick her up for dinner. Max's acumen was better than her own because it took her an entire dinner to realize the banker was a jerk. When he took her home, he wouldn't take no for an answer, and it was only when Max growled—showing sharp, white teeth—that he had backed off.

So she trusted Max's reactions and what she was seeing now was trust and liking. His mouth was open in one of his exasperating, slobbering grins as he watched the dynamic between her and the human Max, tail wagging furiously.

He was actually closer to human Max than to her because though the man was standing utterly still, one hand was still scratching behind Max's ears.

Small Max was a slut for attention, but he wouldn't be reacting this way if Big Max were giving off bad human vibes.

"He's very important to me," she said finally, still watching the man's deep brown eyes, unwavering and intelligent.

His head dipped. "Understood. He'll be safe with me." Max gave a sharp, happy bark. Her dog couldn't possibly know what they were discussing but as far as he was concerned, every minute not spent in her tiny backyard and in the presence of his mistress and a new best friend was a happy minute.

Paige sighed. The decision was made, she was just stalling.

"OK." She handed him the walking-with-Max equipment. Leash. Something less fun than the leash. "That's the pooper-scooper." She eyed him suspiciously. "You know how it works?"

He turned it over in his hands, biting his lips against what looked like a smile. "No, but it looks pretty straightforward. I think I can figure it out."

She glanced at her watch and winced. Ouch. She had to hurry if she was going to be at work on time. Plus she was hoping for Silvia's call. "I'll meet you at your door in twenty minutes and hand you Max's food bowls, some dog food, and a Milk Bone." Max barked at the sound of his favourite words of all time. "If you give me your cell number I'll program it into my cell and I'll give you my number when I bring you Max's stuff, so you can call if anything happens."

"You can give it to me now," he said.

He was naked except for swim trunks. "But you don't have your cell with you."

"I can remember a ten-digit number. Trust me."

She gave him her number and, sure enough, he repeated it back to her perfectly. Whatever his wounds were, they certainly hadn't damaged his brain.

He could contact her if Max got to be too much

of a handful. And she had to give him a fallback option. "I'll give you the key to my backyard when I stop by. If you get tired of him, just open the gate and make him walk through. He'll drag his feet and look heartsick, but just ignore him." She gave her dog a quelling look which he happily ignored. Some slobber fell to the sand. "He can get really annoying."

The man went very still. "You don't know me and you're going to give me the key to your backyard?"

Paige smiled. "First of all, I'm leaving you Max, and he is much more precious to me than the backyard I'm too busy to care for, and where Max digs up all the plants anyway. There's nothing there to steal, not even flowers. And Uncle Mel sent you here. My godfather. Uncle Mel more or less walks on water as far as I'm concerned. If you were a serial killer, he'd have let me know."

His face had turned somber. "Not a serial killer, promise."

If he *was* a serial killer, he was a lonely one. Paige recognized loneliness and she was seeing it right in front of her. He was so lonely, even the company of her wildly rambunctious dog was welcome.

"Okay," she said softly. "I'll drop the things off and I'll see you tonight. And as a thank-you for taking care of my dog, I'll even cook you dinner."

Dinner was definitely a word Max recognized. He gave an excited bark.

"I second the motion," the other Max said in his deep, sexy voice.

Chapter Two

Man, Cookie Lady was fucking *gorgeous*.

Max was really glad he'd seen her first on the beach, loose and relaxed, because when she stopped by to leave keys and food for the dog, she was all wrapped up tightly in Corporate Woman gear and seemed another woman entirely.

That luscious golden-brown hair pulled back tightly into a French braid. Conservative dark suit. Sensible shoes. Briefcase. Glasses. Nothing at all like the laughing woman in a sundress and sandals, hair loose around her shoulders, playing with her dog.

She had pulled a reverse Marian the Librarian, buttoning up, but it was too late because Max had already seen the skimpy-sundress, bare-legs, hair-down, glasses-off version, and it was stunning.

Noticing women was something new. In the

Sandbox and after getting blown up, and while being put back together again, he hadn't desired anyone. There wasn't anyone to desire in the field, and in the hospital, man, you do *not* get a hard-on for the lady who cleans your bedpan and wipes your butt.

And besides, this past year, not much was working south of the border, including his legs.

But his legs—or one leg, at least—were now working, and everything else came back online, in one big rush this morning. On a beach. While wearing swim trunks that outlined him just fine.

Shit, that was close. Standing there in the surf with this beautiful, laughing woman who was trying and failing to show contrition for her dog—so close he could smell something flowery over the brine of the ocean, so close he could see the green flecks in her blue eyes, so close he could touch that clear, lightly-tanned skin . . . he had to curl his hands into fists.

Not reaching out and touching her? Well, it took a SEAL's self-discipline. Because what he wanted more than anything was to go with the rush of hormones suddenly flooding his system. Pull her down in the gently whooshing early-morning surf and roll right on top of her.

He could feel it, he could almost taste it. Just

31

pulling her down with him, lifting that light skirt, hand smoothing up her thighs, ripping off her panties and losing them in the surf, putting his hand between her legs . . .

His long-dormant dick had lengthened and thickened and was well on its way to rising, ready to celebrate breaking its two-year dry spell. He had to will all the blood that had gone AWOL from his head to scramble down to his cock all the way back up, so he could make rational conversation with her without scaring her off.

He hadn't had sex in so long, the desire was as intense as when he'd been a kid with a perpetual hard-on. Hot desire prickled in his veins, made his hands tingle, and filled his chest with heat.

But when he'd been a randy teenager, just about any female who didn't make you run screaming from her—and who had the right plumbing— would do.

This time those intense feelings were focused tightly on *her*. Paige Waring. Cookie Lady. Mistress of Max. Pretty and laughing and luscious.

And then the kicker. A real shock. An invitation to dinner! And sex afterward!

It had been like a punch to the chest, even though the small part of his brain that was still capable of rational thought realized that a dinner invitation wasn't an invitation to sex. That was just dickful thinking.

It was a pity invite. For the crippled soldier, all alone.

Didn't matter.

He didn't feel like a crippled soldier now. Now he felt like a man with a mission. To get the delectable Paige Waring into his bed just as fast as was humanly possible. And since there wasn't a limit on his time because he wasn't on active duty anymore—his heart gave its usual sharp pump at the thought—he was going to keep her there a long, long time. Because man, sex was *back.* Big time.

The dog tugged at his leash, dancing in the waves. He wanted to play.

Well, so did Max. After two years of misery and pain, he was ready to play again.

It was hard to keep Max out of her mind. The human Max, Maxwell—not her furry friend.

Paige had an incredibly frustrating day, trying to piece together corrupted research files from the Argentina Research Station and waiting for her friend Silvia, who worked there, to contact her.

The Argentina research project was interesting, and a little creepy. As a plant geneticist, Paige was fascinated by what nature could do all on its own. But now her company, GenPlant Laboratories— an offshoot of a major food multinational—had spliced a human growth hormone gene into corn, creating a new variety, HGHM-1, intending to produce a type of corn that grew so quickly you could have three crops a year, each crop double the tonnage.

Their research fields were in a vast company landholding four hundred miles south of Buenos Aires and one of her best friends, Silvia Ramirez, was the local project leader.

They'd been playing phone tag for days. Silvia had sent a file of preliminary results, but the file had somehow become corrupted, almost impossible to reconstitute.

Without the files and without Silvia to help her, Paige was stymied. HGHM-1 was the company's top priority at the moment, and she didn't have any other urgent projects which needed her attention.

So Paige spent all day with basically nothing to do but think of her new neighbor. Not obsessing really. Just . . . thinking about him.

He was in pain. He suppressed winces when he put too much weight on that thin, mutilated leg, but she could tell it hurt him.

He hadn't said a word about it, though, pretending absolutely nothing was wrong. In fact, offered to look after her dog.

It had been a real surprise to her when she opened her mouth to say "no" and "yes" had plopped out.

Much as her Max exasperated her, she loved her dog. The only time she left him with strangers was when she had to leave town on a business trip, and then only at the certified kennel she'd carefully checked over.

So telling a man she didn't know that she'd leave her dog with him for the day was way out of character.

The thing was, for a second there, human Max had looked so lost and lonely. The best remedy for that was time spent with her Max. Her Max would run you ragged chasing after him and keep you laughing all the while. No time to feel lonely. Max was joy incarnate.

The other Max wouldn't be lonely for long, though, once he put himself back together. There was a whole world of women out there who'd love to play with him.

The man simply exuded sex. It came out of his pores. She wondered whether her Max could smell the pheromones coming off him, though maybe males didn't notice hormones from the same gender.

It was an interesting thought.

When Max caught her just before she stumbled into the surf, it had been like receiving an electrical charge. For a second there, she thought she could actually hear electricity crackling, though probably what she heard were her neurons frying. Held tightly against that super-hard, overly lean body really messed with her system. If she'd been one of her test plants, she'd have wilted from overload.

Certainly her brain had left her body. It was already crazy that she'd let him keep Max for the day.

Of course, the man was a naval officer, used to enormous responsibility. He was a SEAL. Or a former SEAL. Those men knew how to do everything, and she was sure he could ride herd over an undisciplined but friendly dog.

Asking him to dinner? Well, that had been a little loony. Not her style at all. She was pretty cool around men. She couldn't remember ever asking a guy out on a date.

Not that the dinner was a *date*, of course. It wasn't, not at all. It was just a friendly neighborly gesture. A thank-you dinner. But once she'd had time to think—to overthink it, Silvia would have said—she realized she'd gone way out of her comfort zone.

She would have called him to cancel, except . . . well, except there was a part of her that looked forward to tonight. That wondered whether the zing she'd felt when she touched him was an outlier.

If she were to plot her emotional reaction to men on x and y axes, the line would wander gently over the lower third of the page. That one experience had been, literally, off the charts. Zipping up to the top and disappearing into the stratosphere.

Her cell phone rang. She snatched it up, hoping it was finally Silvia, and heard static.

Then, faintly, "Paige?" Silvia, sounding as if calling from the back side of the moon. "—Sent you—"

Paige clutched the receiver. "Silvia! Finally! The data file you sent—"

But she was talking to empty air. They'd been disconnected. Again. Paige flipped her cell closed with a frown. Silvia wasn't answering emails, was never online according to Skype, she wasn't Twittering, and her Facebook page hadn't been updated—something she did at least three times a week.

Silvia, the most gregarious person Paige knew, seemed to have dropped off the face of the earth. She would never leave Paige wondering where she was. If Silvia were capable of getting in touch, Paige knew, she would.

And the file she sent had been hacked and corrupted. Paige was sure of it. But who to complain to? Silvia's attachment had been personal, not part of the regular updates of the Argentina Research Station's reports to the head office. Officially, the attachment didn't exist.

Well, this had been an unproductive day. Worrying about Silvia and mooning over her next-door neighbor.

She hung up her lab coat, unbraided her hair—her own personal signal for being off-duty—and walked out the big two-story glass doors of the research complex.

Worry drummed in her heart. For her friend, and because she had a file-restoration app a lovesick nerd had once designed for her in grad school, in the hope of luring Paige into his bed. The ruse hadn't worked but the app did.

It looked like the file had been degraded by a pro, but NerdApp had restored bits and pieces. One sentence had leaped out at her, chilling her to the core.

Strong evidence of a human carcino—

The sentence was incomplete, but the only word in the English language that began with those letters was "carcinogen."

Something in what Silvia was studying was

giving humans cancer. And Silvia was nowhere to be found.

There was absolutely nothing Paige could do, not at the moment. The head of her department, Dr. Warren Beaverton, was in Estonia for a conference. And though Dr. Beaverton was excellent at what he did, outside generating lab data he was a useless human being with barely enough backbone to stand up straight.

And right above him was Vice President for Research Dean Hyland, who, on a scale of humanity, one to ten, ranked minus-five. And who, being corporate, knew less than her cleaning lady about genetics. She had no idea how he'd gotten his degree. Bought it, probably, from some online company based in Montenegro.

Instinctively, Paige knew she couldn't involve either one.

Something was really wrong. At times, when Paige lifted her extension, there was a slight humming sound before the click of connection.

She didn't have to read thrillers to know what that meant. Her phone and undoubtedly her office computer were being watched. It would take nothing to tempest her keyboard so they could follow stroke by stroke what she wrote.

Silvia was smart and so was she. If they could

just communicate briefly, they could figure out a way to talk without being overheard. They could set up a message board, they could invent new Skype names, they could communicate via throwaway cells.

But first, Paige had to be able to talk to Silvia.

And Silvia was nowhere to be found.

At least she had the two Maxes tonight to take her mind off her worries.

Chapter Three

Max stood on the doorstep, trying to keep his jaw from dropping, drinking in the sight of Paige in the open doorway. This was the third version of Paige Waring he'd seen, and if the first two bowled him over, this one took his breath away. *Kapow!* Dead man standing.

The laughing beachcomber and staid business-woman were gone. In their place was this sexy knockout.

That shiny, light brown hair—enough for about six women—shimmered around her shoulders, reflecting the light with every move she made.

She'd put makeup on that highlighted her large blue-green eyes and made that lush mouth a work of art. She had on a simple, elegant, sexy, frothy turquoise summer dress, white and turquoise bangles, and open-toed sandals showing bright pink toenails. Even her fucking *toes* were sexy.

A stronger version of the perfume he'd smelled this morning mixed with warm skin would have brought him to his knees—if he were able to bend both knees.

She was a wet dream come to life, she lived right next door, and she was about to feed him.

Max leaned down to unleash the dog and to give him time to hide his reaction, because staring slack-jawed at a woman was definitely uncool.

The instant the snap of the leash was undone, the dog bounded forward. He was crazy-eager to get to his mistress, though Max had learned today that crazy-eager was the dog's default setting. He'd been crazy-eager to chase squirrels in the small, dog-friendly park at the far end of the beach, he'd been crazy-eager to play Frisbee on the sand, he'd been crazy-eager to play fetch with a stick in the surf.

He was crazy-eager about everything, and keeping him out of trouble had kept Max on the move and in a good mood all day.

Max jumped his mistress, trying to reach her face and lick it. Paige stepped back, almost falling under the dog's weight.

Max snapped out of his Paige-trance.

"Max!" He put command in his voice. "Sit!"

Immediately, Max plopped his butt on the floor.

The discipline lasted a second as he shivered with excitement, then hind muscles bunched for another leap on Paige.

"Stay!" Max commanded, and surreptitiously slipped him a doggie treat. He'd never thought to try that with his men. Give them a command, then slip them a Mars bar when they obeyed.

Now it was Paige's pretty jaw that dropped. She gazed wide-eyed down at her dog then up at him. "Oh my gosh! He obeyed you! That's amazing, how did you manage that?" She narrowed her eyes at him. "And don't you dare say it's because you're a man."

He clenched his jaw closed because, well, it was true. He was used to commanding men. Corralling her dog into something resembling discipline came easily to him.

"I won't say that. Promise." Max wasn't a fool. He wanted to keep on her good side. "Here." He pulled his hand from behind his back to show her a bouquet of flowers. "Believe it or not, your dog picked them out. He sniffed at all the florist's bouquets and decided on this one. Just sat down in front of it and wouldn't budge until I bought it. I have no idea what the flowers are."

She was smiling as she took the bouquet, sniffing appreciatively. "Thanks, though it wasn't necessary. Let's see, we have black-eyed Susans, African daisies, Gladioli, Zinnias and Asters."

His eyebrows rose. "That's impressive. I know daisies from roses, but that's about it. I know edible mushrooms and those that will poison you." And how to make deadly oleander tea.

"Don't be too impressed," Paige called out as she walked into a small, pretty, light-filled kitchen and came back out with a vase. "Knowing plants is my job. I'm a plant geneticist." She looked at his face and laughed. "I get that blank look a lot. No one knows what to say to that. Must be like your line of work. Come on in and sit down; can I serve you a glass of wine?"

The dog was whining and wriggling at his feet. Max looked at Paige. "Thanks. I'd love a glass of wine. What are we going to do about Max? I think we've reached the limits of my one-day training course."

Paige turned back to the kitchen, her words trailing. "Well, I do happen to have some *treats* for a *good dog*." As if the words were a trigger releasing a spring, Max leaped up and scrambled into the kitchen, nails clicking madly on the tile floor.

Well, it was good while it lasted. No one could expect a dog barely out of puppyhood to stay still forever. Particularly after only one day of training.

Max was jumping up and down, making light yips of joy. Paige bent down open-handed, and he ate the treats delicately from her palm, then licked it. Paige laughed and ruffled the fur on the top of his head as he looked up at her adoringly.

Max understood perfectly. The instant he'd seen Paige on the doorstep, so pretty and smiling, something in him—something painful and dark and twisted—cracked open, just a little.

Amazing.

The groundwork had been laid by a sunny day with an energetic, affectionate dog, and now the work was complete in the presence of its mistress.

Paige exuded calm. Sexy, radiant serenity. Did such a thing exist? Hell if he knew. But if it did, she had it in spades.

The way she moved, those luscious yet slender curves, some kind of perfume that moved straight into a man's nose and zapped the thinking part of his brain—those were there. But there was also some kind of serene force field around her. She moved in her pretty orderly space like some kind of angel sent to earth to remind him that life was good, was worth living. That life wasn't battle and death and loss. Blood and pain. That life had things that were worth fighting for.

Paige and her funny, hyperactive dog—hell, yes,

they were worth fighting for. What he was watching was a scene that was unthinkable in certain parts of the world. A serene, successful, single woman who lived alone with a dog.

Where he'd spent the last years of his career, right now a woman like Paige would be lashed and then stoned, her dog whipped and despised.

He was really glad he'd worked so hard to create a world where that kind of horrific cruelty could be defeated. He didn't regret anything. Particularly not now, in this light-filled room with a beautiful, smiling woman.

There was just something about her. The world needed women just like her. Needed women who could make things better just by being.

And right there, in Paige's colorful kitchen—sipping a glass of excellent chilled white wine with her dog dancing around her feet, watching her move so gracefully—something happened to Max.

He'd spent years in very bad places. Culminating in that last year in Afghanistan, which broke his heart and his body. And then the hospital, lashed to the bed by pain and weakness. Dark years, years with feral beings around him, years feeling that the world was hung together with fraying ropes and fraying hopes.

Right now, right this moment, watching the evening light flood the pretty apartment, something powerful moved through him, some force that was strong enough to shift the darkness in him that was heavy as iron, hard as rock. Something made of light, intangible yet very real, very strong.

Whatever it was, it was intimately connected with the beautiful woman humming to a tune on the radio, set to a soft rock station. Suddenly, he wanted to know all about her, find whatever it was in her that could lift those iron weights in his soul. Find out how she could fill a room with light.

"What's it like, being a plant geneticist? What do you do? How does a plant geneticist fill her day?"

She turned to him in surprise, soft hair shifting on her shoulders. A fleeting expression crossed her face, one he was unable to decipher, the merest hint of darkness, as if a bird's wing had come between her and the sun. Then it was gone.

But when she answered, her voice was light and amused, and he wondered if he'd imagined the darkness. It was almost impossible to connect this woman with any kind of darkness.

The full, luscious mouth turned up at the corners. "It's sort of hard to explain, and boringly technical."

"I went to school," he said softly. Actually he had two master's degrees. One in military history and one in political science. From the days in which he tried really hard to understand the world. Those days were gone. Now he just tried to defend his little corner of it and survive. "I could try to follow."

She stirred something with a wooden spoon, tapped it against the pot, and put the spoon on a ceramic dish. Man, whatever it was she was cooking, it smelled heavenly.

She switched the burner off. "Okay, it's done, but it will take about ten minutes to settle. Why don't we sit at the table and enjoy our wine?"

"Sounds good."

She'd set two places, at right angles instead of across from each other. They were so close he could smell that flowery something above whatever was cooking on the stove. So close he could touch her without any effort at all. He picked up his glass and took another big gulp.

Goddamn it. Even the fucking wine was perfect.

She sipped her wine, head tilted to one side as she studied him.

"Coming back to what we were talking about, I'm really sorry if I gave the wrong impression. I didn't mean you *can't* understand what I do, in the sense of being unable to. What I meant is that, like most jobs, what I do day to day is the tip of the iceberg, and you'd have to know what I did yesterday and what I plan to do tomorrow to get the full picture. The short version is I research how Mother Nature designed plant life, and then think of ways to improve on that. The big picture is really exciting because in a way we're unlocking the secrets to life itself. But the day-to-day stuff is really tedious and boring. In the research lab we spend all our time peering into microscopes, checking cultures in petri dishes, and meticulously recording minute changes—punctuated by days in the field, checking crop rows, measuring growth by millimeters. Not exciting in any way unless you're a botany nerd. I imagine your job is hard to describe too. If you could tell me without having to kill me afterwards."

She smiled and Max tensed.

Here it was. The SEAL thing.

Women just couldn't get past it. Some women treated SEALs like action figures with guns, men able to leap tall buildings in a single bound. The thing was, SEALs weren't supermen. They weren't a special breed of man with superhuman abilities. They were just determined, relentless men who developed specialized skills by working like fiends. What they could do they learned to do the hard way. They worked hard, fought hard, often bled and died.

They were warriors, but they also learned languages and orienteering and history, and had to know how to dig a well, apply a splint, and engineer a road.

Most people couldn't get past the fighting thing.

He couldn't count the women who'd watched his face avidly as they asked him how many men he'd killed. Sometimes they looked at him in disgust as they asked it, as if he were some hired gun. A barely domesticated animal.

Sometimes the avid curiosity morphed into a desire that had a sick taste to it, and that turned his stomach. Because clearly they liked the idea of fucking a killer.

Either way, there could be no explaining what he did.

"I wouldn't kill you," he said softly. "No matter what you've been told. It's a myth."

Oh man. He couldn't kill her, he couldn't hurt her in any way. Seeing Paige sitting next to him, with that soft, lightly-tanned, smooth skin, pretty face open and smiling, friendly and kind . . . she was everything he'd ever fought for. The idea of hurting a woman or a child had always made him physically sick. Paige, hurt . . . *God*.

Paige looked him straight in the eyes, watched him openly. He had no idea what she was seeing, but she suddenly nodded her head, as if confirming something. "No," she said. "You wouldn't hurt me."

"Damn straight," he answered.

There was an electric moment of silence. Max let out his breath in a slow exhale. There was a lot of meaning behind her words. At one level, of course he wasn't going to hurt her, kill her. But the deeper meaning was she felt he wasn't a man to be feared.

Max could hardly remember not being big and strong. By the time he was twelve, he'd shot to six feet and looked sixteen. No one messed with him, and if they did, they were sorry.

The life he lived, particularly after joining the navy and passing BUD/S, had made him even bigger and stronger and meaner-looking. He *was* mean. Fuck with him and you'd regret it. But he chose his battles. He was not out of control and he resented it when a woman treated him like someone in an action movie or a violence addict.

"So," Paige said softly. "Why don't we not talk

about our work and talk about something else? Like Max here."

At her feet, Max's tail thumped. There was something about the way the dog was sitting next to her, totally focussed . . .

Max shifted the tablecloth, and—yup. The dog had his head on Paige's thigh. Something he could identify with. He'd like to have his head on Paige's thigh, too.

He frowned at Paige. "Are you feeding him under the table?"

She winced. "Busted."

"That's not good," he said primly, taking the moral high ground, trying hard to keep a straight face as he watched her reaction.

Her skin was fascinating, it signalled every emotion. Right now she was slightly flushed with embarrassment as if she'd been caught with her hand in the cookie jar.

"I know," she said earnestly. "Don't think I don't know it's wrong, I do. After I got Max at the pound, I read up. I'm a researcher, I know how to gain expertise. I read thousands of pages on dog care, and everyone stressed that dogs shouldn't eat from the table. It's bad for them and fosters bad habits." She thunked her forehead with the palm of her hand. "I *know* this. But—just look at him.

He pulls at your heartstrings. How can I resist?"

Max leaned over. Doggy Max swivelled his muzzle to him, suddenly alert to the fact that maybe another chump was at the table. Someone else to scam.

His tail thumped more slowly now, as if his energy had been suddenly depleted. He whined and shivered, looking pathetic, whipped. He inched closer to Max, but cautiously, as if Max might have a hidden stick with which to beat him, and wasn't the man he'd spent the entire day with, playing on the beach.

As Max watched, the dog slowly, tremblingly lowered himself to the floor, laying his muzzle on his front paws, as if too weak to hold up his head.

Max raised his head. Paige met his gaze then rolled her eyes.

"Don't tell me, I know." She sighed. "You'd think he just came out of some concentration camp where they whipped and starved him. Instead of having just been fed."

"You fall for it, though," he accused. "Hook, line and sinker."

"Over and over again," she agreed. "What can I say? I'm a total wuss."

They met each other's eyes again and burst out laughing.

It surprised Max. The laugh came straight up from his belly. Genuine, carefree, unstoppable. The first time he'd laughed, really laughed, in . . . in years.

And hard on the heels of that laughter, something else, something sharp and alive, moving fast, like a shark in the water. Dangerous. Subterranean. Irresistible.

Sexual desire, of a nature and intensity he'd never felt before, whooshing in like a tsunami onto a dry beach.

He watched her at the table—so pretty and alive, so whole, so easy to be with—with her golden-brown hair and eyes the color of the Pacific a few steps outside the door. Her light golden shoulders gleamed. They were covered by the thin straps of her dress with no signs of a bra. Was she wearing one? He didn't dare lower his gaze but he had excellent peripheral vision. He didn't think so.

Oh God.

Just a thin layer of cotton covering those breasts. Perfect, round breasts. His palms itched with the desire to touch them, run his fingers over that smooth, smooth skin.

Everything itched. Desire skittered under his skin like fire, so intense it was almost painful. It was as if he'd never had sex before, every molecule of his body turning around and aligning itself to hers, like iron filings to a magnet.

"Don't tell anyone at work that I have no backbone when it comes to my dog," Paige said, pouring some more wine into his glass. "I have a reputation as a hard-ass."

She looked up at him and froze, her eyes widening, that pretty mouth rounding into an "O" at the expression on his face. It was the exact moment he imagined that mouth around his cock. He gritted his teeth against a groan at the image in his head.

Paige was no dummy and she was a woman. They seemed to have a whole slew of extrasensory perceptions that went into alleyways where men couldn't follow and which allowed them to read men's minds.

His mind wasn't hard to read. What he wanted, fiercely, was right there on his face. He wanted *her*.

He was as hard as a rock, so hard it felt as if his dick were a separate thing, not part of his body. A stone cylinder glued to his belly, heavy and intractable.

He didn't plan what happened next—it just surged up out of the moment, unstoppable, irresistible.

Reaching out, he covered her hand with his. Her skin was as soft as it looked, the hand warm and delicate. At the touch of her hand, he became even harder, more blood racing to his cock. It felt like his entire body simply went off-line as his dick came online.

Everything he'd felt this past year—pain, anger, despair—vanished in a wash of incandescent heat blazing throughout his body, from his toes to the top of his head. Blasting away everything except pure, red-hot desire for this one woman.

He looked at his hand over hers and felt more heat wash over him. His hand was larger, darker, stronger, angled over hers. A mental image of the two of them exploded in his head. This is exactly what they'd look like in bed. His larger, darker, stronger body over hers, moving deeply in hers . . .

He closed his eyes at the image and breathed the intensity out.

He opened them again to find her watching him, looking slightly anxious. But she was also deep pink with some strong emotion he hoped to God was at least one millionth of the lust he felt, her mouth open as if she couldn't pull in enough air.

God knows he couldn't. There was no air in his lungs, just a burning sensation. Heat suffused him, inside and out.

They stared at each other. She had the most amazing eyes, a light blue with green streaks, shimmering as if the ocean were at her feet and reflected in her eyes.

He breathed in a gasp. Said words that were wrenched straight from his chest without any prior thought at all. "I want you."

Oh, fuck. The words were out there, stark and simple, and he couldn't call them back. He barely recognized his own voice—low and guttural, as if the words came from somewhere deep inside him. And they had. They came from his very core.

He'd played the sex game all his life. He liked women and he liked sex, and though he wasn't as slick as some, he knew how to say enough sweet honeyed words to get a woman into his bed. Some wanted romantic words, some wanted sexy talk. Some didn't require much talking at all.

He'd never just come out with it like that. Crude and simple. *I want you.*

He scrabbled for more words, better words, but they just weren't coming. In his head was heat and the image of them tangled together, skin to skin, so close they could feel each other's heartbeat. He had a sensory hallucination for a second where he could *feel* what it would be like entering her, parting her lower lips with his cock . . .

He tightened all the muscles in his stomach and groin because he was a second away from coming.

He opened his mouth and all that came out was air.

Since there weren't any more words he could say, he simply sat there, trying to control his breathing. Trying to give the impression of a man who was in control, who *had* control, when it was slipping through his fingers.

There'd been a flicker of something in her eyes. God, what?

Her small hand flexed under his. For a terrible moment, he thought she was going to refuse. Slide her hand out from under his and say no.

At the thought, it was as if his chest filled with barbed wire. He was a strategic thinker—in the battlefield, under fire, he could always see the next step and the one after that.

Right now? He had no sense of what he'd do if she said no. None. He wanted her so much, it felt unthinkable that they weren't going straight to bed to start having sex just as quickly as their legs could carry them.

Shit, if she said no, he couldn't even drop to his knees and beg her. His fucking leg would crumple. He'd fall over flat on his ass.

But the god of wounded warriors smiled on him, after a whole year of fucking with him.

"I know," she said softly. "I can see that you want me."

He froze. She could see it? How? He felt as big as a house, but she couldn't see him below the waist. Obviously his face showed his ballooning need. He hoped whatever she saw didn't scare her.

He took in another breath in a gasp. Tried to get all the words out before speech was beyond him, because they needed to be said.

"I don't know what you'll decide, but if I do get lucky, then I need to give full disclosure. I haven't had sex in two years. I was deployed in—well, a bad, sandy place for a year, and I spent the year after that in hospitals and rehab clinics trying to put myself together. I don't have any condoms with me at all. Coming here it never even occurred to me because until about two minutes ago, sex wasn't part of my life anymore. And now I can't think of anything else but sex with you. But this no-condom thing has to be taken into account. I do know I don't have any diseases. None. Bloodsuckers at the hospital drained me of half my blood, taking tests, and I'm clean."

"Oh!" She gave a faint smile. "I—ahm. Me, too. I had a checkup just a couple of months ago. I haven't had sex for a year—too busy, really. And

. . . the work I do, it sometimes takes me to test fields and research stations in remote parts of the world. Some in countries that are not, ahm, always completely stable. So my company offers its female researchers birth control. We get monthly shots. I've just had mine."

Max scowled, sex wiped instantly from his mind. "Your company sends you to *dangerous places*?" he breathed, the thought driving him slightly insane for a second.

Max had close-up intimate knowledge of what bad places were like. He knew hellholes the way a suburban dad knows the potholes on his street. The idea of smiling, delicate, pretty Paige in some of the places he'd been horrified him.

"What the *hell* are your bosses thinking, sending you—"

She shut him up by placing her mouth over his, swamping him with heat. Her mouth tasted exactly as he thought it would—sweet and hot. Fresh and exciting.

It was a brief kiss, two mouths meeting, but he broke away gasping as if burned. He looked at her narrow-eyed as she watched him, head cocked to one side as if he were a puzzle.

She was the goddamned puzzle. Max knew kisses, he knew sex, he knew women, and he knew his reaction to women. This was all completely new.

Fuck.

He'd nearly come in his pants with a mere kiss. A kiss that lasted two seconds, tops.

It wasn't supposed to be like this. Max was The Man. Cool and in control, in bed and out. Not a man so excited that a touch to the mouth damn near set him off.

Probably it was two years of abstinence. Yeah, that was it. Two long years with only his fist in the Sandbox, and in the hospital nothing at all because his dick was a dead piece of meat between his legs. It had been painful to breathe. Sex just hadn't been on his radar.

Maybe what he'd just felt was some . . . some anomaly in the space-time continuum. A one-off.

Try it again.

He touched his mouth to hers and again felt that electric shock.

She'd closed her eyes. They slowly opened when he lifted his mouth. The pupils were a little dilated and she looked dazed. Good, maybe he wasn't completely alone in this, whatever this was. Because it wasn't sex. Or at least it wasn't sex as he knew it.

Again.

She watched him, watched as he moved his face closer to hers, closing her eyes at the last second. This time the kiss was longer, deeper, nerve endings concentrated in his mouth as he tasted her—one long, slow stroke of the tongue, her mouth silky soft and delicious. She tasted of wine and sunshine and woman.

When he lifted his mouth, she made a soft sound. "Max?"

Under the table, a scrabbling of furry limbs and a soft woof. He snapped his fingers and patted the air. "Not you, boy. Me."

Paige smiled.

"I'm right here," he whispered, reaching out a hand to cup her neck and bring her back to him. Another kiss, deeper, longer, sweeter, hotter.

When he pulled back she searched his eyes. "Where are we going with this?"

For the first time, he chanced a smile. He no longer felt as if his head were going to explode any second now. The smile felt odd, unused facial muscles working. "To bed," he whispered. "I hope."

Hand still cupped around her neck, he bent forward until their foreheads touched. "I think I remember how it's done. But I have to warn you, I don't have smooth moves and smooth words." They'd been blasted right out of him.

Her lips curled up. "Maybe not smooth words, but those are the right words. I don't like players."

Nail it down. Get it right. For all he knew, in the two years he'd been out of the scene, the rules had changed.

"That's a yes?"

Paige pulled away, angled her head, observed him for a full minute. He let her. If he passed muster, he was just about to become the luckiest guy in the universe.

"Yes."

Yes!

Chapter Four

This was so unlike her, Paige marvelled at herself. She was really picky and fussy when it came to men. How did she end up saying yes to a man she hadn't even known for twenty-four hours?

Because of all those muscles? Even if he was very lean it was obvious he was a big man. Give him another couple of months and she was sure he'd bulk back up. Muscles were good, though she'd never really thought of herself as a Jersey Shore kind of gal.

She wasn't. She was cerebral. True, his size was a plus, and that macho air—which she usually disliked—surprisingly worked for her. But macho wasn't enough. He was an officer, he was a SEAL. Presumably he had smarts, and so far he seemed bright enough, but they'd barely conversed much beyond generalities.

So—not so much the muscles or the macho or the mind.

Nope.

He'd been kind to her dog.

She'd have berated herself for her stupidity if it weren't for the fact that her entire body was tingling as he brought her hand to his mouth, eyes never leaving hers.

His mouth was warm, but she knew that. When he'd kissed her, the warmth of his mouth had spread all through her. There was a tiny bite of beard around his lips. He'd recently shaved but he looked like he'd had a heavy beard.

He kept her hand in his and rose. She rose with him, and into his arms, the most natural thing in the world. He was very tall. She was so close to him she had to tilt her head back.

He had that grim look again, only maybe it wasn't grimness. Maybe it was just his default expression—the expression of a hard man who'd seen bad things. And though he didn't seem like the type of man to talk about it, she imagined his leg was hurting.

"I'd give anything to pick you up and carry you to the bedroom," he said. A long finger was tracing the contours of her face. Just the merest touch, but it felt exciting and tender at the same time.

"It would be romantic and it would get us there faster. A twofer."

She laughed. "Well, I've never been carried anywhere, so I guess I don't know what I'm missing."

"And I don't know where your bedroom is," he pointed out. "So I couldn't carry you there anyway."

One hand was still in his, the other had gone around his back. She didn't have any spare hands so she indicated with her chin toward the back of the house. "Second room to the right. The first is my study."

He kissed the tip of her nose, kept his face close to hers. "Well then, Paige Waring. Why don't you lead us to it?" His wine-scented breath washed over her.

So. She was going to do this. Amazing. She watched his face for another long moment. Not making up her mind, because it wasn't her mind that was involved here. Just checking her body that this was what it wanted.

Oh, yeah.

His face was so interesting. Hard planes, weather-beaten skin that made him look older than he probably was; dark, observant eyes; hard-looking mouth that had been surprisingly soft when kissing her.

And there was . . . something. What? What made this man out of all the men she'd ever met the one man she'd go to bed with after the shortest acquaintance in her social history?

Whatever it was, it was potent, because now that the decision had been made—and her body, having been duly consulted, enthusiastically shouted *Yes!*—she couldn't wait.

"Come with me then, soldier."

He smiled. "That would be sailor, but you bet I'm coming with you."

He limped. If Paige hadn't had her arm around his waist she wouldn't have noticed, but there was a slight hesitation every time he put his weight on his left leg.

Max trotted right behind them, tongue lolling out of his mouth, wondering if this was a new game.

"We're being followed," she whispered.

He glanced down at her. "I noticed. I think the kid needs to stay outside, don't you?"

She nodded. "Wouldn't want him to lose his innocence. He's only eight months old."

"Yeah, too young for this."

They reached her room and he gently closed the door in Max's muzzle. There was a puzzled bark from the other side of the door. "Sorry, big guy,"

Max called out. "Wait till you're old enough to have a beer. Now." He put his hands on her hips and looked her up and down. "Oh God," he whispered. "I don't know where to start."

She smiled. "From the top."

The setting sun outside the window shone directly into the room, bathing it with a golden light. Everything in her room seemed to glow, as if enchanted. She had a small collection of silver vases which gleamed on her dresser. There was utter silence, broken only by the silver surf splashing on the beach. A moment out of time, magical.

He seemed to understand the magic of the moment too, holding her eyes as he slowly undid the buttons of her dress until it hung open. It was too hot for a bra so she stood before him in panties and an open dress.

He closed his eyes briefly then opened them, gaze dark and hot. "Did you wear those panties just to drive me crazy?"

She looked down. Pale pink silk and lace. They were pretty and they were expensive, too. She had to wear an anonymous lab coat at work and it always gave her a thrill to know she had on sexy, uber-feminine undergarments. She met his eyes. "There's a matching bra, too. I can put it on if you like. So you can take it back off."

He sighed. "Tempting as that sounds, I'll pass." He placed his big hands on her shoulders, leaving them there for a moment. A cool breeze fluttered her curtains, filling the room with the scent of sunshine and ocean. His hands were warm and heavy, the skin of his palms slightly abrasive as he smoothed them over her shoulders, shucking off the dress.

It was pointless trying to cover herself with her hands, so she stood straight under his scrutiny. That warm, dark gaze felt like hands caressing her as he looked her up and down, finally meeting her eyes again.

"Man," he breathed and she nearly laughed. As a compliment, it was more effective than any flowery phrases had ever been. The heavy hands drifted down her sides, thumbs hooking in her panties. A swipe of his hands and they fell. She stepped out of them and stepped out of her shoes.

Though her heels were low, it felt as if he grew much taller once she was in her bare feet, standing before her fully dressed while she was naked.

"Here, feel how much I want you," he whispered, voice low and hoarse. Shockingly, he took her hand and placed it right over his groin. Instinctively, her hand curled around him, his penis so hot she could feel the heat through the material of his jeans. At her touch, his penis moved beneath her palm as blood raced through it, becoming even harder.

He stood still under her touch, the only sign of his arousal a dark red wash over his cheekbones.

That convinced her more than anything else that she had nothing to fear—his utter stillness. He was watching her carefully, as if to take his cues from her.

"Now you undress me." That deep voice grew even lower.

"Okay." Paige stepped closer, so close her naked breasts brushed against his shirt front. She reached up and undid the top button of his white shirt.

To her surprise, her hands were trembling, with excitement, with trepidation. This was so unlike her other sexual experiences, where things happened fast. There was a solemn, deliberate pace he'd established, each step toward the lovemaking like a little ceremony. Definitely foreplay, though he wasn't even touching her, just watching her.

And yet it was almost unbearably exciting. She was so aware of everything—of the gathering shadows in her room, of the silence, of the sound and feel of her breathing. Her skin tingled with anticipation as she slowly unbuttoned his shirt. He watched her intently, face expressionless. If she hadn't noticed the high color of arousal in his face, if she couldn't feel the thick column of his penis against her stomach she could almost think he was unaffected by her movements.

Almost.

Her fingers were at the last button before his belt and she stopped, hands hovering over the buckle. She looked up at him and he nodded.

Taking a deep breath, she unbuckled the belt, unzipped his jeans, the back of her fingers brushing against him, hot and hard. His hips jerked and she looked up at him, startled. "Get me out of these clothes fast, please."

O-kay.

She was feeling a sense of urgency herself, like swimming in a river that was picking up speed, rushing toward rapids. She had to stand on tiptoe for a second to push the shirt off his shoulders. Half a minute later, she kneeled to pull off his jeans and briefs and take off his sneakers.

When she rose, he was naked. The most powerful man she'd ever laid eyes upon. His body was utterly unlike any other naked male body she'd ever seen. Almost as if he were a male of a different species. His body was a reflection of the life he'd led. Broad, hard muscles defined by battle and not a gym.

He was thinner than his body type would indi-
cate, no doubt because of the injuries. Each muscle
was hard and tightly defined, like an anatomy
drawing in living flesh.

And the scars. Oh, God, the scars. She'd seen
them on the beach but out of politeness had kept
her eyes trained on his. Now she could look all
she liked.

She sucked in her breath, fingers reaching out.
The leg was bad enough, but this. . . . The scars
were everywhere, some thin and white, some
with thick raised keloid tissue. She touched them
delicately, each scar representing untold pain. She
traced a thick scar over his left side, right under
the brown nipple. Obviously his rib cage had
stopped what should have been a killing blow.
There were two round, puckered scars even she
could recognize as bullet wounds low on his hip.
Together with the one on his shoulder it made a
little trifecta of pain.

He was alive by a miracle.

He stilled her hand, flattening his over hers.
Under her palm, she could feel hard muscle,
prickly chest hair, the strong beat of his heart.

Their eyes met. "I'm so sorry," she whispered.

"It's over," he said. "Right now, all I want to

think about is this." He smoothed a big hand over her hip, across her belly, laying his palm lightly on her mound. "Open for me, Paige," he whispered.

There was no question. Her feet shifted, his hand slid between her legs, cupped her. She huffed out a little breath of excitement. It was as if a sun bloomed there, between her thighs. His fingers stroked her, her flesh so sensitive there she broke out in goose bumps.

One finger circled, slid inside, and her knees weakened. She clenched around his finger and the color deepened over his cheekbones. He bent down and kissed her, not touching her anywhere but with his mouth and his hand between her legs and oh, when his tongue touched hers, she clenched tightly again around his finger. He sucked in a breath when he felt it, the breath coming from her lungs.

Another slow swirl of his tongue in her mouth. "We need to take this to the bed before I fall down," he said against her lips.

She smiled, mouth so close to his she felt his breath. She was vibrating with heat, with excitement, and couldn't formulate words. "Hmm."

Max turned, stretched out on the bed, held out a big hand. "You're going to have to be on top.

Sorry. This is going to be a huge incentive to me to gain more flexibility in my leg. I like the missionary position."

"I'll just bet you do," she said with a half-smile. Oh yeah, this was a man who'd like to be in command.

Paige looked down at him, at this huge, dark man on her pristine white bedspread, taking up half the bed. Almost every muscle he had was tense, in relief. One muscle, in particular. Was it a muscle? She knew her botany but not her anatomy.

Whatever it was, it was huge and hard as steel and utterly fascinating. His penis was dark with blood, the thick tip even darker, and almost reached his navel. She could see his heartbeat in the tip, trembling slightly with each beat of his heart. Though she would have sworn it was impossible, it thickened even more under her gaze.

She was supposed to put that inside her?

But then her vagina pulsed once, sharply. Her body was readying itself for him, all by itself. Her body wanted this, no question.

How strange. With her previous lovers, she realized, she had to almost coax herself into arousal— but not now. It was as if some outside force were taking her over, or maybe a really primitive part of her, one she'd never been aware of, was coming to the fore.

He curled his fingers up. "Come to me, Paige." That low, deep, utterly male voice was irresistible. Feeling carried by forces beyond her control, she placed one knee on the bed and swung herself over him.

If you'd asked her, she'd have said she preferred the missionary position, too, at least at first. If you'd asked her, she'd have said it was awkward being on top right away, she'd feel clumsy clambering over him, wouldn't know where to put her knees and elbows.

But nobody asked, and she found herself flowing on top of him like water, the only thought in her overheated head to try to touch as much of him with as much of her as possible. In a moment, she was stretched out on top of him, his arms holding her tightly, kissing her savagely, as if they were long-lost lovers reunited after years of separation.

One hand was holding her to him, the other reached down to open her up. Oh God, she gasped when he touched her again, she was even more sensitive there than before. Every nerve ending in her body congregating right . . . *there*.

She moaned and he stiffened under her, kissing her more deeply, holding her more tightly. She was opened up over him and he started sliding along her lips without penetrating, so slowly she could feel in turn that broad head, the steely shaft, his thick pubic hair against her. Then back, slowly. Forward. Back. The motions speeding up. With each passage, she grew hotter and wetter. He was moving faster now, passing over her clitoris with a little explosion of feeling each time.

Explosions of feelings everywhere. Her mouth, her hands, clinging to his hard shoulders as if she'd fall off a cliff if she didn't hang on tight, the insides of her thighs lightly abraded by the hairs on his legs, the hard muscles of his stomach brushing against hers with every movement.

Faster. Harder. Hotter.

She was on top, but not in control. He was doing everything—kissing her so hard she was breathing through his mouth, his hips moving so fast the bed started creaking, the friction burning her up.

He must have felt something: her muscles going slack as she began that luscious slide into orgasm, her breath caught in her lungs, that inward turning . . . something. Because the moment she started clenching around his penis, he lifted her slightly, thrust his hips up, and, oh God! entered her.

He was already moving, hard and fast, somehow timing his thrusts to her orgasm as they rocked together in some primordial rhythm that sucked her under, as if the climax were some warm tidal sea where she lost her sense of self completely, connected to life by her mouth to his and him rocking inside her.

Floating, rocking, detached from earth. Slippery and hot, clenching around him—not only with her vagina but with her arms and legs—until they were one creature, one being, fused together.

The pulses were starting to die down when he made a noise in her mouth, his movements inside her becoming short and hard—so fast she thought the friction would burn her up—and he started coming. He swelled inside her, impossibly, and came in huge hot jets and that set her off again, this time in tight clenches so hard she could feel it in her stomach muscles.

They slowed, quieted, and all the tension of the orgasm left her body in one huge whoosh, leaving her sprawled all over this huge man.

They were sticky with sweat and their juices, a feeling she'd ordinarily hate. With any other man, she'd have gotten out of bed as fast as possible to head into the shower.

Not now. Because, though they were sweaty and sticky, there was an amazing feeling of closeness, as if she'd become part of his body or he part of hers. It had never occurred to her before how incredibly *intimate* sex was.

It wasn't just a pleasant pastime. It was a melding of bodies.

She felt every part of his body. His heart thumping against her breasts, the beats hard and steady. The crinkly chest and body hair like a little mattress, or like lying on a lawn. She smiled at that thought and opened her mouth to tell him when she felt him draw a huge breath, lifting her up.

"That was fun," his deep voice rumbled. "Let's do it again."

Paige laughed, her stomach muscles brushing his.

He was serious, still hard inside her.

He gave one experimental thrust, as if asking permission, moving easily now that they'd both come.

Did she want another round right now? Hmmm. She felt really relaxed. Sex with him was exciting but really . . . intense.

Another smooth stroke, a kiss dropped on her shoulder.

Another. Oh God, he was heating her up.

She opened her mouth to say *okay* when her stomach suddenly rumbled.

"Well, I guess I have my answer," he said good-naturedly.

And then his stomach rumbled.

He tilted her chin up with a long finger and waited until she opened her eyes. He smiled. "I vote we go eat ourselves silly then come back to bed. What do you say?"

And Paige Waring, staid scientist, said, "Sounds like a plan."

Oh man, he was in heaven. Max sat up and leaned back against something really soft. Silk, maybe. Or satin? The headboard was really comfortable and looked like something a Pascha would have. The bed, too. Real girly stuff. Amazingly frilly sheets with a sort of flounce around the bottom.

He sniffed appreciatively. Everything smelled so nice, too. Even over the smell of sex, which made him horny.

Everything made him horny now. It was as if his dick had had an "off" switch that had now been switched back on. Permanently.

Paige was taking a quick shower. She'd seen the interest on his face when she said that and shook a finger at him so he stayed in bed like a good boy.

There was plenty of time.

He hoped.

Paige came out—the bathroom door opening, flowery-smelling steam billowing out—wearing a thin silk robe, wet hair hanging down her back. Shower Paige. To be added to Beach Paige, and Scientist Paige, and Dinner Date Paige and Naked Paige.

He liked the last one best.

She smiled at him as he swung his legs over the side of the bed. "I don't have anything that could possibly fit you, so I guess you should put these on." And tossed him his briefs.

He caught them one-handed, and swallowed. Put them on, followed her to the living room. Max the dog was leaping in delight at seeing them again after all of an hour's absence. "So . . . no clothes of absent boyfriends around?"

Not very subtle, but he suddenly had a burning need to know.

"Nope." She gave him a sunny smile. "Nary a one."

"So . . . this thing we're having . . . "

"This *thing?*" A little frown appeared between her ash-brown eyebrows."

Max felt like choking. "Yeah, this thing. This affair." Words were sticking in his throat like razor blades, each one sharp. "Whatever it is we're having, it's exclusive, right?"

Her head cocked and she just stared at him. A little sweat trickled down his bare back.

"Just you and me," he clarified. "Exclusive."

"Just you and me," she repeated, and nodded. "Yes."

He let out his breath. "So . . . we're a thing?"

Paige closed her eyes. "You're missing a good chunk of vocabulary."

"Yeah." He knew. He could barely think, let alone speak. The only thing he knew was that Paige was his, was a part of his life now. He'd seen a glimpse of the sun and he wasn't going to let it go.

"Okay." She opened her eyes and looked at him. "I will forgive your total inability to express yourself adequately and state that we are now 'going out.' Do you want me to say we're 'going steady'?"

Tension left his body. "Will you go to the prom with me?"

She laughed and took one step forward. He took a step forward. They met and he kissed her. And kissed her. He didn't consider himself a master kisser, but this felt like something else, like a big fat dividing line. Before and After.

Before was darkness and solitude. After was warmth and light.

Max jumped them. After was also the dog, wriggling with happiness at their feet.

Paige broke away, breathing hard. Her lips were red, swollen, glistening, just as her little cunt had been. The thought nearly unmanned him.

They had a "thing" now. She'd said so. She wasn't going anywhere, and neither was he. So why the urgency? Why this prickling feeling that everything would dissipate like smoke unless he grabbed her now?

She stepped back, watching his eyes. Maybe understanding his compulsion? With a flutter of silk she disappeared into the kitchen, coming back out with a tray. The dog was leaping and dancing at her feet, giving small yips of joy at the smell of food.

"I think at this point we need to put him outside—otherwise we'll never hear the end of it."

"Oh yeah," she sighed.

She snapped her fingers and Max wriggled happily. When she opened the door and pointed outside, he collapsed on the threshold, legs splayed, whining as if shown the door to hell itself. Paige snapped her fingers again. He rose trembling to his feet and slinked outside. Amazed that she would do this terrible thing to him. She closed the door in his reproachful face.

Max started barking immediately, loud barks guaranteed to wake any neighbors within a mile. They looked at each other, listening to Max. When they heard the sound of his claws tearing at the wooden door, Paige stepped close.

"Max! Bad dog! No barking!"

She might as well have been talking to the wind. The intensity of the barks increased.

This was ridiculous. He slapped the door. "Max! Stop!"

The noise stopped immediately. There was a faint whine and a yip and then nothing.

"Does one have to go to officer school to be able to do that?" she asked, tilting her head up to him.

Max smiled down at her. "It helps."

"I don't want to be commanded." There was a little pucker of worry between her eyebrows and he smoothed it away.

"I don't want to command you." Oh man, no. "Why would I want to do that?"

She shrugged, the light silk sliding off one shoulder. No, he didn't want to command her, but he did want to do something else.

It filled his head until he could think of nothing else. Max was forgotten, food was forgotten, the only thing filling his head was Paige, naked underneath a thin silk robe. It wouldn't have made any difference if she'd been wearing chain mail.

She looked down at him, blushed, then looked up. "I thought you were hungry?"

"Mm." Heat filled his head, his hands itched. The only thing that could make them stop itching was touching her. It took only a second to untie the robe and slip it off her shoulders and then she was in his arms, naked, soft breasts against his chest.

She'd seen precisely what his body wanted. It was visible to all, sticking out from his groin. Men really had nowhere to hide.

But—but she was affected, too. The signs were less visible, but there, if you knew where to look. Dilated pupils, a slight sheen on her face, her left breast trembling with the beat of her heart.

And there, that sweet spot between her legs. He ran his hand down her back, between her buttocks, lower and . . . yes. Oh yeah. Soft and hot and wet. The female equivalent of a hard-on.

Suddenly, his leg wouldn't hold him anymore, and not just his leg. His entire spine had melted, gone liquid, flowed into his cock, and then solidified.

Kissing her, he reached out with his foot, hooked a chair, dropped his briefs, sat down, and pulled her down on top of him. Just opened her up, pulled his cock away from his stomach and shoved it into her because if he didn't, he'd die.

They sat like that, a little sexy tableau, Woman

on Man. Paige's arms were around his back, face buried in his neck, his cock buried to the hilt in her.

"Whoa," he said and stopped, because what could he say? He hadn't planned this at all. He thought they'd eat together and maybe he could coax her into another round in bed eventually. Or maybe tomorrow morning if she fell asleep immediately. This—this was unplanned and completely unstoppable. His body had reacted faster than his head.

He looked down past her shoulder. Bright shiny hair, pale golden skin, strong sleek back, the indent of a small waist, buttocks sitting on his thighs.

It was, hands down, the most erotic sight he'd ever seen.

"Are, um, we okay here?" Because maybe she'd actually wanted to eat instead of being jumped.

In answer, she lowered her mouth to his shoulder, took a little nip, then kissed him.

His cock leaped inside her at the tiny bite. He lifted his hips while holding hers and slid in and out, once, testing.

She remained lax against him, eyes closed, a faint smile on her face. She sighed.

Okay.

Oh, yeah.

Another slide in, pulling out. And again. She

lifted her face slightly and took his earlobe in her mouth, and took another little bite.

He lost it.

Holding her tightly, he slammed into her, establishing a hard rhythm, trying and failing to hold back. He couldn't. It was as if his life depended on getting as deeply into her as he could and staying there as long as he could.

Thank God she was with him, growing wetter by the minute—otherwise they'd catch on fire.

Harder, faster . . . they were rocking in the chair now and a dim part of his brain hoped they wouldn't topple over, because there was no way he could stop.

Paige moved her head again and kissed him, her mouth as soft as her cunt, and it set him off. Rocket man.

He held her hard against him while a hot wire sparked down his back and exploded through his cock, and he came in hot, fierce spurts that went on forever.

Just as his spasms were dying down, she exhaled sharply in his ear—raising goose bumps all over his body—and clenched tightly around him, as if her cunt were trying to hold on to him.

Oh man, he wasn't going anywhere—he was

staying right here, feeling her entire body shaking with her climax.

When it was over, he was holding her tightly, panting. Maybe holding her too tightly. Was he hurting her? He slowly relaxed his grip, shifting to make her more comfortable.

They were wet where they were joined and every move made a small noise. He rubbed a hand over her satiny back, exhausted, as content as he'd ever been in his life.

"Uh oh." Paige wriggled on him a little. He swelled inside her, as if he hadn't just had the most explosive orgasm in his life. "Are we ever going to eat? Or are we just going to sit here until they find our dead bodies?"

It was a thought. At some point in June his XO would arrive. Wouldn't find him, would check with Paige, and there they'd be. Two corpses, still together, covered in cobwebs.

He sighed. "We'll eat. Sometime next week. Maybe."

Chapter Five

April 5

My gosh, good sex is better than Prozac as a mood lifter,
Paige thought five days later as she walked back
to her apartment after taking Maximilian for an
afternoon walk. He was unusually frisky, leaping
and barking and making her laugh. The kids on
the beach made her laugh. The cool little wavelets
frothing over her feet made her laugh.

It was Friday, Maxwell was on his way home
from a doctor's appointment, and they'd spend
the evening and the night together as they had
every evening and every night for the past four
days. And the weekend—she shivered. Two full
days with him. Forty-eight hours. Non-stop.

Oh yeah. Sex with Max was better than any
mood-lifting drug known to mankind.

Even the dark cloud of worry about Silvia was

manageable. She hadn't heard from Silvia since last Monday, B.M. Before Max. When she still had the capacity to fret and worry. It seemed to have left her body, together with all her sexual inhibitions. And all that empty space? Filled by her new lover.

Maybe Silvia had pulled a Paige? Maybe she'd found herself a super lover and had disappeared for a week somewhere?

After all, she was in Argentina, a country full of Latin lovers. Of course, there was no Latin lover on earth who could compete with Max, but still. Paige imagined having a laughing girl-fest with Silvia over a glass of wine at that swanky place on De Mott Street. *I was worried about you*, she'd say, and Silvia would smirk, her dark eyes dancing with amusement.

"OK. Got it. Not to worry," Paige said out loud to the imaginary Silvia, bending to ruffle the fur behind her dog's ears. "I should take a leaf from your book, big boy, and be a little less anxious. Though I'd try not to have that goofy expression on my face."

He was panting and yipping, tongue lolling out of his mouth, in dog heaven. A long walk with his mistress and at the end of it food. What else was needed to be happy?

"Indeed," Paige said, not even annoyed with herself that she was talking out loud to her dog. "What else is needed? Besides fantabulous sex?"

Max yipped in agreement, and she laughed as she opened the door and almost tripped over Max, who was scrambling to get inside, barking wildly because it was food time. Thank God the only neighbor was Max, who had a real soft spot for her Max.

Though, come to think of it, it appeared that human Max was also *her* Max. Now wasn't that delicious?

She shook her head as she reached under the sink, doggy Max's enthusiasm reaching frantic proportions. They'd definitely started *something*, but it was too early to say just what. It was enough that, so far, whatever it was, it was pretty wonderful.

Max was bouncing off the walls. Though doggy Max was like a marine when human Max was around, obeying instantly, he reverted to the slacker teenager he really was in the presence of his mistress.

Paige had one obedience trick in her arsenal. "Only *good dogs* get food." She usually said that in tones that would have been used by an old-time school marm. Sometimes it actually worked, depending on how hungry Max was.

The jumping stopped but the barking didn't, so she sighed and filled his food and water bowls.

Max had said he wouldn't be back before six, which gave her time to get some work done in her study, have a really nice, long, leisurely bath, and start cooking. Heat washed over her as she wondered whether they'd end up eating the food at midnight, as they often did.

After amazing sex.

Oh, God. She sat down abruptly, her legs giving out.

For a moment there, she'd had a sensory memory of being held tightly by him as he moved in her, hovering in a blaze of heat on the knife's edge of an orgasm . . .

She gave a shiver and simply sat for a moment, because her legs wouldn't hold her, flushed red with the memory of this past week.

Max watched her, head cocked, probably wondering what his insane mistress was up to.

Reliving the most intense sexual experiences of her life, that's what. But she couldn't tell him that. He was only eight months old.

Get a grip on yourself. It was so hard to reconcile what she knew of herself with the messages her body was sending her.

Paige was cool and cerebral. A little detached.

Always had been. She'd never been ruled by her hormones like her roommate in college had been. Moira had had a real good time in college. Real good. But she'd dropped out because Study of Gross Male Anatomy hadn't been on the curriculum and nothing else had interested her half as much.

Paige had been a straight-A student all the way.

She'd always liked sex, it was one of life's greatest pleasures. Somewhere above *Spaghetti all'Amatriciana* but definitely below that amazing massage she'd had at the Broken Tree Spa overlooking the Pacific. And it had always been a pleasure she could do without when there was no one suitable around.

So that was her experience of sex, which was worlds away from this compulsion, like a dark creature living inside her that filled her head with heated images. Every time she moved, she was reminded of Max, particularly when she sat down.

She, who was so very self-sufficient, couldn't wait for Max to get back from San Francisco.

Not just for the sex, either. She wanted to hear what the doctor said about his leg. She wanted to tell him what an incredible dickhead the project leader was being. Maybe she'd share her worries about Silvia. If he laughed them away, she'd feel better about it. If he took her worries seriously, she might think of contacting someone.

She trusted his judgement absolutely.

That was something new, too. Paige never trusted anyone's judgement as much as she trusted her own. But the few times Max disagreed with her opinion, he made her think. For such a macho man, he had the capacity to reason things out in a way that made sense to her.

She missed him. She wanted him home right now.

It was as if she had this tropism, like a plant to the sun.

She wanted him home, *now*.

Her vagina clenched.

Whoa. She definitely needed to think of something else. Some work ought to do it. There was some data she needed to enter into a spreadsheet and some reports she had to catch up on. Work cooled her down, centered her.

She dove in and was lost to the world when her cell phone rang.

"Hello?"

"Paige!"

She sat up, electrified. "Silvia! Where are you? I've been trying to—"

"Paige, I have to be quick! I've sent you info on

Twitter. To Barbie, go check it now. Make sure you put it somewhere safe. Something terrible is happening, Paige. I think we're going to have to go to the FDA. Maybe the FBI."

Paige's eyes widened as she clutched her cell phone. "Where have you—"

"No time, Paige! I've been running away from them all week. I think I've finally found a place where I can be safe. A friend is going to help me cross over into—" The connection was broken and Paige stared at the cell phone's display. She checked the call register. It wasn't Silvia's cell phone number, which was memorized in her SIM card. Silvia was either using someone else's cell or had bought a disposable one.

Something terrible is happening.

The urgency in Silvia's voice spurred her. She accessed Twitter and scrolled. She and Silvia had set up a private communication system—@Barbie1 and @Barbie2—to complain about their bosses. Two years ago, Paige had had what they called a "seagull boss"—he flew in, he crapped all over everything, and then flew out—who was angry at the failed results coming from his pet project. In one notable incident, he threw the hard copy of the failed test—all two hundred pages—in the air, accusing her of not doing her job. Of being a Barbie doll hired for her looks.

Instead of being kicked in the ass, he'd been kicked upstairs, but not before writing an epically negative report on her.

Silvia had been there, and ever since then, they kept a close eye on all the assholes. Currently the biggest asshole in sight was the man overseeing the Argentina project out of Buenos Aires.

Paige looked at the message Silvia had left for her @Barbie1. It was nonsense with a tiny url in it. Clicking it brought her to a site dedicated to the restoration of Assyrian artifacts, and then to a specific section of the site. Smart girl.

She isolated the section, which was huge—at least six hundred pages, over six hundred kilobytes. But the kicker was in the first ten pages. Paige skimmed the intro to the section, her heart starting to thump in panic.

The test fields of HGHM-1 in Argentina had been planted five years ago, the minimum time the FDA required before applying for permission for human consumption of a new variety. Test results on animals had shown no anomalies. Human testing had not yet begun. But Silvia had gathered data from hospitals and clinics in the surrounding area. The data was preliminary, not all of it collation-ready, but serious enough to warrant an immediate halt to the test trials.

Cancer rates in a radius of two hundred miles had increased by 400 percent over the past five years. Argentinian newspapers were calling it "The Cancer Epidemic." Silvia was the first to connect it to the test fields, which had been kept confidential. Even on a hasty reading, Paige could see that there was a strong case to be made for the fact that her company's new plant variety was massively carcinogenic.

The project had to be terminated immediately, the plants uprooted and destroyed. A whole department of the company would have to shut down, a $30 million investment wiped off the books, the legal department advised that probably a multi-million dollar lawsuit was in the offing. Heads would roll.

Silvia had also sent her a personal message.

On Monday, a car tried to drive me off the road. It was that twisty, winding road I sometimes take to get to Santa Maria. The car tried to run me off the road twice, but there were other cars on the road and it drove off. I was shaken. When I got home, my door was open. They'd trashed

*my apartment. They took my computer. I took
one look and ran. I've kept my cell off so they
couldn't track me, and turned it on only to try
to call you, but they must have some kind of
homing device, because a few seconds into the
call, I get static. By "they" I think it's a little
rogue operation inside the company's security
division. I don't dare use any friends' cell
phones. These guys mean business.*

*I'm in BA right now, staying with friends for
a night or two, then moving on. I'm sending this
to you from an internet café.*

*I need to get home somehow. Can you help? I
don't think security at headquarters is involved,
but you never know, so don't contact them. Right
now, I'm thinking FBI.*

*I'll be checking for a message from you a
couple of times a day. Remember it's GMT +3.*

*God, Paige. Help me. I need to come home. I
need to put this into someone's hands.*

Her own hands were trembling. Her mind was
racing as she eliminated the restoration of Assyrian artifacts section and downloaded only Silvia's
file onto her hard drive and then onto her thumb
drive. She watched the bar filling while trying to
figure out who could be after Silvia.

The most obvious choice for bad guy was the overall project's team leader, Jonathan Finder. He had the psychological profile for it, too. Ambitious and greedy. This was his project and he was making his name with it. It was going to have to be scrapped and would probably cost the company huge amounts of money in reparations. It was the kind of blow that could destroy a career.

Paige had always considered him a lightweight, but even wusses could be driven to violence by fear and greed.

Paige didn't even know where Finder was. He wasn't at her lab, but that didn't mean anything. GenPlant Laboratories ran facilities all over. Four research centers in the continental United States, including the high-security facility on Santo Domingo, and three outside the country. One in India, one in Thailand, and one in Argentina. Finder could be in any of these.

Was he capable of running a rogue cover-up operation?

If she only had something she could take to someone. Even an incriminating email, *something*. If she could go to the section head, Larry Pelton, with something other than wild conjecture, maybe she could stop Finder. Larry definitely had the authority to block Finder, especially if Finder were using GL resources to hunt Silvia down.

It was true that she and Larry had an unfortunate sentimental history, but she was sure he would overlook that.

She'd had no desire for a two-night stand. One night had been enough. She and Larry had avoided each other ever since that disastrous date when he'd tried and failed to stuff what felt like a marshmallow inside her, and they both ended up staring at the ceiling.

That was nothing compared to what was at stake. Her main worry was how to help Silvia right now. How to get her to a safe place and then get her back to the States. She had no idea what to do, who to turn to.

Then she thought of Max. Of course! He was a former SEAL. He'd know what to do, or at least who to contact. The legal implications were something she could think about later, but right now, the most important thing was to keep Silvia safe. Surely he'd know how to do that?

His cell phone number was programmed into hers. She felt a huge surge of relief as she pulled out her phone, checking her watch. 5:00 pm. He'd be on the road. It was dangerous to call someone while they were driving. A text message would be better. It gave off a signal, and he could choose to pull over to the side, and then they could talk.

The message was simple.

SOS – P

There. She felt better already.

He'd help her, and he'd know what to do. Together they'd figure out a way to save Silvia. Now she needed to put that file in a safer place. Where? Max had given her his cell phone but not his email address.

If there was a conspiracy inside the company, who to trust? It was entirely possible that people in the upper echelons knew the truth, and frankly, Paige didn't trust any of them.

There seemed to be a career point above which science started mattering less than profits.

She'd send the file to Larry and to . . . the police? It was a police matter, but no one was hurt . . . yet. The FBI? Silvia had mentioned the FBI. That made sense. Certainly the FBI would know what to do, who to turn to. There must be an FBI office in San Francisco. She logged on to the FBI.gov site and found the link to the San Francisco office, copied the address, and opened her Gmail account.

The drumbeat of anxiety over Silvia's fate was beating in her head as she typed. Max sensed her anxiety and scrunched close to her, leaning against her leg and laying his muzzle across her feet. He always sensed when she was upset.

Paige dropped a hand to briefly scratch his head, then bent back over the keyboard.

Suddenly, to her astonishment Max scrambled to his feet, hunching his shoulders and growling low in his throat.

"Get your hands off that computer," a male voice said.

Paige whipped around, wide-eyed. Two men were in the doorway, one tall and thin, the other stocky and shorter. The tall one had a gun pointed straight at her. She froze, utterly incapable of movement, trying to process these two men who'd appeared from nowhere.

"I said, hands off the fucking keyboard!"

She jerked her trembling hands up as if the keys were on fire. Oh, God! What now? Another minute or two and she could have sent the file to the FBI and to Larry. As it was, the only copies of Silvia's file were on her hard drive and her thumb drive.

The two men came forward. The man with the gun kept it trained on her. The unarmed man came around to stand beside her. He bent forward to see the screen, and Paige got a horrifying whiff of sweat, suntan lotion, and some awful cologne. Instinctively she recoiled when he lowered his head to hers.

Max's growling grew louder, lips curled back from his teeth.

The man tapped the keyboard, closing her FBI search, checking her email history. "Okay," the man said over his shoulder to his armed partner. "This hasn't been forwarded. There's a copy on her hard drive. Deleting . . . now."

"No!" Without thinking, Paige batted his hands away. He gave her a casual backhanded blow that nearly toppled her out of her chair.

Max attacked.

Max, her joyous, friendly dog—barely out of puppyhood—snarled like a hellhound and leaped for the man's throat.

An attacking dog is a fearful thing, like a primal nightmare hurtling out from the darkness. The man shot an arm up to protect his face and stumbled back, giving a high-pitched scream. "Shoot! Shoot the fucking dog, goddamn it!" he shouted.

Paige's head was still woozy from the blow, but when she saw the armed man raise his hand with the gun in it, she screamed and launched herself at him just as he pulled the trigger. The report was loud in the room, stunning her.

Max gave a loud, pained yelp and fell in a boneless heap to the ground, red staining his head.

Paige went wild, shrieking with rage, clawing for the gunman's eyes, feeling flesh under her fingers.

This time the blow was harder, knocking her to the floor next to Max. The world turned black for just a second, then slowly came back into focus. She looked up from the floor at the two men, one holding a red-stained forearm and the other with the gun glaring at her, the two long scratches on his face sullenly bleeding.

Good! she thought viciously, wishing she and Max had inflicted more damage. She reached out blindly and gathered Max into her arms, burying her hands and face in his fur, tears seeping out of her eyes. *Oh God, Max.* Her faithful friend, her . . . she stilled. There was something . . . a faint throbbing under her fingertips.

Max was alive!

Please, don't let him gain consciousness now, she prayed. The man Max attacked had been terrified. One twitch of Max's paw and they'd finish off the job.

Max was completely limp in her arms, but her gorgeous, smart, loving dog was alive. These monsters hadn't killed him.

Suddenly, she was yanked to her feet with a jerk that almost dislocated her shoulder.

"Come with me," the tall man with the gun said, pulling her after him. In her living room, he pushed her down into an armchair.

She'd never seen these two men before, but she could guess who they were. They looked exactly like every other security moron employed lately by GenPlant. Ill-fitting suits with lumps under their jackets, *check*; dour, dull expressions, *check*; a slight hint of sadism, *check*.

They were here and had pulled a weapon on her. Paige understood very well that this probably meant they weren't expecting her to live to testify against them. More goons just like them had presumably been sent to Argentina to find Silvia, but Silvia had managed to elude their grasp. Paige wasn't going to be so lucky. If she wanted to come out of this alive, she was going to have to think fast.

And if she wasn't going to get out of this alive, someone had to know what happened.

She slipped the thumb drive way down into the cushions of the armchair. If anything happened to her, Max or the police would find it. Maybe in time to save her, maybe not. She might die and Silvia might die, but at least the truth would come out.

The tall man brought out a kitchen chair, turned it around and straddled it, gun hand along the top of the back. His index finger stayed within the trigger guard. It was pointed loosely at her.

"So. What do you know about this Argentina thing?"

"I don't know what you're talking about."

This time the blow came from behind. Unexpected. Hard. When she opened her eyes again, it took her a moment or two to focus. Her head throbbed.

"Okay, that was dumb of you, and I understand you're not a stupid woman. You've got a PhD. So let me tell you upfront that we can keep this up all night," the tall guy said. "No problem. And we can get real inventive. You're a pretty woman. Smart, too, if you work in a lab. So you can connect the dots. My friend and I, we can do what we want here. No limits. We'll get what we want. The only question is: will it be the easy way or the hard way? Your choice."

His eyes were a pale blue, so lifeless they could have been marbles. There was no mercy in them, no emotion at all, not even the pleasure of someone who liked inflicting pain.

Nothing.

Paige was working hard to stop her trembling. These men were barely above animals. Animals had an instinct for fear, and attacked when they sensed it. So she had to control herself.

If she could keep them talking for just another forty minutes, Max would be here. She couldn't defeat these two men but he could. Even with a busted leg, these two idiots would be no match for him.

"So. We know your friend Silvia Ramirez has been trying to contact you all week."

"And she's escaped you all week, hasn't she?" Paige narrowed her eyes at the men. "You didn't lay a hand on her."

"We will. Don't worry about it, our men down there are good."

Not good enough to capture a woman on her own. Paige didn't say the words, but her expression was clear.

"She hasn't been able to establish contact with you, we know that. We cut her off every time she got you on the phone."

"You were listening to my calls," Paige breathed. That was how they'd done it. The instant they heard Silvia's voice, they cut the connection. Thank God she'd texted Max! "How long have you been doing that?"

Another slap to the back of her head, softer this time. A smack more than a blow. A little something to establish authority. "We ask the questions here, bitch, not you," the thug behind her growled.

The man with the gun studied her, as if she were a bug under a microscope.

"We deleted the file you received. Did Ramirez send you anything else? Another file? Did you receive anything in the mail?"

Ordinarily Paige was a lousy liar. She hated lying because it gave her cognitive dissonance. She was a scientist. Reality was her field of study. Lies were a distortion of reality, and used up significant amounts of space on her mental hard disk. You had to keep track of lies, remember them, coordinate them. Not worth the effort, she'd always thought.

She didn't have to lie now. Silvia hadn't sent anything else and nothing had arrived in the mail.

Paige looked the tall man straight in the eye without blinking. "No, I didn't receive another file and I haven't received anything in the mail."

He held her gaze for a long moment, then shifted his eyes to the man behind her. "She's telling the truth." He waited a beat. "Ramirez tried to contact you all week. Why?"

Paige told a version of the truth. "Because we're friends."

The tall man narrowed his eyes. "She was on the run, desperate. She wasn't trying to contact you to make a date to meet for drinks. Why was she trying to get in touch? To send the file. Anything else?"

Paige said nothing and his mouth flattened.

"Let's try this another way. What do you do at the company?"

That was easy. No cognitive dissonance there. "I'm a plant geneticist. My main field of study is biolistics. Currently I'm applying the agrobacterium method—known as the 'Gene Gun'—in vivo, for the transformation of monocot species, by shooting genes into plant cell chloroplasts."

Silence.

"We need to take this to the lab," the man behind her said. "The one on the island."

Paige's heart started thumping, a frantic tattoo of panic. They couldn't take her to the main company headquarters labs twenty miles away. It was a huge, bright complex, with thousands of employees coming and going at all hours of the day or night. A place where she was well-known.

No, they meant the other complex. GenPlant Laboratories kept facilities on the small island she could see from her deck. Santo Domingo Island. Certain varieties highly susceptible to unintentional cross-breeding were studied there.

Paige had been there once. It was mostly deserted, the main buildings dedicated to micropropagation under artificial light, automatically watered. It was a series of concrete bunkers with huge underground facilities and only a few researchers who worked sporadically in labs confined to one wing. There wouldn't be anyone now on a Friday evening.

It was a perfect place to hide a prisoner.

It was a perfect place to kill someone and get rid of the body.

Once she was on the island, she was lost.

"No," she said. "You can't go there. Company rules—"

She didn't finish the sentence. Something punched her arm, something covered her head, and blackness descended.

Her last thought was, *Max. Help me.*

Chapter Six

Max found himself whistling in the SUV, coming back from the doctor's visit—never his favorite activity. He'd grown to loathe doctors and nurses and physical therapists over the past year. His lost year. The year of putting himself back together.

Good people, all. Probably. And they *had* put his broken pieces together, there was that. But they had never believed he could go back to the way he was before, and Max found that unacceptable. He'd been a hard man and he was determined to come back even harder, no matter what the medical pukes said.

Fuck 'em if they thought he couldn't do it. If they thought he'd injure himself if he pushed himself harder. Well, by God, he'd pushed himself and come out the other end without causing a permanent injury, like they kept nagging he would.

Even his goddamned bad leg was better. The orthopedic surgeon was surprised. *Whatever it is you're doing,* he said, *keep on doing it.*

Well, Max had every intention of doing it. He was up to a one-mile swim, every day. He'd get up to two miles—and then three—and hit that fucking island that was always just out of reach. It was off-limits, he knew that, some kind of research lab. But his goal was to get close to it and swim back. Six miles. Every day. He could do it. Maybe by the end of the year.

And he had his own physical and mental rehab routine now. He'd swim and then spend the day with that damned dog, throwing Frisbees and laughing. It was impossible to be depressed with that mutt around.

Not to mention the mistress, Paige. Oh yeah. He was really looking forward to spending every evening and every night with Paige.

Because it was entirely possible that sex with Paige Waring was what had improved his leg. God knows it improved everything else. And he had every intention of keeping on doing it, just like the doctor ordered.

That was the reason he was whistling. And the reason he was pushing the speed limit. To get back to her.

Man, one week, and his entire outlook on life had changed. Since Afghanistan it had been one grim, gray day after another. Holding on. Surviving. Getting better one painful inch at a time. Putting one foot in front of the other, and considering it a victory, since it had been touch-and-go as to whether he'd ever walk again when he woke up in Ramstein. Touch-and-go as to whether he'd even have a leg, or so the surgeons told him. The operation to save his leg had taken seventeen hours.

His entire life since he'd been a kid had been aimed at joining the navy and becoming a SEAL. It was all he'd ever wanted. Now that he'd never be a SEAL again, the future had been closed off, this impenetrable black iron wall clanging down right in front of him.

He still didn't know what the long-term future held, but his immediate future was spending his evenings with gorgeous Paige Waring in her pretty apartment and spending his days with her dog.

Not bad for a man who only a week ago hated the thought of waking up in the morning.

It was sex. That was part of it. Granted, hotter and better sex than he'd ever had, but sex was fleeting. No one knew that better than him.

Up until now, he'd thought sex was fucking. Who knew sex could also be lovemaking? And that lovemaking was *better* than just sex? Though they'd smoked the sheets up, there was affection there. Real, tangible affection. Warmth and connection.

He liked her. A lot. And was beginning, for the first time in his life, to think of the "L" word. Much scarier than "like."

She was smart and funny and just so goddamned pretty. But beyond the prettiness there had been other things he wanted to explore and knew he would. Because now that he'd found this, tasted it, there was no going back.

She kept him on his toes. She made his heart beat faster and his blood boil. And at the same time, he found a strange kind of peace with her, as if he'd come home after a long and weary journey.

It was going to take him a long, long time to grow tired of Paige Waring. Maybe the rest of his life.

The sun was low in the sky, the light washing over the landscape. The effect was spectacular, every color kicked up a notch until it glowed. If he hurried, they could watch the sun set from Paige's deck. Maybe he could coax her into sitting on his lap. Oh yeah. His dick stirred at the thought.

Man, his dick was making up for lost time. No

sex at all for two years and now it wouldn't stay down.

But that was okay because it was happy and so was he.

Everything about this moment was just so fucking perfect. Doctors not riding him for overdoing it, for a change. A beautiful woman waiting for him. A ridiculously likeable dog waiting for him, too. A glorious sunset.

When was the last time he looked forward to something? Noticed a beautiful sunset? Noticed fucking *colors?* And when was the last time he'd felt so goddamned *good?*

There was a wonderful evening ahead of him. He'd deliberately had a light lunch because he was looking forward to whatever it was Paige was going to cook for dinner. And then, oh man, spending the night with Paige. Making love until they were sated—or at least she was. Max felt like he could go forever, now that he'd reconnected with his dick. And then sleeping in on a Saturday morning, that slender soft body curled up next to his. And maybe they'd spend all day Sunday in bed.

The future rocked.

He was really looking forward to days playing with her stupid mutt on the beach, waiting for her to come home. Maybe one of these evenings he'd try to rustle up some dinner himself, just for some comic relief. There was a hospital nearby in case it all went south.

Maybe tomorrow evening they could go into Monterey. He could take her out to a nice restaurant, maybe out to a movie. Maybe—what the fuck—maybe dancing? Though he didn't know how to dance and would trip over his own feet, not to mention the bum leg. But she looked like a woman who might like that—dinner and dancing.

And God knows, whatever made her happy was okay by him.

Because, well, she'd given him his life back.

He was . . . he was *happy*. Looking forward to seeing her again. Looking forward to life.

He pulled out his cell and punched in her number. To tell her he was about an hour out. To ask her if she needed him to pick up anything in town.

Who the fuck was he kidding? He just wanted to hear her voice, hear that she was happy he was coming back to her. Hell, maybe hear the sound of that mutt barking in the background.

NO SIGNAL.

Damn. He really wanted to hear her voice. Tell her about the doctor's visit, about the cheeky squirrel staring at him from the branch of a tree outside the clinic while the doctor was bent over his leg.

Shit.

He tried again fifteen minutes later.

NO SIGNAL.

Five minutes later.

NO SIGNAL.

Max drummed his fingers on the steering wheel. Damn but he wanted to hear her voice. Right now. She had this most amazing voice. Soft but clear, just a little husky in bed.

Last night she'd whispered, *"Now, Max"* right into his ear, just as her little cunt started pulling on him, her breath washing over his ear. He'd started moving faster, harder, and it had set her off.

Oh, Christ. *Don't think about that.* Because his entire body had flushed with heat and his cock stirred again at the memory. It had been like that all day, with a real embarrassing moment on the doctor's cot when he'd remembered her kissing his scars and he'd started getting an erection.

That earned him a real odd look from Dr. Mc-Bride, former college linebacker. Max had had to think of Afghanistan to get his cock back down again.

Oh God, he missed her. He wanted to be back in

her apartment *now*, on her deck. Petting her dog, sipping a glass of wine with her. Watching this spectacular sunset. Right now. Right . . . fucking . . . now.

The cell phone's buzz startled him. The signal was back.

A text message. He glanced at the display. It was from Paige. Not only was her number memorized on his SIM card, it was emblazed in his head.

His blood stopped cold when he saw the message.

SOS - P.

Fuck. She was in trouble.

Max stepped hard on the accelerator.

A loud, angry buzzing filled her head, the ground underneath her thumping up and down. She bounced each time, coming down jarringly hard on a wooden surface that had knobs and lumps on it. It hurt. Her arm hurt. Everything hurt, particularly her head. It felt as if someone were hammering spikes into her skull.

She tried to cushion the bounces but her hands wouldn't move. Was she paralyzed? No, her fingers could move, but her hands couldn't.

It was impossible to think with this loud buzzing noise, the jarring motions rolling her back and forth and up and down. Sometimes the ground beneath her suddenly dropped and she fell with a painful jolt.

It was dark, but bright pinpricks of light came through.

None of this made any sense. Where was she? What—

And then it all came back in a sickening, painful rush. The two men. Max, shot and bleeding. Silvia, on the run. The file Silvia had sent, with the terrible data.

She was lying on her side, hooded, her hands in restraints, totally unable to counter the painful jolts.

Men's voices over the deep buzzing noise. An engine. A boat engine. The smell of brine penetrating the smelly material of her hood. She was on a boat with those two men. They were taking her to Santo Domingo.

She surreptitiously tried to see if her cell phone was still in her pants pocket. If it was, she could be traced through it. A sudden surge of hope pulsed through her as she rolled with the rolling of the boat, trying to bring her wrists around to touch her pockets.

Nothing. Her cell phone was gone. Whether they'd thrown it away or left it behind in her apartment, it was of no use to her.

The deep buzzing of the engine changed tone, lowered. The boat swung sideways. They were landing.

She breathed through the sudden panic. Once she was on that island, she was lost. No one could find her—not even Max, even if he knew where she was. The facility had over fifty thousand square feet of research labs, culture labs, propagation houses, and equipment sheds, plus a huge hangar-like building called the Repository, a bank of varieties for future testing.

There'd be plenty of privacy. No one would hear her screaming. The two men could do to her what they wanted, with no one the wiser.

For all anyone knew, she would disappear off the face of the earth.

She could only hope that Max had found the thumb drive. But even if he did, how could he know where they had taken her?

The boat's engine cut and it rocked gently on the water. A strong hand wrapped itself around her upper arm and pulled sharply, taking her by surprise. She'd been planning on pretending to still be unconscious but when he pulled her stumblingly upright, she automatically scrambled to find her footing.

One of the men was at her back and prodded her roughly onto a plank. At the end, unmistakeably, was solid ground.

She was on the island.

And she was lost.

Chapter Seven

"Paige!" Max pounded on the door with his fist. "Paige, open up!"

There was no sound. No quick footsteps, no voice, nothing.

Max raised his fist again, then brought it quietly to rest against the door. He rested his forehead against it, disgusted at himself.

Shit. He was a SEAL. He'd trained for years. This was not how to stage an infiltration. What the fuck was the matter with him? He knew better than this.

There was no way of knowing what that SOS message meant, but one thing was certain—Paige needed him. If she was in real trouble, if someone was holding her hostage on the other side of that door, he'd just thrown away every single tactical advantage he had. Just wiped it out.

If there was someone behind that door, that

someone now knew that an angry male was on the other side. He could hurt Paige, kill her.

Max broke out in sweat. Maxwell Wright, whose heart rate never increased in battle, was sweating like a pig, the sweat of anxiety. Super-cool SEAL, tested and tried in the battlefield. He was good in combat, he had the medals to prove it.

Now look at him. Sweating, panicky, ready to barge into a dangerous, unknown situation—which ran counter to every single thing he'd ever been taught. Any instructor worth his salt would have kicked his ass.

He knew better than this. He had to do better than this. Paige needed him. Whatever was wrong, a quiet, controlled response was better than a sweaty, panicked one, hands down.

If his drill instructor had just seen him, he'd have screamed in his face and told him to drop to the grinder and pump out a hundred push-ups.

Intel. He needed intel.

He stood an inch from the door, breathing hard, staving off panic. *Think! Goddamn it!*

The bottom rim of the huge, golden red sun was close to touching the surface of the sea. The air was filled with golden light, but in an hour it would be dusk, the light gray and unrevealing. Whatever he learned here, it had to be now, with the light.

Carefully, he made his way around the perimeter of the house. It had the exact same layout as his own. Living room with adjoining kitchen, hallway with two rooms and a bathroom. When he reached the study window, he heard a whine, looked in.

Max! Max huddled on the floor in a pool of blood. The dog raised his blood-streaked head when he saw him and gave a half-hearted bark.

Now he was certain that there was no one in the house—otherwise, even wounded as he was, Max would be barking harder.

Max went back to the front door and froze. How the fuck had he missed this? He had to get his act together because he'd missed what he should have seen right off, if he hadn't been crazy with fear for Paige.

Scratches on the backplate. Paige's front door lock had been picked.

Evidence, right there, that someone had come for Paige. Was holding her somewhere, right now. Could be hurting her, right this minute.

The panic dissolved and icy calm took its place. Years of training steadied him, gave him the right place in his head to go to. A place of discipline and training and determination.

Once Max entered that place, he was invincible. It would take an RPG to take him down.

He had the key to Paige's place. A minute later, he was in the house, bending down to the dog.

"Good boy," he said soothingly, touching Max's head. Max whined once when he touched the open wound. A furrow, caused by a bullet. Max licked his hand as he studied the wound. It was only a flesh wound. It had bled a lot, but the bleeding had stopped.

Max went into the bathroom, got a towel and disinfectant, and carefully cleaned the shallow wound as best he could. The dog licked his hand. "It's okay, boy. You'll be okay." The furry tail thumped once on the floor.

Max noticed blood on the muzzle, unconnected to the head wound.

Oh, yeah. Good for him.

"Bit the fucker, did you, Max? Good boy. You're the best. I hope you tore his fucking throat out." But looking around, he saw that, besides a few drops of blood near Paige's desk, no one's throat had been ripped out.

Well, that could be remedied.

"Where'd they take her, boy? Where's Paige?"

Astonishingly, Max rose unsteadily to his feet. He stumbled, fell. Before Max could reach down to pet him, reassure him, the dog rose again and stood.

He was standing, though he must have been weak from blood loss. He was standing, though in all likelihood he was lightly concussed. He was hurt, but, by God, he was standing.

He was as brave as any SEAL.

"Where's Paige?" Max said again, feeling like an idiot. The dog was smart, but not that smart.

To his surprise, though, the dog moved slowly, painfully into the living room, stopping at a flower-covered armchair. Max followed.

Now that he'd calmed down, Max could read the situation in front of him as clearly as if seeing what had happened an hour or so ago. There were two chairs dragged in from the kitchen, one in front of the armchair, one sitting right behind it. Two men, then, flanking Paige. The seat of the armchair was still dented where she'd sat.

He looked more closely. There was something about the crease on the left-hand side of the big seat cushion, corresponding to Paige's right hand. He dug and came out with something small and metallic.

A thumb drive.

Smart, smart Paige. She'd had the presence of mind under threat to leave him something. What? He was distracted by Max. The dog's coordination was improving by the minute. He was trotting back and forth between where Max sat in front of Paige's computer and the front door, whining, pointing his nose at the door, clearly exasperated with the human Max who wasn't getting it.

Paige went out this door, Max was communicating with every fiber of his doggy being. *What's the matter with you, you moron? Come on, let's go get her!*

But human Max needed more intel. Going blind into a situation was not good. Max stared at the screen, willing himself to understand what Paige wanted him to know.

He scrolled briefly through a couple of files randomly. All work related. When he opened them he simply stared, understanding one word in ten. Some were data spreadsheets. Some were graphs. Some lab results. The physics and genetics and biochemistry were way beyond him.

OK. He'd stand in awe of her education some other time. Right now he needed to know what was in here that could help him find her, and fast.

When he'd gone over the files three times—fending off Max, who was scrabbling at his leg and whining loudly—he decided to look at them in chronological order, something he should have done immediately.

The first one—Christ! It had been loaded less than an hour ago. Maybe the last thing she did before the two fucks picked her lock, shot her dog, and spirited her away.

He finally clicked through and saw a personal message, which he'd missed in his scrolling. From a woman named Silvia, who was apparently a friend. He read through the message and finally reached a grim understanding.

The company Paige worked for was sitting on a bomb that was about to blow up in its face. A bomb that, at a conservative estimate, was about to cost them millions, maybe billions. Something like this would eventually come out, but from what Max was able to see, right now the only thing standing between the bomb and the world was two super-smart women. One was being chased all over Argentina and the other had been kidnapped.

He opened his cell, engaged an encryption app designed by the friend he was calling, and waited.

"Yo. World's Finest Hacker. Black Hat, White Hat, take your pick. How may I help you?"

Oh yeah. Cory Mayer, former Delta operator. Max had met him on a cross-training exercise. Cory had been a gifted shooter, but it turned out he was even more gifted with a keyboard, which had turned out handy when an IED had exploded under his badly-armored vehicle outside Nasiriyah seven years ago. He'd left his legs back in Iraq—but not his brains. He'd since recycled to become everyone's go-to guy for intel.

"Yo, Hackerman. I've got myself a time-sensitive situation here. A possible kidnap victim, works for GenPlant Laboratories. What can you tell me about the company?"

"Hm. How you been, Maxie boy? You getting over your scratches?"

Max nearly smiled. Though Cory's voice was slow and honeyed he could hear wild tapping in the background.

"Doing fine now, except for this woman. She works for the company, does research work for them. I think she's come across some information that will hurt the company."

"Oh ho!" Cory chortled. "Are we talking babe material, here?"

"Yeah," Max said curtly. "And it's a woman I care about. A lot."

There was silence at the other end, but the pounding sounds intensified.

"Okay." When he came back online, Cory's voice was curt and serious. "Here's what we've got. Big company, last year's profits were half a billion dollars on three billion sales. Has come up with some killer apps—two new types of antibiotics that can overcome resistant e. coli infections and pesticide-resistant fruit trees. And that was just last year. Seems to be humming right along."

Okay. "It's got research facilities in Argentina. What can you tell me about that?"

Another minute as Cory worked his magic. "Yep. A big research facility four hundred miles south of Buenos Aires."

"Anything wonky there?"

"Not that I can see."

Max knew there was but it was clearly still hidden. Not even Cory, brilliant as he was, could see things that weren't there yet.

"How about their security?"

After a minute, Cory said, "Oh."

"What? What?"

"Not good. Someone's been hiring from Magnum Secure lately. Hiring heavily. I'd say now a good 70 percent of their security staff comes from there. Bad juju, Max."

Very bad juju. Magnum Secure was a notoriously corrupt private contractor that had operated extensively in the Sandbox. He'd come across MS operators a lot, and they were aggressive and greedy. The owner seemed to recruit men who cared for nothing but the bottom line. If someone in Paige's company had been filling its security department with ex-MS contractors, Paige was in trouble.

None of the operators would draw the line at hurting a woman.

"The woman in question's name is Paige Waring, Cory. Like I said, she's a researcher there. I'm at her house now and there are signs of a struggle. I think she's been kidnapped because she holds some information about something that went wrong at their lab in Argentina. Where do you think they'd take her? To headquarters? It's about twenty miles from here."

"Pulling up satellite images now . . . no. I don't think so. It's a busy facility. There's a huge parking lot with cars going in and out constantly. My images are from fifteen minutes ago and there's a lot of movement. Dunno, Max, just seems too public for a kidnapping. I can't even see any outbuildings where someone could be held."

The dog's whining was stronger now, with a note of urgency in it. He was pawing Max's leg. The dog went back to the front door, looking over his shoulder at Max, and barked.

Was Paige being held nearby? Is that what Max was trying to tell him?

"Listen," he told Cory. "I gotta see about something. Can you send those images to my Gmail account and we'll talk in five? And see if you can find any databases with other property the corporation might own nearby."

"Sure thing," Cory said. "A woman, huh?"

"Yeah. Smart and kind and pretty. Exactly the kind of woman fuckheads like to hurt."

Max could almost hear Cory's teeth grinding. His mom had been beaten to death by his dad. He was guaranteed to give Max his best.

Max opened the front door and the dog flowed out, nose to the ground. To Max's astonishment, instead of making a grid back and forth to try to pick up Paige's scent, the dog ran around the house and headed straight for the beach.

What the fuck?

He'd been prepared for Max to lose the scent right away. They'd have driven her away in a car. When Max headed for the beach, nose still to the ground, his heart sank. Sweat broke out in every pore.

Had they killed Paige and buried her on the beach? Their stretch of beach was usually deserted. The beach narrowed along their stretch and the bed was rocky. The popular beach was two miles down—long wide stretches of sand and no rocks underfoot.

Oh God, now he could see it, as plain as day. Three sets of footprints, two on either side of deeply furrowed tracks. Two men holding up an unconscious woman. Then halfway down the beach, two sets of footprints, one much deeper than the other. The depth of a man carrying an adult woman.

Max had followed his nose straight to the water, so at least he wasn't going to find Paige's body in a shallow grave. The dog was at the water's edge, moving back and forth anxiously, unable to follow the scent into the sea. The sea that might contain Paige's body.

Max rejected that idea violently. Shook it right the hell off. He'd just found her, he wasn't going to lose her. Not an option.

Coming closer to the water the footprints were muddled. And there was a long indentation in the sand, with a heavy furrow in the middle. The kind of print a boat with a hull would make.

He refused to even think that they were putting Paige on the boat to dump her overboard. It was still daylight. Would they risk someone seeing them on open water when there were other, easier options available? Why put Paige in a boat? Ten miles east and you could get onto the largest freeway system in the world and disappear.

They had to keep her alive for a reason. And they put her on a boat for a reason.

Max was going to find her and hurt the men

who'd taken her, and then he was going to bring her home. That was his mission and he hadn't failed a mission yet.

"Max!" he called and slapped his thigh. The dog looked up from where he was nosing the sand, completely recovered and quivering with anxiety. "Come with me!"

The dog hesitated, torn. He wanted to stay where there was the last sign of his mistress, but she wasn't there. On the other hand, maybe the male human could help. He slowly trotted to him.

Max headed for his apartment because he knew Mel would have everything he could possibly need. He needed speed because someone could be hurting Paige right now. He nearly ran back, ignoring the grinding pain in his leg.

Mel had security cameras front and back, something Paige didn't but would have—just as soon as Max got her back. He'd install security cameras right away, alarms at the doors and windows and fence, and front and back door electronic security systems not even he could penetrate.

Mel's cameras worked on a forty-eight-hour loop and they were digital, hi-def cameras. So when Max moved the tape back, he watched, every muscle in his body tensed, as three men drove up in a tan SUV. Two men got out, one stayed in the car.

Max watched as the taller of the two men picked Paige's lock and they walked in. He fast-forwarded to when the two men walked out, dragging a semi-conscious, hooded Paige.

They stopped at the SUV to talk to the driver who backed the SUV and drove away.

While they were talking, the camera caught the faces of all three men. Max froze the camera, studying the three men carefully, knowing he would never forget those faces—they were dead men walking.

He flipped open his cell and called Cory back. He didn't even have a chance to say anything when Cory said, excitedly, "Max, GenPlant Labs has a super-secret facility on an island not far from where you are now. The island is called—"

"Santo Domingo Island, yeah. Listen, do you think there's any chance of satellite coverage of the island? Say, from about an hour ago to now? Can you hack Keyhole?"

He knew what he was asking. Keyhole was the NSA's top-secret series of eyes in the sky so powerful they could see the balls of flies. Keyhole intel was beamed down in code so highly encrypted it took a bank of servers to decode.

But Cory was a genius.

"Please," Cory said. "For you, anything. But I'll

do you one better. There's a big oil consortium looking for shale oil via a new imaging technology. They've covered all of Central California with something like four thousand bird-sized drones. Each drone records a tiny area and a computer puts a composite picture together. That picture would be much clearer than Keyhole."

Max didn't even question how Cory could know that. And didn't bother asking Cory to hack into the central computer putting together the mosaic of drone photograms. He could hear Cory pounding the keyboard. Cory knew what to look for.

Five minutes later, Cory whistled.

"What?"

Cory's voice was grim. "Not looking good, big guy. I'll send these images to your cell. I'm looking at a boat that landed on a pier on the south side of the island at 17:47. The time stamp will be on the footage. Then we see two guys pulling out what looks like a hooded female—she's stumbling and they're dragging her along . . . "

Max could picture it all too well, the two men who'd been on the security footage manhandling Paige. His hands fisted.

"You're going to get these fuckers, correct, Max?" Cory asked. "They're really manhandling her." For a moment, all Max could hear was Cory's rough breathing. "One of those fuckers just back-handed her. She fell to the ground. God*damn* it!"

Max closed his eyes and grappled for control. "Oh, yeah," he said softly. "I'm going to get them. Count on it."

"Good. I'm watching them disappear into the main building. Straight up from the jetty. The good news is that they entered the building through what looks like the front door, so we know where she was at 17:54. The bad news is that the central building is enormous. There are several outbuildings, and we have no way of telling if there are underground corridors. No way of knowing where she might be now."

If she's still alive. Cory didn't say it but it hung there in the air.

Max wasn't going there. Not touching it. "What can you tell me about the island? How many people are on it—can you tell?"

"It's hard to say. There are no cars, of course. There's a jetty on the south side, but only for small boats. That's where they landed. I can't imagine boats carrying much more than ten people moor-ing there. Hang on, wait a minute. Let me check." Max held his cell to his ear, clutching it so hard it was a miracle the plastic didn't break.

The urge to spring into action was so strong it

prickled under his skin but he knew better than to be impatient at the planning stage. Paige was in danger, but she wouldn't be helped by him barging in unprepared and getting his ass capped.

"Okay." Cory came back online. "There are two guards stationed on the north side of the facility. And two more at the jetty. I went back in time to check their routine and they patrol every half hour, fifteen minutes to each quadrant. They're armed—looks like AK-74 rifles. Sidearms, too, but they're holstered and I don't have enough resolution to tell what they are. They stick close to the buildings. If that's a normal research facility I'll French-kiss you."

Max nearly smiled. "Thanks, buddy, I'll pass."

"No way to know how many people are inside or where they're holding your friend. Sorry. The drones don't have IR capability. That's going to come online next month, or so I heard. But right now what's under the roofs is unknowable. And it'll be dark soon."

"Yeah. I better get going. Thanks. I owe you."

"Just bring that woman back safely. Check your cell, you'll see the images. I'll be on standby. Let me know if I can help with anything. And don't forget my buddy PJ. Pretty high up in the SF FBI office."

"Yeah. Listen. I'm going to send you a file. Forward it to PJ."

"Got it."

"You're the best."

"Yes, I am. Bring her home, Max."

"You bet. Count on it."

Max carefully studied the images Cory sent him, then went to Mel's locker, where he knew he would find everything he needed. Mel had given him the combination, and sure enough, it was full of gear.

The right gear, bless Mel's black heart.

As in all missions, Max had to balance out gear and weight. Too little gear was bad, too much gear was bad. It had to be Goldilocks Gear, just right. His hands were already picking things out.

Mel had a sweet little suppressed MP-5 that felt like home in his hands. He picked up a Glock 45 and holster as backup. Three magazines each. Night vision binocs. Emerson folder. Four flashbangs. Restraints and duct tape. Waterproof bag. Wet suit and tanks.

Some C-4, det cord and detonator—because there were few situations where blowing something up didn't help.

He went out onto his deck and checked the island with Mel's powerful x140 binoculars, running a slow, careful sweep east to west, then west to east. He saw the jetty with a small boat moored there. Two guards were standing together about fifty feet away. One was smoking. They had their backs to the ocean.

Sloppy. Real sloppy. If he survived the swim, he could take them down easy.

He was deliberate in his actions, not hurrying, though the drumbeat of fear and rage was in his ears. He gave one last long, slow look at the island, at where his Paige was being held, then put on his wet suit. He checked it, checked the tanks, though he knew it wouldn't be in Mel's locker if it wasn't in perfect shape. Force of habit from a man whose life had always depended on the trustworthiness of his gear.

Time to go.

He stepped down from the deck onto the sand, but stopped when he heard a bark. Max on the deck, watching him. To his dying day, Max would swear the dog looked at him with reproachful eyes.

It was crazy, and it would make his task—already nearly impossible—harder. But he was going to have to search a huge building for Paige, with no idea how to track her. Max could be invaluable.

"You want to help me, big boy?"

Max whined and trembled with eagerness.

He went back into the house, dropping a hand to Max's head to scratch behind his ears. "OK, boy. We're going to go get her together. We're a team."

Mel's locker had a small inflatable dinghy, something he probably used when the grandkids came. It took only a few minutes to inflate.

At the beach, he watched Max. The dog bent to track his mistress, nose rooting around the sand, stopping at the water's edge, then looking back up at him.

He pointed. "In." Max leaped into the inflatable.

He looked at the dog, the friendliest mutt on the face of the earth up until about two hours ago. Now, with blood on the side of his head from a bullet and blood on his muzzle from having mauled a man in defense of his mistress, Paige's dog stared up at him with cold, determined eyes. A warrior.

Yessir.

That made two of them.

Man and dog looked out to the island, to where the woman they both loved was being held captive.

It was three miles away. Nothing, in his SEAL days. One of their training exercises back in the day was being dropped ten miles from shore and having to swim back.

But since coming back from the dead, Max had never been able to swim more than a mile. Even that was stretching it. He'd stop in the water, cold and exhausted, knowing if he went any further he'd never make it back in.

This was three.

Towing a small inflatable with thirty pounds of gear and forty pounds of dog.

He shifted his weight onto his good leg. The bad one was aching, shooting messages of pain which he ignored.

The sun was huge, red, glimmering, halfway into the ocean. Soon it would be completely submerged, giving way to night.

Time to go.

"Let's go get Paige, Max," he said, pushing the inflatable into the water. The dog answered with a short bark.

He put on his fins, adjusted his face mask, and slipped under the surface, clutching the tow rope. Going after his woman and prepared to die in the attempt.

Hoo-yah.

Chapter Eight

Paige sat in a chair in a large empty room. Most of the room was in darkness, the only illumination coming from the big ceiling light directly above her.

At one point it had been a propagation lab. The room still had trestle tables set up for the exacting work, but everything else was gone except for a few chairs. For the first half hour after they'd pushed her into this room and taped her to the chair, she'd desperately tried to free herself. But all she managed to do was tire herself out and make her headache worse.

Each time the iron legs of the chair scraped against the concrete floor, the sound echoed in the room. However hard she wrenched, the tape held. Wrists and ankles bound with duct tape, she was also bound to the chair, the tape wrapped around her waist, thighs, and shins.

In her desperate attempt to free herself, she'd almost tipped over. She stopped immediately. Being bound to a tipped-over chair, unable to move, would be even worse than her current situation, not to mention the fact that if she fell wrong, she could knock herself out. Whatever was coming, she had to keep her wits about her to deal with it.

So she stilled and tried to reason her way out of this situation.

The problem was, she had so few data. She had an analytical mind, but it needed facts to work with.

Fact: Silvia had stumbled upon a terrible side effect of a GenPlant experiment. Paige knew that the company wasn't a corrupt fly-by-night operation. It would halt the experiments immediately. But obviously someone in the company wasn't so honourable and had hired goons to back him up in a rogue operation to keep the experiment going.

Fact: She had no idea who that was, though if she had to bet, her money would be on Jonathan Finder.

Fact: She had no idea what had happened to Silvia, or if she was even alive.

Fact: She had no idea what was going to happen to her.

Fact: Max would come for her. It wasn't a wish, it

was truth. Something about the past week they'd passed together had given her that certainty. He'd come for her as fast as he could, but he had no idea where she was. Now she regretted bitterly not talking to him about her worries over Silvia.

Why hadn't she? He wasn't a good-time boyfriend, there for laughter and sex, gone with the wind when there were problems. Everything she knew about him told her that.

She could have told him, and with hindsight should have told him, but . . . this past week had been so wonderful, so extraordinary, that she'd instinctively kept the world at bay to create a little bubble for them.

How wrong she'd been.

He'd have found her dog by now. Paige hoped with all her heart that he'd found a wounded Max and not a dead Max, but he'd understand that something violent had happened. He was probably calling hospitals in the area, maybe involving the police. But there would be no clues. Even if he found her thumb drive, it wouldn't have any concrete clues.

It seemed like hours went by and no one came for her. She simply sat, bound to a chair, trying not to panic. She had no wristwatch and no cell phone and no way to judge the time passing.

Were there guards posted outside the door? Even if there weren't, she couldn't move. And even if, by some miracle, she were able to free herself and evade the men who'd brought her here, she was trapped on an island. There was no way she could swim back to shore. It must be three miles. She'd die trying to escape.

She tried to calm herself with yoga breathing exercises but they weren't working. Her heart pounded fast and heavy. It was hard to breathe, as if something were crushing her chest.

Footsteps sounded outside and she straightened, heart rate doubling, sweat breaking out on her back.

Across the big room, the steel door unlocked with a snick and slowly opened. Paige tensed, breath caught in her lungs.

A man slowly walked into the room, identity unclear in the murky light. He stepped into the cone of light and Paige slumped in relief. Larry Pelton.

"Larry! Oh, thank God!" She wrestled one last time with the duct tape. "Get these things off me! Two men who work for GenPlant kidnapped me and they're after Silvia, too. We have to hurry!"

Larry walked up to her, reached out a hand. At first she thought he was going to rip the duct tape but he didn't have a knife. The only person she could imagine ripping that tape with his bare hands was Max, and Larry was no Max.

Instead, he put his finger to her throat and watched as his hand drifted down to the first button of her shirt.

"So pretty," he mused.

Paige was so shocked she didn't move as his hand slid into her shirt and cupped her breast. He leaned down and with his other hand grabbed the hair at the back of her head so she couldn't move, and kissed her.

Larry Pelton had been one of the world's monumentally bad kissers. Epically bad. She often thought, during their very brief liaison, that he should have his kissing license taken away. His tongue slipped into her mouth like a warm slug, retreating before she could bite him.

The door opened again and two men came in. Two armed men. The men who'd kidnapped her.

Larry smiled as he lifted his head, fisted hand in her hair tugging so hard it hurt. "Paige, my dear." He shook his head in sadness. "You and your friend Silvia have been giving me so much grief. It's going to be a real pleasure making you pay."

During Hell Week—132 hours of continuous torture—Max ran two hundred miles in combat boots and full combat gear, swam fifty miles, did a thousand push-ups, and endured hours and hours of surf torture, all on four hours' sleep. It was so grueling 70 percent of the candidates rang the bell before day two.

He did it by refusing to quit.

Simply refusing. He'd rather die.

By the end of the week he was in constant pain, and when Hell Week was over on Friday afternoon, he collapsed where he stood. At the medical exam, he had shin splints and four torn ligaments. The doctor had simply looked at him, patted his shoulder and said quietly, "Good job."

No one was going to pat his back now. It didn't make any difference because what was waiting at the other end was much more valuable than his Budweiser.

Paige.

A living Paige. Laughing in his arms.

He could face the future, even a future outside the Teams, if he had her by his side. The thought of living without Paige in his world terrified him. It would be like having all the lights switched off and living in darkness for the rest of his life.

If he had to swim to hell and back for her, he would, gladly.

He paced himself, knowing he couldn't use

his combat swim technique, which was fast and powerful. He simply didn't have the strength or the stamina. Max had trained all his adult life and he knew his body intimately. At his peak, he could almost guarantee that as far and as fast as a human could swim, that's how far and how fast he could.

But he'd come close to death. His injuries had been deep and grievous. He'd lost forty pounds of muscle and hadn't put it all back. Thinking he'd power his way to Paige was a good way to kill himself.

The thought was grinding and humiliating, but if he had any chance of surviving this, he had to do it the smart way.

His strokes were slow to conserve power, using his arms more than his legs because his left leg was almost useless.

He swam, tugging the tiny rubber boat with Max and his gear in it, emptying his mind of everything but the will to get to the island.

He surfaced for a second to get his bearings. His injured leg couldn't kick as hard and it threw him off course.

That was what he told himself, but the truth was he was reaching the limits of his strength. And he was only a third of the way there.

It was almost night, though there was just enough pewter in the sky to clearly see the island, a dark triangular shape in the distance.

Max clung to the side of the inflatable, breathing deeply, staring at the island. He glanced at his hand holding onto the tug rope. It was shaking.

The dog made a soft whining sound, shifted slightly to bring his muzzle close, and licked his hand. The dog wanted Paige back as much as he did. He was wounded—he'd been shot in the head—and yet he was unwavering. He'd jumped into the inflatable without hesitation and had remained utterly still while, underwater, Max towed him. Dogs don't have good eyesight; the way they make sense of their world is through their noses.

For the dog, Max had suddenly disappeared, and the inflatable dinghy with the uncertain footing simply began moving. It must have been terrifying, but Max saw no signs of fear in the dog, only determination.

He looked down at his hand. The trembling had stopped.

He had his team. He had his mission.

Go.

He slipped under the water again.

* * *

"You weren't very helpful to my men," Larry said casually. He'd brought a chair to sit down on, not straddling it like the goon had done back at her house, but sitting down properly, one elegantly-clad leg over the other. "They told me. That's why you're here." He *tssk*ed. "You made me come all the way over here when it really wasn't necessary, Paige."

The hair stood up all over her body and she realized, in a single swooping sensation, that the two men had had orders to kill her. She hadn't given them what they wanted and they'd understood they didn't have the technical knowledge to grill her, so they'd just grabbed her and carted her here.

The facility was deserted.

Larry could do what he wanted.

Her life was quite unmistakeably on the line.

"So, Paige. Let's have our little talk now." He shot back a cuff and checked his wristwatch. A Patek Philippe, because Larry liked his stuff. "My men in Buenos Aires should be calling at any moment to say they've got Silvia. When we've wrapped things up here, I can consider this entire episode closed."

"Are you crazy?" Paige asked, then clenched her jaw. Antagonizing Larry was not smart right now.

She made her voice reasonable. "Think it through, Larry. The data Silvia has is unofficial, yes, but it's hard data. HGHM-1 is a massive failure and will be shut down the instant the news is out. You can't hide something like this forever."

Larry smiled, the smile of a parent listening to a young child explaining the tooth fairy. "It doesn't need to be forever, my dear. There is an end point to this. HGHM-1 is officially a success. News of the fantastic test results will leak tomorrow. Gen-Plant stocks will soar. My broker is going to leak the news and says the share price will probably increase tenfold. Nowadays it's really hard to find good investments. Money will pour in. I've bought a hundred-thousand shares in the company worth a million bucks, a lot of it on spec. Multiply by ten and you've got a cool ten mil, in a week."

Paige stared at him, frowning. "But—but it's *not* a success. Even if—" she swallowed. "Even if you get rid of us and bury Silvia's data, it will come out sooner rather than later. The figures I saw speak for themselves. Anyone in the company would recognize them and close HGHM-1 right down. It's just a question of time."

As she spoke, a sense of relief washed through her. There was no incentive, really, in killing them because there'd be no stopping the process. Killing them would bring him nothing—expose him to huge risk—and that was her best defense.

"Ah, my dear," Larry said, smiling. "All I need is just a little time. When news leaks out, as it will starting tomorrow—and the share price goes through the roof—I'm going to sell at the top and bail. There's a job waiting for me at Laster Labs. New job, new life, over ten million stashed safely in Aruba. Life's a bowl of cherries, sweetheart."

She shook her head. "It's not that easy. When the shares tank, as they will, as they must, they're going to look carefully at all employees who bought and sold big blocks of shares. Insider trading is a federal offense, and—"

"Ah, ah, Paige, my dear." Larry shook his head. "I'm not stupid. My broker split the purchase up into fictitious accounts, staggered so that there's no suspicion. My broker also fronted me the money to organize this—" With a flick of his wrist he included the two thugs behind him. "What do soldiers call it? This *op*." His lips pursed around the word and made a slight smacking sound on the "p."

Paige's head fell back. "You *are* crazy."

His smile grew. "Not at all. Sane as they come, and soon to be filthy rich."

She looked at him carefully, in his casual, expensive clothes. Closely shaven, pricey haircut, fabulous shoes. It would be nice to think that the monster in him showed, but it didn't. His eyes were twinkling, a half smile on his face. As a matter of fact, he looked exactly the way he had looked at a company mixer when he'd attracted her enough for her to accept a date.

He looked perfectly ordinary. There was absolutely no way to tell that he was willing to kill two people—maybe more—or to let an experiment gone terribly bad continue and have her dog shot, all for money.

"So. Let us begin." He looked down at his neatly pressed trousers and flicked at an imaginary piece of dust, then looked back up at her, suddenly serious. He blinked, blue eyes pale and empty. And *now* Paige could see the monster in him. "Paige. My dear. Where is your dear friend Silvia?"

"I don't know."

She saw the blow coming but was unable to avoid it, was only able to brace for it.

Larry drew back his fist, punched her on the side of the head, and sent her crashing to the floor.

"Wrong answer, bitch."

Chapter Nine

Afterwards, Max would have little recollection of swimming to the shore of the island, just one long period of pain and exhaustion while wet. Just like Hell Week, which was a painful blur in his mind, punctuated by a few memories of extreme pain.

Coming up out of surf torture and running with his swim buddy to the grinder—artillery shells popping, smoke from grenades billowing, confusing them. They hardly needed smoke grenades because their breath created clouds of vapor around their heads in the biting cold.

They hadn't slept in ninety-six hours.

Crushing out a hundred-fifty push-ups, each one so painful he broke out in a sweat, though it was freezing cold and he was wet. Thank God for his combat boots encasing his ankle, because it was swollen, maybe sprained. He didn't want to look. There was blood on his uniform and he had no idea what from. At the last push-up he collapsed to the ground and rolled over, deliberately pissing his pants just to feel a little warmth on his legs.

"Wright!" One of the instructors placed a bullhorn over his face and screamed. Dougherty. The recruits called him the Antichrist. "Look over there at that bell! Nice shiny bell! Ring it and this is over! Ring it and I'll personally buy you a fucking room at the fucking Del, where you can sleep for a week on perfumed sheets! What do you say?"

"No, sir!" Max mumbled.

"Can't hear you, Wright!" the bullhorn roared.

"No, sir!" Max screamed.

He didn't ring the bell. He'd never ring the bell.

Right now, his movements in the water were slow and he was cold: signs of dangerous exhaustion. He'd known men who had simply passed out in the water from exhaustion and drifted down to their deaths.

Wasn't going to happen.

He passed the two-mile mark, stopping to come up for air, treading water, and to observe the situation. His injured leg had stopped working. He was advancing almost exclusively with his arms, muscles trembling with fatigue.

He reached into the small dinghy for his waterproof bag and pulled out the binocs. They had night vision, and with the press of a button, IR.

He scanned the area carefully, in quadrants, and saw no signs of life around the jetty. If they were expecting trouble, they were expecting it from a boat, not from a lifesaver on steroids.

Another mile to go. But, to be on the safe side, he should make landfall at least fifty meters from the jetty. He saw a little outcropping with bushes where he could hide while getting out of the wet suit and gearing up.

Another mile.

He treaded, waiting.

There was a place inside him. He'd found it during Hell Week. It had been with him on countless missions. He'd lost it when he was blown up and then found it again when he refused to become a cripple.

He needed to find it right now if he had any hope at all of swimming this last mile, when the thought of letting go and drifting down, down, down was so enticing.

That place was still in him, but there was now someone else there, too. Paige.

For the first time in his life, there was another person *inside* him, as much a part of him as his hands and legs. She was indispensable, his heart.

The future, any future without her was unthinkable. It would stretch out forever, gray and flat.

This was the first time he'd ever known fear, real fear. A SEAL wasn't afraid to die. SEALs were trained to tackle the worst, most dangerous situations. And no matter how hard the training, how excellent the equipment, shit happens, and it happens a lot in battle. Every warrior in the history of the world knows that.

Every single SEAL he knew had in some way come to terms with his possible imminent death. There had been a few who made it to BUD/S, he suspected, who welcomed death, would go forward smiling to embrace it, because they couldn't even imagine life when they were no longer young and strong.

Luckily, the trainers recognized that and weeded them out. The Teams needed men who weren't afraid to die, not men who wanted to die.

So if death held no terrors, not much else did either.

Except right now, the thought of losing Paige— that terrified him. Losing the light she brought into his life, that sharp mind that kept him on his toes, that vital essence that was purely her. That terrified him.

Paige was It. He'd dated and fucked for more

than half his life. He liked women and they liked him, but he recognized now that his head hadn't been in the game—his cock had.

There was a connection there between him and Paige that was bone-deep, blood-deep, a connection that, if severed, would be like severing an artery.

And it was the image of Paige, the memory of her kissing his shoulder before falling asleep, how she'd instinctively slow down to accommodate his leg, how she sleepily smiled at his touch first thing in the morning without opening her eyes . . . those were the things that kept him going when his body quit.

He was going to get out of this alive and he was going to bring Paige home.

And, later, after he'd made love to Paige, oh, about a thousand times just to make sure she was really safe, he knew what he was going to do with his life.

He couldn't be an active SEAL. That was off the cards. But he still had skills, rare skills.

He would never forget the gut-wrenching terror of knowing someone he loved was in hostile hands. That terror would shape the rest of his life. He was going to put his skills at the disposal of those whose loved ones had been kidnapped. He was going to dedicate his life to bringing them home, just as he was going to bring Paige home.

He moved on.

His movements in the water were mechanical, jerky, wasteful, and inefficient. But there it was—a blackness deeper than the blackness of the water right in front of him, rising up out of the ocean.

The island.

A hundred meters, fifty meters, ten meters, five, two . . . his flippered feet touched the rocky bottom and he hauled himself out of the water in the tiny cove he'd detected, hidden from the jetty by bushes. He took two stumbling steps up the rocky shore, pulling the dinghy up behind him, hearing Max leaping out. He couldn't stand up. He fell to his knees, then toppled to one side.

He woke to Max's frantic tongue lapping his face. His non-reflective watch told him he'd only been out for a few minutes. He gritted his teeth against the grinding pain of his leg and managed to stand up. His leg was trembling. It felt like he was walking on ground glass. He was overdoing it. He could lose his leg.

Didn't matter. He could live without his leg. He couldn't live without Paige.

In minutes, he was out of the wet suit and geared-up. The whole time, Max watched him soberly, sitting on his haunches, waiting for the human to get ready.

The instant Max moved toward the jetty, the dog shifted to his side, keeping pace with him, keeping close. Instinctively, the dog understood teammates stayed together.

Max knew how to meld with the night. He moved like a shadow to higher ground, up above the jetty, waiting patiently after each move to see if he'd been spotted. Hurrying and getting caught wouldn't help Paige.

He scanned with the night vision binocs and saw two men higher up. One smoking, again.

Bad for your health, you scumbag, he thought. *And so's this.*

He went for them.

Even limping badly, it was no contest. They didn't have a chance. They sucked at being security guards, though they did understand the muzzle of a gun to the nape of the neck. There were two guards, but Max was in a team of two, as well. His brave furry friend kept vigil over one of the guards, face-down in the dirt, paws straddling his head, growling low while Max trussed up the first asshole, then the other. Wrist and ankle restraints. Then good old duct tape over the mouth, and he and Max were good to go.

He took their weapons, disassembled the rifles and tossed the pieces into the shrubbery. Took their sidearms, Beretta 92s, and threw them and the magazines into the ocean.

He snapped his fingers and Max heeled. They both moved forward toward the front entrance of the building.

Max kept his nose to the ground. All of a sudden he stopped, snuffled around, then moved forward purposely.

He'd picked up Paige's scent.

Max called the dog back softly. He quivered with impatience but obeyed.

Though his leg was on fire, Max painfully lowered himself behind a bush and observed the door and the guards.

The security system was fairly sophisticated but doable.

If this had been a sanctioned op with air support behind him, Max would have preferred to infiltrate by rappelling down onto the roof from a helicopter, but he didn't have that choice here.

And anyway, Max had been following his nose and had been headed for the door. Paige had walked through that door a couple of hours ago, and so he and his teammate would, too. He had to follow the dog's lead here.

These guards were a little less Bozo the Clownish. They meant business. But then so did he.

He waited, looking for an opening. One of the guards suddenly spoke into a cop-style shoulder mic, swiped a card down the side of the big door, and entered.

Good. So he wouldn't have to blow the door down.

Ten minutes later, the guard came back, put his head next to the other guard's head, and said something. They both laughed.

A wave of coldness swept over him. Were they laughing at the idea of holding a beautiful woman hostage? By his side, Max woofed out a very soft, brief growl.

His partner was growing impatient. Fair enough, so was he.

He was tired of being nice. He shouldered the MP-5, gritting his teeth as he tried to find stability on his bad leg. Goddamn it, wasn't working. It wanted to buckle.

He leaned against the trunk of a big pine and took aim. It had to be a head shot because they had body armor.

Phhht! The asshole with the card dropped as if he were a puppet whose strings had been cut.

Max shifted immediately to the second target

and dropped him before he realized what had happened to his partner.

Max limped to the first target and took out the swipe card.

The dog had already bounded to the door, taking an indifferent sniff of the two dead men as he passed. He pointed his muzzle at the door, arrow straight.

Paige was in there somewhere.

There were no biometric data necessary, which was fortunate, though Max was perfectly willing to press a dead man's thumb against a plate or hold a dead man's retina against a scanner. They obviously felt that the water was protection enough.

Wrong.

The building wasn't a commercial building. There was no corporate lobby or even an entrance, really. Just one big corridor that led to other corridors.

This was where Max the dog did his thing.

He leaned down to run his hand over Max's head and said, in a low voice, "Find her, boy. Find Paige."

The dog took off, nose to the ground, and Max followed as fast as he humanly could. Pain jarred him right up to the top of his head every time he put weight on his leg, but he ignored it. There'd be time to take care of his leg later, once he had Paige safely home.

He would never have found her without Max. The dog moved unerringly down corridors it would have taken him hours to check and clear.

It was a labyrinthine building, built for work and not for representation. It was also empty. He encountered no one as he followed Max. At each corner, he'd stop, listen, check with his small angled mirror, then lead with his rifle, but all he encountered was air and a dog turned to him, waiting for him to follow.

There was a drumming need in him now to find Paige, the sense that a clock was ticking down. He hurried as fast as he could, shutting out the grinding pain, the drumbeat of his heart loud in his head. He needed to get to her *now*. Because something was happening *now*.

Finally, Max lifted his muzzle and stopped in front of a door. It was in the middle of a long, wide corridor with very few doors, which meant the rooms were large.

He put his ear to the steel door and heard faint voices. Male voices. Then a softer voice.

Paige!

He tested the door, opening it just enough to

slip the mirror in and narrowed his eyes as he watched. The dog stuck his nose into the crack and started wriggling. He could smell his mistress and wanted to go to her.

Max put a hand down to calm the trembling dog.

Max studied the situation in the mirror for long moments, trying to remain dispassionate. Looking at the vectors, figuring the odds, checking line of sight and angles. Because that's what he was trained to do and that's what he did well.

He didn't allow himself to think about what he was seeing.

Paige, bound to a chair, head hanging low. Blood trickling from a cut in her forehead. Paige, with a black eye and swollen jaw. Bruised and battered.

He put his reaction away, tamped it right down, put it in a box and locked it.

Observed.

Three men, two armed. All three with their backs to him.

The unarmed one sitting on a chair to one side of her, one leg crossed over the other, foot casually swinging. The interrogator.

The two armed fucks standing, holding their Berettas loosely by their sides. At that distance, they could never miss. She was tied up. They'd have plenty of time to kill her.

The man in the chair swung his leg idly, got up, walked over, and bent his head close to Paige's—much as a lover would. She moved back in revulsion and he laughed. The sound carried in the big room. He said something else and she spat at him.

It was like a frozen tableau. Nobody moved; it seemed nobody breathed.

The man next to Paige wiped his face, murmured something to her, then clicked his fingers. His voice was suddenly clear and echoed in the room. "Let's end this."

The two armed men raised their gun hands.

Max opened the door wider and lobbed a flashbang right into the geographic center of the triangle formed by the three men and, pulling the dog away with him, flattened his back against the wall next to the door, opened his mouth, and covered his ears.

There was a way to deal with sociopaths, Paige was sure. Unfortunately, she had no idea what it was.

There was no reasoning with Larry—none.

In his money-crazed head, he had the perfect plan for instant riches and the only two people stopping him from raking in amazing wealth were herself and Silvia. To him, once he got rid of these two pesky women, it was going to be smooth sailing. A hole in one.

He was going to kill her. Or, rather, have her killed, as she just couldn't see him pulling the trigger himself. It was there, in his face and in his body language.

Most of it was because he'd convinced himself that she stood in the way of a lifetime of champagne and Rolexes, but a part of it—she understood quite well—was because she had refused him. She'd wounded some deep insecurity in him and she was going to pay.

She'd told him everything she knew, bits and pieces coming out with each blow. The pain was like razor flowers blossoming at odd points of her body. Her jaw, her shoulder, a wrist she suspected was broken when he punched her so hard she fell to the floor again.

The only thing she didn't tell him was about the thumb drive.

If she'd had the slightest hope that he'd let her live, she'd have told him. No question. She ached all over, the pain deep and vicious. Anything to make this stop.

But he wasn't going to stop, and since she was as good as dead, she could leave this earth with the hope that even if they caught Silvia, too, Max could find the thumb drive, figure out what was going on, and go to the cops with the story.

Max wouldn't stop until he found the truth, though in all likelihood they'd never find her body. You can drag rivers and ponds but not the ocean. They'd weight her down, slip her body over the side of that boat, and no one would ever know what had happened to her.

He'd take care of her dog, though.

Oh God. How ironic. She'd never thought to find love, not the wild, pulse-pounding kind. She'd thought maybe someone would come along at some future point. A fellow research scientist, maybe. Some nice guy who didn't turn her off. They'd date for a year or two, then start discussing marriage.

Never, ever, would she have thought love could come in another package. Tall and broad, a warrior. A wounded warrior who woke up every sense she had and made her feel alive down to her fingertips.

And now she was going to lose that love the instant she found it.

"Tell me!" Larry said, moving his face close to hers, spittle flying from his mouth. "Goddamn you, you bitch, *talk!"*

He'd asked her a question and she had no idea what it was. Never mind. She didn't even have the strength to raise her head. When she moved it, spikes hammered into her brain and she lost her vision for a second.

She gathered her senses for one last effort and spat at him.

Larry wiped his face and stood up, waving his hand at the two goons behind her. "Let's end this."

They were raising their rifles. Oh God. This was it.

Max, she thought, a solitary tear falling down her battered face. *I love—*

The world exploded.

A flash of blinding light so intense she continued to see it behind closed eyelids, and a noise so loud she heard it through her diaphragm like a punch.

Was she dead? Is this what death was like? So bright and so noisy?

She couldn't think, she could hardly breathe. She opened her eyes, blinked, blinked again. All three men were on the floor, red seeping from their heads. Hands were tugging at her—a knife flashed, a big black one—and she shrank back, hoping it would be quick . . .

But the knife didn't cut into her flesh—it was

cutting into the hateful tape binding her. And there was, there was . . . there was *barking*. How could that be?

Suddenly the world righted itself. Max! And Max!

The last strand of tape was cut and she stood up, then fell into Max's arms because her legs wouldn't hold her. His couldn't either. They fell to the floor in a heap and she landed on warm, hard male.

"Oh God," she breathed, her lungs clogged with emotion. "You came for me!"

Max looked awful. Pale and drawn and drained, but smiling as he kissed her. "*We* came for you. Did you doubt we would?"

Her dog was barking, frantically licking her face, front paws on human Max's chest, wiggling and whining with happiness.

"No." The word came out as an explosion of joy. "No, I knew you'd come, both of you."

"Woof!" her Max said.

"Woof!" her other Max said.

"Damn straight," she answered and embraced them both.

Epilogue

One year later
Outside Eugene, Oregon

"Silvia will be here in about an hour," Paige said, flipping her cell phone closed.

Max gave a sly smile. "Cory's really happy. He just bought himself a tie. I never thought I'd see him in a tie, but once he found out she's coming, there was no stopping him."

"A tie and those new titanium-blade legs. He's going to be irresistible." He was, too. Silvia had quietly tried to pry the guest list for their wedding anniversary party out of Paige and hadn't stopped asking until Paige gave in and said Cory'd be there.

"Just as long as he doesn't con me into a race," Max said sourly.

"Because he'll win. And you hate losing." Man, did she know her husband. He'd acquired most of the use of his bad leg back, but no one could keep up with Cory's blades.

"Maybe I'll dare him and if I win he has to join us. That would be an incentive." Max's company, Search Inc., was very successful. He put together different teams for every search-and-rescue job but Cory was always part of it. Search was growing so quickly, Max wanted a partner and he wanted it to be Cory.

Search wasn't the only thing that was growing, Paige reflected. She placed a hand on her belly and smiled up at her husband.

"Did you get that shipment off?" he asked. "Of . . . things?"

Max still didn't have a complete grasp of what she did and rarely ventured into her propagation lab, a little unsettled by the silence and rows and rows of tiny containers.

"Yes, it's safely gone. And I just got ten new orders." She'd been surprised at the success of her own company, a small propagation laboratory that was growing exponentially. It felt so good to be her own boss and leave the corporate world behind.

She looked out over their home, a restored nineteenth-century homestead that she loved, her gaze taking in her lab and Max's high-tech bunker next to it, where he and his teammates planned their "extractions." It was soul-satisfying work. Last week they'd rescued a four-year-old boy.

The house glowed with candles and everything was ready for the guests, who would start arriving in about an hour.

"It's all good," Max said softly, almost to himself, then smiled down at her. He bent to kiss her, the kiss growing heated, until she pushed at his chest. He lifted his head, dark eyes glowing.

"No," Paige said. "Absolutely not. I just put my makeup on."

Max gave an exaggerated sigh, but didn't stop smiling. "A man can try."

A sharp bark sounded and Paige looked down at her dog. He lifted his muzzle and she could swear he smiled at her.

"Is that a *smile?*" her husband asked.

"I think it is. A smug one."

"Well, he's a father, after all. Puppies will do that."

Paige nestled her head against her husband's shoulder and sighed with happiness. "Well, we'll see how you react to your own puppies." She smiled into his startled face. "We're having twins."

SEALs
and Why We Love Them

Dear Reader,

Anyone who has read my books knows I often write about SEALs, simply because I admire them so very much.

I'm a romance writer and so part of what makes my writing heart tick is the appeal of my characters. On that level, any SEAL is off the charts. They are almost caricatures of manliness—brave and strong, with that relentless male focus that can be so effective, and yet can sometimes drive those of us who are married or in a relationship crazy. (I can hear you smiling.)

Their macho is in their minds—not their muscles. I've read lots of books about SEALs and memoirs by SEALs, and what shines through is the incredible intelligence of these men (for they are all men). They are smart in every way there is. They are book-smart *and* street-smart, an unusual and unusually attractive combination. Reading the memoirs, in particular, you find that these men take an often chaotic world and make some kind of sense of it.

The world they operate in is neither orderly nor rational nor kind, and they must act in ways that are orderly, rational, and, yes, kind. They are bound by rules their enemies do not in any way respect, so we're asking them to go out and fight for us, put their lives on the line for us, and—oh yes, forgot!—please do that with one hand tied behind your back.

I really admire human excellence, particularly the kind that isn't innate, the kind you have to work really hard for. The med student who spends her weekends practicing tying sutures on the bedpost; the pianist who practices those extra hours to be able to put soul—and not just technical perfection—into that Bach sonata; the scientist who runs that test for the ten thousandth time and it turns out successful, when everyone else would have stopped at the thousandth iteration. That is, perhaps, the quintessence of being human.

And, contrary to popular myth, SEALs are human, very human. They are not supermen. Bullets do not bounce off them. They bleed and they hurt and they die. They do what they do in the shadows and they do it for us.

Hats off and my heartfelt gratitude.

Lisa Marie Rice

Reckless Night

A Dangerous Passion Novella

Malua, Sivuatu
Oceania
December 23

Manuel Rabat opened his present with a heavy heart, knowing it would be absolutely perfect because his absolutely perfect wife, Victoria, was a world-class artist.

Even the fucking wrapping paper was perfect. Handmade wrapping paper. Florentine-style marbleized paper in brilliant swirls of turquoise and emerald green. A work of art in itself, something his brilliant wife probably shot off casually on some morning in which she had a little spare time.

But the gift, ah. The gift was not something shot off casually. It was the work of many painstaking hours of labor that his wife had put in because . . . she loved him.

It still astonished him.

He looked down at the small square canvas.

A portrait of his hand. His right hand on a table, a small vase of flowers in the background. He stared. It was utterly perfect. He had big, strong hands and she captured that strength, the raised veins, the scars, even the yellow calluses on the side of his hand from a lifetime of karate.

His hand wasn't beautiful, but it was large and powerful and she caught that perfectly, and set it against the delicate crystal vase of flowers in the background, the flowers at the edge of maturity, just ready to drop their petals. The contrast between the powerful male hand and the delicate bouquet was stunning.

The canvas looked ancient, like some Renaissance painting by one of the old masters that had time-travelled to their home, the dark background and earth tones of his hand offsetting the pale pastels of the flowers.

He pointed to the vase of stunning flowers. "What are those, my love?"

His wife smiled. "Peonies."

They looked like roses, only fuller, even more beautiful.

And the perfect finishing touch, giving it a patina of ancient mystery—gilt flourishes around the edges, making a golden frame within the carved wooden frame. And . . . if you looked closely, the perfectly symmetrical pattern revealed itself to be tiny interlinked "d's." Her secret signal to him, the only time she allowed herself to even think his name.

Because his name wasn't Manuel Rabat, not at all.

In a previous life, what felt like a century ago, his name had been Viktor "Drake" Drakovich. A name that had been feared and envied in many places and hated everywhere.

A name that even now would bring hit men out of the woodwork if there was even a hint that he was alive. Criminals from all over the world would come crawling out from under rocks to travel to Oceania to have the privilege of killing him.

Drake had died back in New York in a conflagration, leaving his billion-dollar arms empire behind. He had no idea if someone had stepped into his shoes, and he didn't give a fuck. That was another life.

He had enough money for ten lifetimes and above all, he had Grace, who was now Victoria.

Grace—Victoria—never ever made a mistake, not even in private. She did everything she could to keep them safe.

It was only in her many stunning handmade

gifts to him that she allowed herself their secret code. A tiny "d" somewhere in the gift. Sometimes it took him an hour to discover it.

"This is beautiful, darling," he said, cursing his inability to express fully what he felt. She'd created a masterpiece, something that, if it didn't go onto the wall in his study, would be in a museum.

Beautiful was a stupid word, an inadequate word, a nothing word.

But it made her glow. She smiled and kissed his temple. "You like it? Once—" That was her code word for the short time they'd lived together in his penthouse atop the Manhattan skyscraper that had gone down in flames. *Once.* "Once I saw your hand on your desk and there was a vase of flowers. Lilies of the valley because it was winter."

It had been snowing the day they made their escape. Sleet and snow falling heavily from the sky, together with shards of rotor blade from the rooftop helicopter his enemy had shot down. "I was so struck by the juxtaposition of your hand and the delicacy of the flowers, I knew I would paint it one day." She kissed him again. "So happy birthday, darling."

Happy birthday.

Drake had no idea whether December 23rd was his birthday or not. It had been on the passport of one of his identities while operating in West Africa as a Belgian, Hugo Van Hoof, and he'd simply retained it.

Who knew what day he'd been born? Or even what year? His earliest memories were of being a street rat on the streets of Odessa. He had no idea who his parents had been.

"My birthday," he said sourly. "And now Christmas is coming up."

She laughed because she knew perfectly well why the idea of Christmas coming up made him so exasperated. Because she'd give him a perfect Christmas present, something so unusual he wouldn't even think of needing it until she gave it to him and he'd give her—what?

It's not as if he didn't have the money to buy her things. He could probably buy her a whole country if she wanted one, albeit a small one. Maybe Andorra? Liechtenstein?

He could buy her furs, diamonds, Valentino dresses. By the ton. Chanel handbags and Gucci shoes, by the truckload. Cashmere scarves, gold-plated golf clubs, a collection of gold Rolexes. A diamond as big as the fucking Ritz.

She didn't want them.

As a matter of fact, in an attempt to keep them low profile, she specifically kept their spending down. *His* spending down because she spent almost nothing.

Every single one of the many presents she'd made him had cost very little except time and work; they had been infused with her talent and love for him and were absolutely priceless.

The thing was, Drake was very smart. He knew how to handle money, he knew how to handle weapons, he had run a fucking empire single-handedly. He could defeat more or less any man on earth in close quarter combat.

But he didn't have a creative bone in his body, not one. When he tried to think of making her a present instead of going out and buying the most expensive thing he could, he drew a complete blank. He loved her as he had never loved another human being; she was his life, his heart, but he couldn't think of anything to get her that was an expression of his creativity, which was nonexistent, and not his bank account, which was considerable.

She wasn't in any way interested in his bank account, which still astonished him.

"Come." Grace—in his head he would always think of her as Grace—pulled at his hand. "Come look at the table I set for your first-ever birthday party."

First-ever birthday party.

It was true. The thought of organizing a birthday party had never even crossed his mind. And if it had, he'd never had friends before to celebrate with. Only employees and enemies.

Grace had changed that, too. She'd invited his airline's chief pilot and his girlfriend, his driver—who was also her bodyguard though he'd never tell her that—the mayor of Malua, their new home, and his wife. Plus the president of their bank who already thought Drake walked on water after he deposited one one-thousandth of his assets into the bank. She'd also invited the manager of the art gallery she'd set up in town and his partner.

Acquaintances. Maybe—who knew? Maybe someday friends. As a matter of fact, without realizing it, they were becoming friends. This had never happened to him before.

The notion felt odd to him, like a new taste. He didn't even know if he liked the idea of having friends. He only knew he didn't *not* like it.

And the thought seemed to please Grace, so that was that.

He'd rarely if ever allowed men into his home, and only after passing three layers of security. He couldn't do that to people Grace had invited to celebrate his birthday, though he'd tried to suggest . . . but then Grace put her foot down.

Their guests were coming in through the front door without being patted down or passing through a metal detector. So dictated Grace Law, which was the law of his land.

Still . . . trust but verify as they said. The door frame of the entrance *was* a hidden metal detector that gave off a vibration to his cell phone instead of an auditory signal. He had security guards stationed discreetly, two of whom would be serving drinks on the patio.

Other guards were posted in hidden stations in their extensive garden and on the floor below.

And anyway, Drake had a sixth and even a seventh sense for who might be carrying in his presence. Guns and weapons had been his entire life up until very recently. He'd be willing to bet his life—and more importantly Grace's life—that he could spot a hidden weapon.

"Close your eyes." Grace smiled at his expression, reached out with index finger and thumb and closed his eyelids. "Come on. I have something to show you."

"Another gift?" he asked in dismay. God. Already the painting was perfect. He couldn't stand *another* perfect gift.

"Not really a gift." Drake couldn't see her, but he knew his wife so very well and he knew exactly what her expression was. Loving, smiling, just a little bit exasperated at her husband who was so competent in so many ways and yet a failure at so many things ordinary people instinctively knew how to do. "Give me your hand."

He held his hand out and she took it gently, then tugged.

"Come with me. No peeking."

He resisted for just a second. Giving up control to another human being went against every instinct he had. All of his life had been spent under the constant threat of violence. He was alive today because he had taken an inborn paranoia and turned it into a science. Otherwise that first assassination attempt in Kiev fifteen years ago would have got him, not to mention the twenty others over the years.

He was alive because he trusted no one.

He trusted Grace. With his life. It still gave him cognitive dissonance.

She loved him and she'd saved his life back in New York. The fact that she loved him was proved to him a thousand times a day.

The imperative—*trust no one!*—vied briefly and violently with the other imperative—*trust Grace!*—and trusting Grace won, as it always did. But it took a second to overcome long-ingrained instincts.

He was certain that Grace was standing there, patiently waiting while he violently and silently fought with himself, a scenario she'd seen dozens of times over.

To anyone who hadn't lived as Drake did, alone in the midst of the most violent criminals on earth, he must seem crazy. But Grace understood him, understood him down to his bones.

And loved him, notwithstanding the darkness and danger she knew lurked right underneath his surface.

It never failed to baffle him and thrill him.

"Okay," he said and heard her exhale.

She led him through a couple of rooms and stopped on what he knew was the threshold of the dining room. There was, as always throughout the house, a delightful scent of living plants, fresh flowers, lemons, and in this room, delicious food.

"Open your eyes, my love," Grace said.

His eyes popped open and he stared.

A fairyland. She'd turned the room into a fairyland, touched by magic. The room glowed with candles, candles everywhere, on every surface. Last year she'd learned how to make candles from a book and instead of producing lopsided messes as anyone else would, she produced a series of gorgeous candles that looked like flowers, candles with bits of seashell or flowers pressed into them, or twisting, sinuous, very modern elegant shapes that caught the eye.

Four huge candle-pillars were in the four corners, looking like alabaster, glowing from within. He had no idea how she'd made candles that big.

Their dining table was long. Down the center she'd cut supple branches and braided them all the length of the table, tall slender columns of wax placed in the interstices of the candles.

The centerpiece was a huge green Christmas tree candle with red hanging decorations.

The napkins were arranged in some amazingly complex way to look like flowers in the middle of the plates.

There was an incredibly fresh smell to the air as well, coming mainly from the open sliding doors leading out onto a patio and the swimming pool.

He had nearly lost his calm when she explained what she wanted in their new home. Open doors? Insane.

He'd spent his entire adult life behind the strongest walls and doors science could devise. An *open* door? So enemies could just walk in?

Drake was hard-wired by this point to give Grace what she wanted but this went against everything he knew about the world.

In the end, of course, he caved, but not before secretly creating a force field of security around the sprawling home on a bluff overlooking the ocean. He had 400 motion sensors and an array of IR cameras everywhere. If a fly shat on his property, or in a buffer zone of 100 meters around his property, he knew about it.

Still.

He looked out the open window, looked longingly at the sliders against the wall, his hands itching to close them . . .

"Relax," his love murmured, rubbing his back, and he did.

"Old habits, dusch—" She lay a finger against his mouth, a slight frown between her eyebrows and she shook her head slightly.

"People are coming," she said quietly.

Of course. Manuel Rabat, a Maltese businessman who'd spent time in America, would never say the Russian term of endearment *duschka*.

"Darling," he finished and she smiled and kissed him. Just a brush of her lips and all those unsettled . . . things inside him that baffled him and kept him off balance suddenly settled and focused and burned brightly with the desire he felt for his wife.

He didn't know what to do with the other emotions—and even acknowledging that he had emotions felt odd and jangled—but, by God, he knew what to do with this.

He fisted his hand in her soft, thick hair and deepened the kiss, everything roiling inside him suddenly still, focused like a diamond point on her, her mouth . . .

Drake was taking her down to the floor when a bell rang faintly.

One of their guests, otherwise he'd have been notified by his security staff.

Grace pulled away smiling, leaned her forehead against his. "Our guests are arriving."

"Yes." Kissing her was the only thing that could possibly make him forget that strangers—and the whole world was full of strangers as far as he was concerned—were coming to his door. Invited by him. Greeted as guests, allowed free rein of his home.

It still felt so foreign to him.

And then Drake watched Grace's face and saw something, something she forgot to hide from him. She wanted this evening. She wanted company and conversation.

He knew she hid her real feelings about the way they had to live, while reassuring him over and over that he was enough for her. That the world didn't matter.

But it did.

Sivuatu was paradise on earth in terms of weather and nature, but there was no cultural life, none. He knew that back in New York, she'd gone to almost every single concert in Lincoln Center, buying tickets that cost $25 and were up in the nosebleed sections because she had little money, but she was there. She went to all the plays in Central Park and to all the off-Broadway plays she could afford.

There was absolutely nothing like that here.

They lived in isolation, because of his paranoia. Absolutely justified paranoia, true, but limiting nonetheless.

Grace filled her life well. She spent her days painting and had thrown herself into gardening. Plants were one thing Sivuatu excelled at. She looked and acted happy.

But then she loved him and would never, ever complain. He knew her well enough to know that.

Right now, she was really looking forward to having guests. She'd enjoyed decorating the dining room. It was clear in the loving care she'd taken. She found pleasure in this evening.

So whatever it cost him in terms of peace of mind, it was worth it. His wife needed the world, or at least the tiny corner of it he felt safe to give her.

That was when the plan sprang full blown in his head. The *perfect* gift for Grace. And he could arrange it tonight!

The mayor and his wife were entering, smiling, looking around in awe. Smiling at Grace. Smiling at *him*.

Drake walked forward to greet them, wondering if this was going to become a new style of life.

Wondering whether he'd pay for it with his life.

"Well." Grace—now Victoria—laid her hand on her husband's shoulder after their guests had gone. Even now that she'd touched him a million times, it still thrilled her to feel him under her fingers.

The first time she'd touched him it had been like laying her fingers against a powerful engine, an extraordinary feeling of sheer power under her fingertips, and it was still that way.

Her husband swung his face to hers, placing his huge hand over hers. "Well."

Grace studied his face. As usual, it gave little away. Her husband had learned to school his expressions in very harsh places. "Your first birthday party. What did you think? It wasn't so bad, was it?"

"No." He gave out a little half puff of surprise, frowning. "No, it wasn't."

"And you actually enjoyed yourself, didn't you? I saw a couple of smiles break out. Surprised the hell out of me." Her husband had a bleak and dark view of life and she was making it her life's work to slowly ease some joy and light into it.

His eyes widened. "I smiled?" She understood his surprise. Smiles were rare for him.

"Oh yeah." She kissed him. "Real, actual smiles. Lips upturned and everything. They made you very handsome. I saw the mayor's wife do a double take."

"Now, that's not possible, dusch—" He stopped, shook his head, corrected himself. "Darling. I'm as ugly as sin now. You saw to that."

She hadn't seen to it so much as overseen it. A brilliant plastic surgeon had altered the major points on his face to avoid being detected by facial recognition software. He had a flatter nose now, a slightly different chin, his stark features a little more ordinary.

"Absolutely not. You could never be ugly." The smile that had been lurking broke free. "I'm so glad you had a good time, though you were so very vigilant, always. Were you expecting someone to pull out a gun and start shooting between the sea bream and the lemon sherbet?"

It wouldn't have surprised her husband if someone had. That much she knew. He was ready for anything. A hint of unexpected violence and her husband would react instantly.

He shrugged. "Actually, the dinner party was delightfully gunshot-free. And everyone had a good time."

He still seemed a little surprised at that. Grace knew that there had been almost no social events in his previous life. Any dinners with other people had been business, mainly with criminals and outlaws, and then only when his business partners insisted. Drake said he hated negotiating at the table. He'd had dinner with his lovers, but that was different.

He'd been extremely open with her about his copious sex life before meeting her, just as he'd made it abundantly clear that that part of his life was forever over.

"Of course they had a good time. You're a fascinating man and—"

"No, darling." He kissed her forehead, looking much more sure of himself now. "They had a good time because you created such an elegant setting, the food was fabulous, and you are a charming hostess. You put everyone at ease. A wild boar would relax at a dinner party you'd organized."

Grace smiled. It was true—to her astonishment.

Being able to put people at ease was this strange new ability that had just . . . materialized.

She'd spent her entire life feeling completely estranged from everyone—an alien in human skin. A struggling artist in a world that cares nothing for art, incapable of playing the games other New Yorkers found so integral to their lives.

Somehow, Drake had changed all that. He loved her as a woman and an artist, loved her exactly as she was, and it was as if his love had shattered iron shackles, setting her free. She found it easy to relate to people now, even though she and Drake led very private lives.

"We didn't have wild boars," she chided gently.

Though judging by his wariness that first hour, there might as well have been. Drake had been stiff and formal, and the whites of his eyes had shown. He'd all but rolled them in his head like a pony's sighting a rattlesnake. Then he'd settled down. Had actually disappeared with his chief pilot for half an hour. She'd suspected them of smoking a cigar but they passed the sniff test.

She stroked his shoulder. "We had perfectly nice people over for dinner with no agenda other than to have a good time. And—" she dropped the little bomblet casually, "become friends with us. With you."

Her husband was the most controlled of men. If she hadn't had her hands actually on his shoulder, she wouldn't have noticed the little jolt at the word *friends*. The notion of having friends was still something that rocked his world.

She nuzzled his neck, never tiring of the feel of him.

They'd met in violence and tragedy. He'd killed four men under her eyes before she knew his name. But from the first moment, he'd thrown a mantle of protection over her. Though he looked frightening and *was* frightening, he'd never frightened her. Not for a second.

She would never tell him and was ashamed to admit it, even to herself, but she'd fallen in love with him the instant she'd seen him. She'd been taken at gunpoint to the alleyway outside a gallery showing her paintings and had seen a powerful man, not tall but immensely broad. He was facing three armed thugs and he hadn't looked frightened at all.

He'd looked dangerous.

And she'd fallen.

But that was another time and another continent and another life. She shivered, as if to shake the memories off.

Her husband was uncannily perceptive. "What's the matter, my love?" he asked gently.

Grace didn't answer, but turned the question around. "What were you and Mike doing when you were gone so long? Were you smoking cigars? That's what I suspected but you didn't smell of cigar smoke. Were you smoking?"

She fisted her hands on her hips and tried to look ferocious.

Her amazing husband, the strongest man she'd ever seen, a man who could never be bested in combat, a man who could outshoot any sniper, threw up his hands in mock terror.

"Never!" He gave an exaggerated shiver. "Would I risk your wrath? I tremble at your feet. You barely let me eat meat. God only knows what the punishment would be for smoking a cigar!"

Grace narrowed her eyes. "If I caught you smoking a cigar, my revenge would be swift and merciless."

"Voilà!" he cried. His dark eyes gleamed. "Behold an obedient, completely smoke-free husband!"

She laughed. Getting him to eat a healthy diet was an ongoing struggle. In New York he'd lived like the Sun King and had eaten like the Sun King, too. He'd had a rotating staff of top chefs on the floor below his penthouse and they sent up elaborate four-star meals three times a day that were the equivalent of mainlining cholesterol.

Now she fed him fish and fruits and vegetables and he grumbled about having to obey the food police, but she knew he was feeling better.

"So, don't change the subject. Where did you two go off to?"

This time the smile was sly. "Ah, my darling. I went off to arrange . . . your Christmas present."

Grace's eyes rolled as she stifled a sigh. The eternal question. What could he give her? He asked her that a thousand times a day, and at each birthday, Valentine's Day, Christmas, he visibly suffered.

What could he give her?

Nothing.

She had everything she could possibly desire. A husband who loved her and whose love was made visible and tangible every second of every day. A beautiful home on a tropical island. Time and space to paint.

What else could she possibly want or need?

Certainly not the expensive baubles he kept trying to give her.

"Not another diamond?" she asked suspiciously. The last one was so big it weighed down her hand and nearly blinded her whenever they were in sunshine, which was every day in Sivuatu. After a week, it went back into its box and into a wall safe that held about a hundred of its kin.

He laughed. "You are perhaps the only woman in the world who doesn't want diamonds, my beloved. Actively dislikes them."

"I don't *dislike* them," Grace murmured.

Diamonds were rocks. Big, shiny rocks whose only purpose was to attract a huge amount of attention. A woman draped in expensive jewelry was the object of envy, sometimes hatred. The opposite of what they needed. To save their lives, they needed to fly under everyone's radar.

Drake realized in theory but not in practice that ordinariness was a protective cloak around them, one she tried to pull over them at every opportunity.

Being ordinary protected them. In New York, Drake had lived large, albeit away from prying eyes, but with an outrageous degree of luxury. And all the tight security in the world, the armed guards and bulletproof windows hadn't been enough to save him because his enemies knew he was there.

They'd gone to a great deal of trouble and effort to convince his enemies that he was dead. So why attract attention with an outrageously fancy home, high living, jewels, and super expensive designer clothes?

It was insane, suicidal.

"Diamonds attract attention, and we don't want that, my love." She twined her arms around his neck and kissed him just below the ear, a spot she knew from experience would make him shudder.

Ah, yes.

"I don't need diamonds," she whispered in his ear. "I need you."

He had his arm around her waist, holding her tightly to him and she felt him rise urgently against her stomach.

To her surprise, instead of taking her down to the ground, or over to the sofa, he stepped away with a secretive smile.

"So. All right." His voice had that slight guttural tone of arousal and she could *see* how sexually excited he was. Nonetheless, he kept himself out of arm's reach and handed her three sheets of paper. "Here's your Christmas present, two days early."

Puzzled, she took the sheets, reading carefully, not understanding until—all of a sudden—she understood.

Her eyes widened as she lifted them to her husband in shock. He was smiling. "Are these—" she held up the sheets of perfectly ordinary photocopy paper. "Are these for real? For—for us?"

"Oh yes," he answered softly. "In another name, of course."

"Of course."

They'd had several identities since their "death," and continued to have them. For example, she ordered hard copy books from Amazon to be delivered to Australia, then flown in to their island by her husband's airline under one fictitious name and credit card, and ebooks set up on her Kindle account under another fictitious name and fictitious credit card.

"These are—" All of a sudden her hands shook, the paper rattling. "These are tickets to *Aida* at the Sydney Opera House, to a showing of *Phantom of the Opera* and to a showing of *Cirque du Soleil*," she whispered. "All in Sydney."

"They are all right?" Drake asked suddenly with a frown. "On the website it said that there were live elephants onstage at the *Aida*. I don't know what that means. Who wants live elephants on a stage? Imagine if they have a bowel movement? And the other shows—apparently they are very popular. These are things you would like to see?"

"Very much," she assured him softly.

"And there is a show of 100 Picassos at the Museum of Sydney. I know you'll like that."

Grace was as tempted as she had ever been in her life. Diamonds didn't tempt her, not in any way, but *this*. An opera, two shows. *Picassos*. Her voice trembled as much as her hands as she put the printouts of the ticket reservations down, trying to conceal her sadness.

"My love, I can't accept these. I won't endanger us. It's not worth it."

They had to stay on this island forever. Drake had made that clear when they escaped the assassination attempt and made their way here to Sivuatu.

He bought the airline company flying into and out of the island and the three shipping companies whose ships docked here. He knew everyone who came to the island and surreptitiously recorded their faces. He had his finger on the pulse of the island, no question.

This island was safe.

He was shaking his head. "How can you imagine, my dusch—my darling, that I wouldn't think this through? I never operated in Oceania, never. I never even operated in southeast Asia. I cannot imagine any of my old enemies in Australia. We will fly over under assumed names on SivAir's executive jet. I have arranged for us to rent a private apartment in downtown Sydney so we won't need to check into a hotel. Australia has very few CCTVs on its city streets, much fewer than, say, London or Paris or New York. When we are outside, we will wear big straw hats and sunglasses. For the shows, I bought us box seats and bought all the other tickets in the box."

She laughed. "Of course you did."

A faint tendril of hope made its way to her heart.

"And while making the arrangements, I had no pickle. No pickle at all."

"Pickle?"

"Pickle of danger."

She forced herself not to smile, ruthlessly beat down the laugh. "No . . . pickle of danger?" The laugh lay treacherously in wait in her throat. She had a sudden image of him in one of his martial arts stances, brandishing . . . a pickle.

"Not one," he said seriously. "I have a finely honed sense of danger, perfected over a lifetime, and I am feeling nothing at the thought of us going to Sydney for three days."

She blinked at him, hardly daring to hope that this would happen.

"So." He picked up the show and opera tickets and handed them back to her. She took them with shaking hands. "Do you honestly feel I would endanger us? That I wouldn't plan this carefully?"

"I don't know." She searched his eyes. "I don't know how far you'd go to please me. It frightens me because it's not necessary. You keep harping on wanting to get me nice presents, simply because I make a few things for you by hand."

"You make me masterpieces. Priceless works of art. But much as I love to please you, you don't think I would endanger you needlessly, do you?"

Put that way . . . "No."

"So." It was his favorite word. He had the faintest traces of an accent. He'd grown up an orphan on the streets of Odessa. In his previous incarnation as the head of a huge crime syndicate, he spoke five languages perfectly and another five well enough to negotiate. His English was nearly perfect and the slight accent bothered no one in Sivuatu as they expected a Maltese man to have an accent.

But she found it so sexy when he said "so." Drawing the word out. *Zooo*.

"So. We are going. We will spend Christmas among the throngs in Sydney, seeing shows and Picassos and, God help me, an opera." This last said with a painful wince and she laughed. "Are you happy?"

He'd done this for her. How could she not be happy?

"Oh yes. Incredibly, wildly happy." She was studying the tickets, imagining *Aida* and the *Cirque*. And the *Phantom*! All those years in New York and stupidly, she'd never gone, though she loved the CD and knew the songs by heart. She stared at the white mask with the red rose logo.

"And are you grateful?"

"Oh yes," she answered dreamily, thinking of the three days ahead of them.

"*How* grateful?" She looked up in surprise at the suddenly harsh, hoarse tone.

And blushed.

They had a fabulous sex life. Drake was an attentive, tender lover who took his time in pleasing her. But every once in a while something in him changed and she caught a glimpse of the truly dangerous man he really was. She hadn't tamed him, not one bit. He just chose to show her a tender side he said he'd only discovered with her.

But sometimes the tiger in him growled and clawed its way to the surface. And then the sex was incandescent.

His entire body was tense, tendons standing out on his strong neck, huge hands flexed. Those dark brown eyes glowed as if there were a power source inside him that had suddenly roared to life. As she watched, a huge shudder went through him. "I said—how grateful?"

Watching his transformation was amazing but even more amazing was what happened to her in those moments.

Something—something *animal* in her awoke, too.

A flush of extreme heat washed over her, head to toes, the heat fizzing under her skin, glowing between her thighs. She could barely breathe, barely form the words.

"Very." Her throat was tight, almost closed. Speaking was hard because speaking wasn't what she wanted to do. "Very grateful."

They weren't touching but it was as if a red-hot flaming rod connected them. She could see his arousal even without looking down at his groin. It was in his face, the flush over those high cheekbones with a hint of Tartar blood, the tight mouth, flared nostrils.

And he could see hers, too. She had very pale skin that showed most emotions. Now it would be flushed. Sweat broke out on her back, a drop curled between her breasts.

"Show me," he whispered darkly. "Show me how grateful you are."

"Okay," she whispered back.

Driven by something entirely beyond her control, Grace took her clothes off. Slowly. Not because she wanted to entice him with some kind of striptease—when he was like this, he needed no enticement—but because her hands shook and her knees felt so weak they could hardly keep her upright. She had to move slowly or she'd fall down in a puddle of heat.

Or blow up.

Thick bands of steel encircled her chest, making it hard to breathe. Spots swam in front of her eyes.

With trembling hands, she reached to the side. Her dress was held at the waist with a small sash anchored by a bow. She undid it and the two panels fell open. Underneath was a strapless bra and panties. She did indulge in expensive underwear, because it couldn't be seen and because it turned on her husband.

He was massively turned on now. She could almost see the waves of arousal coming off him like smoke. He nearly vibrated with desire.

"Off. Dress."

Now she knew how aroused he was because he was losing his faculty of speech. And syntax.

Slowly, she pulled the emerald green linen sheath off her shoulders, letting the dress fall to the floor.

His eyes flared and he waved his hand impatiently at her.

Deep breath. His big hand had all but sent waves of heat her way, hitting her groin like bolts of fire.

She reached behind her, unsnapped her bra. The light silk fluttered to the floor. At any other moment, she'd have admired the pale green silk on the dark emerald green linen, but her brain was too blasted to notice aesthetic niceties. All she felt was heat turning her bones liquid.

"Panties," he said, his voice guttural. His dark eyes studied every aspect of her body so intensely it was as if he were touching her instead of watching her.

Panties. Oh God. Taking off her panties was going to require balance and her legs could barely hold her. She gripped the edge of the chest of drawers with one hand, while pulling down her panties with the other. They, too, fluttered softly down to land around her ankles.

"Off."

Still gripping the corner of the chest of drawers, she lifted one sandaled foot, then the other. While he watched, one foot nudged the soft silk panties over to the pile of clothes.

She was naked and about ready to fall over.

Drake didn't move. He simply watched her with molten eyes, still fully dressed.

"Do you want me?" he asked hoarsely.

"You have no idea," Grace whispered.

"Show me."

Show him?

She looked down at herself. Her nipples were

hard, cherry-red. Her left breast fluttered with her pounding heartbeat. Of course, he couldn't see her liquid knees, couldn't feel how tight her chest was.

There was only one other thing she could show him.

Grace parted her legs, one knee slightly bent. Looking down, the angle was wrong for her, but surely he could see the lips of her sex glistening? With her legs spread, the air felt cool on her wet sex.

"Show me more," he insisted.

O-kay.

Still gripping the corner with white fingers, Grace ran her free hand slowly down the center of her body. Her skin felt hot to the touch, slightly damp. One finger between her breasts, then the flat of her palm over her belly.

Drake's gaze followed her hotly, riveted on her hand.

When she stopped her hand along her lower belly, his gaze snapped up to hers.

He didn't even talk, just jerked his head downward.

More.

She nodded jerkily.

They were both beyond words now.

Grace opened her hand and slid it between her legs, closing her eyes as she touched herself. She needed Drake's touch, she craved it, her vagina wept for it. At least her fingers quenched the red-hot heat, if only a little.

She ran her index and middle fingers along the lips of her sex and moaned a soft exhale of breath.

Drake shuddered again, throughout his entire body.

Slowly, because if she moved quickly, her legs would give way, Grace slid her middle finger inside her and breathed out again in a harsh gasp, as if she'd been hurt.

It wasn't pain she was feeling.

Drake moaned too.

She slid her finger out a little, then back in. It wasn't anything like feeling her husband's member inside her, but it was something. Anything was better than this empty, hungry heat that cried for his touch.

When she slid her finger back in, her vagina clenched around it, hard. Her legs instinctively tightened, her stomach muscles pulled.

She looked down, saw it, looked up at her husband. He saw it too. Her hand slid away and she showed it to him. The palm of her hand and especially her middle finger coated with her juices.

She licked her middle finger.

It was as if he suddenly burst free of restraints. He lunged for her, pulled her against him while somehow, at the same time, freeing himself, pulling his huge, erect penis out from his pants.

With one arm her husband, the strongest man she'd ever seen, lifted her up, settling her legs around his waist, and entered her with one hard thrust.

They were kissing wildly and they both exhaled as he pushed hard into her.

With no effort whatsoever, one hand behind her head, the other holding her by the hips, Drake walked them to the bed.

Every step moved him inside her, inside her highly sensitized tissues, even the slight movements almost as exciting as his thrusts.

She was whimpering by the time he reached their huge bed. Bending over slowly, still embedded inside her, he gently placed her back on the bedspread and sprawled on top of her. When bending, she could feel the iron-hard muscles of his stomach against hers through his silk shirt.

It was exciting, being completely naked against him, his penis deep inside her, while he was fully dressed. She could feel the unyielding muscles of his back and shoulders under the silk shirt against the inside of her arms, the back of his hard thighs, encased in the polished cotton pants, against her legs.

She felt completely open, completely vulnerable to this hard, tough, highly dangerous man who would never hurt her.

His penis was like a hard, hot club inside her.

He was huge. When they made love, his foreplay lasted forever because he wanted to make sure she could take him without pain. He'd been able to enter her in one stroke only because she'd been so excited and so very wet.

She pulsed around him, another hard pull of her vagina and he winced.

"Not yet, my love."

The words ran around her empty head, not making much sense. But there was only one answer to her husband. "Okay," she panted.

Grace lifted herself, eyes closing as she felt him lengthen even further, something that should have been impossible. Already it felt as if he were reaching up into her heart.

She pulsed around him again and felt him jerk inside her.

"Wait!" He moved around on top of her doing something that pushed him even further inside her.

A shoe thumped on the floor, coupled with a

huge thump of her heart. Her entire body stilled, centered totally on where he was inside her, so hot and heavy.

Moving on her, in her, another thump and she exploded in a climax, writhing under him, clinging to him with her arms and legs as she clenched around him explosively, pulling hard on his penis with her internal muscles.

Her back arched and sounds came out of her mouth, animal sounds, sounds almost of pain while the firebomb of heat kept her pulsing against him, clenching rhythmically, shaking with the intensity of it.

Finally, the pulses died down, became less intense, less on the knife's edge of pain. Became a sensual pleasure, like rocking on an endless warm ocean. And then stopped.

She was coated with sweat from head to toe, utterly incapable of thought, incapable even of directing her muscles. Her arms fell to her sides, her legs opened, no longer able to cling to his hips.

She relaxed utterly, rocking on that endless ocean, simply breathing and enjoying the aftershocks of intense pleasure.

Finally, she was able to open her eyes, only to find his dark brown eyes staring into hers from less than an inch away. He was so close she could feel the wash of his breath over her face.

He smiled, a slow curling of his lips that made her toes curl.

"Ah, my love. If you climaxed that hard when I took off my shoes, what's going to happen when I take off my pants?"

Sydney, Australia
The next day

Drake stood at the huge picture window of the luxury penthouse apartment he'd rented. It had been expensive, but that was nothing. As a matter of fact, if this trip went well, and Grace enjoyed herself, there might be other trips to Sydney and he would buy this apartment or one like it.

They wouldn't come often. It is not good to tempt fate, as the Americans said. Maybe twice a year. He could just buy this flat under an assumed name and keep it for their use.

Because, well, Grace was excited and happy, and next to keeping her safe, that was his priority.

The apartment wasn't a fortress like his penthouse in Manhattan had been. The windows weren't bullet-resistant, as they had been in Manhattan. The truth was, though, that with all his security in Manhattan—the armed guards 24/7, the elaborate electronic sensor system, the bulletproof windows—it hadn't been enough to keep him safe.

The assassin's attack had almost taken his life and would have if not for Grace, who'd saved him.

New York had been dangerous for him in a way Sydney was not.

New York was a nexus for the kind of men who bought what he had had to sell. No doubt there was some kind of arms trade in Sydney but it was small scale and didn't involve the major global players. He should know. He'd been at the top of the pile.

He looked out over the exquisite harbor, the brilliant setting sun painting everything with a vivid glow, bringing out the intense colors of the ocean, the light reflecting like diamonds off the many beautiful buildings.

Seeing things from an aesthetic point of view was new. It was his curse and his pleasure, and entirely Grace's fault. All his life, it had never occurred to him to look at things and see their beauty. All he had ever done was scan his environment for threats and, God knows, there had been enough of them.

Threats.

He sent out his senses, reviewed the situation. They'd flown over in his company's private jet. They'd entered the country under different identities, he'd rented the apartment in the name of a shell corporation that could never be traced back to any specific human being, and the tickets had been bought in the name of yet another identity.

They'd worn broad-brimmed straw hats and large sunglasses from the airport to the apartment, which was perfectly plausible since it was nearly 100 degrees outside.

Heat at Christmas. He'd spent his entire life in the Northern Hemisphere with the exception of two visits to Johannesburg. A balmy Christmas season still surprised him.

It had been 92 degrees in Sivuatu when they'd left.

He admired the scenery while continuing to scan for threats, but nothing pinged his radar.

Of course, it was perfectly possible that his radar had been permanently ruined by the most frightening emotion known to man—happiness.

Happiness could kill him.

Happiness terrified him and fascinated him. He'd never been happy in his previous life. Though he'd been the top player in a dangerous game for a very long time, his ascent there had been brutal and he'd had to remain vigilant every second of every day to stay alive on the top of that heap.

What he'd had had seemed enough. Power and the luxuries money could buy.

But then, of course, there was the blood price to be paid—hatred and fear and envy. Murderous rage. Men on three continents whose only thought was to assassinate him and take his place.

Vigilance was in his DNA, but he'd had little reason to exercise it since he'd died and started his new life with Grace.

Was he getting soft?

He mulled that over. A safe life, someone to love . . . would that be his downfall? Men had been known to grow soft, lose their edge, and then their life.

He searched inside himself carefully because he was betting not only his life but Grace's.

No. Certitude settled in his chest. They were safe. This could be done. This might even be the new normal.

A safe, happy life with the woman he loved. Un-thinkable before now.

"Darling?"

Drake whirled and his heart turned over in his

chest. How could that be? They'd been together a year. He'd had her hundreds of times. He knew her body and her soul inside out. And yet, there it was.

When he saw her unexpectedly, his heart would give this huge thump in his chest like a heart attack, only not. He knew because he'd gone to a cardiologist and had his heart checked. The doctor had smiled and said he would live to be a hundred.

It was Grace who did this to him.

There she was, in a beautiful dress she'd had made from a bolt of pale turquoise Chinese silk her seamstress's son had sent from Shanghai. It had cost practically nothing. The seamstress was superb but inexpensive.

Grace had made her own jewelry—glass beads with intricate swirls of color strung on strands of silk. She had a cream shawl in case the air turned chilly later on, simple sandals, a simple small black purse. Her entire outfit cost about half what he usually spent on wine at dinner with one of his mistresses back in Manhattan and she looked like a million dollars.

"You look beautiful," he said softly and she looked up at him in surprise.

His entire body felt on edge, skin too tight to contain it.

"Thank you," his love said with a smile. She walked up to him and touched his cheek. He covered her hand with his and brought her hand to his mouth. He touched his tongue to her palm and watched her pupils dilate.

Ah, yes. She felt it, too.

Grace stepped back sharply, as if against a magnetic current.

She shook her head. "I know what you're thinking. And much as I'd like to play with you, we have reservations for dinner and the opera."

"Yes, ma'am." With some difficulty, Drake reined himself in. Over the course of the past year, he'd grown used to having Grace whenever he wanted. There had never been any constraints other than if she was feeling desire or not.

She felt desire right now, it was clear. A faint rose under her light tan, breathing irregular and fast. Oh yes, she desired him too.

But he *could* have her, any time he wanted. It would be selfish of him to indulge himself now and miss the dinner date, when dinner and the theater were his Christmas gifts to her.

Drake had a great deal of control over his body. He'd held perfectly still while a bone had been set and stitches had been taken without anesthesia. He could deal with the tiny bite of deferred lust.

He held out his arm like the gentleman he wasn't.

"Ma'am? I thought we'd walk to the restaurant. It isn't far."

He enjoyed the inrush of breath, the blinding smile she turned up at him, the blush of joy. "We can walk to the restaurant? That would be wonderful. It's a beautiful evening. But—but is it safe?"

For the millionth time, Drake realized what he'd asked of Grace. To give up almost everything for him. She'd told him she used to love taking long walks around Manhattan. They hadn't gone for a walk—a real walk—since they escaped the assassination attempt over a year ago.

He tucked a shiny red-brown lock of hair behind her ear and bent to kiss her cheek. "We can walk."

They took the elevator down and plunged into the happy Christmas crowds on the street. Grace's head was swiveling to catch everything. He knew she was storing up images, colors, shapes, and nuances of light.

His head wasn't swiveling but he was alert. They walked a pedestrian street filled with happy crowds. Some kids were breakdancing and they stopped to watch. They were very good, a delight to watch. Fluid and lithe, awash in the joy of youth and health. Unobtrusively, Drake let an Australian hundred dollar bill flutter into the silk top hat on the ground.

"Your spidey sense telling you everything is okay?" Grace's amused voice sounded behind him.

He turned to meet her smiling eyes. "Hmm? My spidey sense?"

Grace laughed, hooked her arm through his again. "Obviously, your knowledge of pop culture is deficient. It comes from Spiderman. He has a spider's senses, greater than ours. Your pickle."

He looked down at her and she laughed again, elbowing him in the side. "Your pickle? Of awareness?"

"Oh." Drake looked around as they walked. No, strolled. *Strolled.* To his certain knowledge, he'd never walked slowly through any city, enjoying the sights. And for the last ten years of his criminal career, he'd never walked at all, but had himself driven from point A to point B in an armored Mercedes with tinted windows and its own air supply. Cut off from the world in a steel cocoon of safety.

Never, ever like this—alive to all the sights and sounds and smells of a great city.

He expanded his awareness. He had a highly refined sense of danger, born of a lifetime of battle. An entire lifetime where a moment's inattention, underestimating an adversary, not noticing the details of a hidden threat could get him killed.

Danger usually manifested in a sense of dread, a tingling at the nape of his neck, cold in the pit of his stomach.

Nothing. He was feeling absolutely nothing like that. No coldness, no darkness. No threat. Just happy human beings as far as the eye could see. Some were hurrying, yes, from point A to point B, but most were ambling along, looking at the brightly lit shop windows, enjoying the last of the sunshine. Many poking their heads into restaurants, planning the evening meal.

How had he missed this his entire life? All this movement and activity, sights, sounds, smells? There was a palpable essence in the air he could only ascribe to happy people all in one place and it was something he had never experienced before. Something he had never even known was possible.

"No pickle at all," he said absently. He took another sweep, encountering only people minding their own business, with no interest in him whatsoever. If anything, a couple of men took appreciative looks at Grace, then turned their heads when he stared them down.

"It's nice, isn't it?" Grace rubbed her head against his shoulder, the kind of gesture that still baffled him. A gesture of affection, totally unrelated to sex. "Being with all these happy people on a sunny day?"

"Yes, my love. It is. It is very nice."

By now Drake had grown used to Grace's uncanny understanding of his emotions. At times, she seemed to understand him better than he understood himself.

It would have frightened him, but the one thing he had come to understand this past year, the thing that now formed the bedrock of his existence, was that Grace truly loved him. He was safe in her hands, in every way.

"I checked the map. The restaurant is not far from here. And the opera is just around the corner." He gave an exaggerated shudder and Grace laughed again.

This was all so delicious. So unusual. So . . . so *new*. He was getting no danger signals at all. He saw very few security cameras and was certain that their hats and sunglasses were sufficient disguise.

So. They might be able to do this a few more times.

It would please Grace and damned if it wouldn't please him.

A quarter of an hour later, they were at the restaurant.

The restaurant was beautiful. *La Mer.* Modern fusion cuisine with French overtones, or so the restaurant site had told him. He had no idea what that meant, but the food smelled delicious.

It was a large, modern space filled with light. The entire back wall was plate glass doors looking out over the glorious harbor. The doors were open. Directly outside the doors was a long, narrow infinity pool, artfully situated so that it looked as if the edge of the pool merged with the ocean.

Instead of air-conditioning, there were big ceiling fans and an ocean breeze wafting through the room.

Waiters bustled by holding plates of food that looked like works of art. Judging from the pleased expressions of the diners, the food tasted as good as it looked.

Grace stopped on the threshold, looking around slowly. Her face glowed as she sighed with pleasure. "This is fabulous! And the food smells so good! However did you find it when you said you'd never been to Sydney before?" She smiled up at him. "What a foolish question. You Googled 'Most expensive restaurant in Sydney.'"

He winced. Actually it had been "Best restaurant in Sydney" and La Mer had come up as first choice on nine out of ten lists.

He'd checked out the floor plan and the promise of an extra 150 dollars had ensured a table at the far end of the room, close to the doors and the wonderful view.

Seated, he sat back and watched Grace order for them. He didn't care what the fuck he ate. It would be good. And it was just so wonderful watching her as she concentrated on the menu with a ferocious frown.

"I hope you like what I ordered for you," she said finally, after endless discussions with their friendly, patient waiter. It had taken Drake less time to negotiate a ten million dollar sale of arms to an Abkhazian warlord.

"All fish," he said with a sigh. He would have preferred meat, but she had him on a strict meat quota and he'd eaten his quota for the month last week. "I'm sure I'll enjoy it," he added politely. "Maybe they will have to catch the fish and it will take so long to catch it and cook it that we will be late to the opera."

She laughed and he smiled at the sound. He loved hearing her laugh.

A wine steward with spiked dyed-blond hair poured them the wine she'd ordered. A South African Chardonnay.

Delicious.

It was a sign of his ease that he would drink alcohol in public. Something he would never have done in his previous life.

That was how he was starting to think of it. A previous life. Another one entirely, not his, not any more.

This was his life now. Walking down a shopping street full of people. A delicious meal in a beautiful restaurant. Later, the opera. His pleasure dimmed a little at the thought, but who knew? Maybe the new Drake—Manuel Rabat—might actually enjoy it. He knew he'd certainly enjoy his wife's delight.

A life of—of *enjoyment*.

Unthinkable before.

Quite possible now.

The waiter slid appetizers in front of them. Fried baby octopus, oysters wrapped in prosciutto, hot clam dip. Some fish he didn't recognize with a ginger and chili sauce. Fried focaccia bread triangles with brie mousse.

"Oh God," Grace moaned as she spread the mousse and popped a focaccia in her mouth. "This is delicious!"

He would have smiled if his own mouth hadn't been full.

Grace looked around again once the appetizers were gone. "It's so strange to have all this Christmas spirit in summer. A hot weather Christmas."

It was. Jazz renditions of Christmas carols played softly in the background. A huge Christmas tree made of lit glass cylinders glowed in a corner. Palm leaves studded with tiny lights were twined around the balustrade of the iron and glass staircase leading up to a loft.

A fat Santa Claus waddled through the entrance, fake beard moving in the breeze generated by the ceiling fans.

It was Christmas but unlike any Christmas he'd ever seen. Hot and sunny. Perfect beach weather.

Australians were an informal people and most of the diners even in this expensive restaurant were in sundresses and Bermudas, with acres of suntanned skin showing.

Grace touched his hand. "We'll get used to it."

"Oh yes," he said softly.

Yes, they would. He hated the cold. He'd spent his entire childhood on the streets of Odessa. In winter, he'd desperately tried not to freeze to death, huddling in doorways and over grates. If he was never again cold in this lifetime, he'd be a happy man.

And . . . well, he *was*. He was a happy man. The thought still stunned him.

"We can make this a Christmas tradition," he told Grace. "Christmas in Sydney. My Christmas gift to you."

"The opera," she sighed and rolled her eyes at his expression. "Verdi, Puccini, Wagner."

Drake shrugged and drank another sip of wine to help make the thought go down.

The piped-in music segued to a lovely saxophone rendering of *Do You Hear What I Hear?* One of the few carols he recognized. The soulful music, gentle and soft in the background, filled his head.

Nearby, a flame ignited at a table as the waiter threw cognac over some kind of creamy dessert and lit it. A woman at the table with the flambé dessert threw her head back and laughed.

Santa Claus was making the rounds of the tables shouting *Ho! Ho! Ho! Merry Christmas!*

The maître d'hôtel stepped away from his station frowning.

Their waiter slid a steaming oval platter of sea-food risotto in front of a diner at the table next to them. Drake looked over with interest because he'd ordered it. Or rather, Grace had ordered it for him. It looked excellent and—

Ice hit his stomach.

His head lifted. He was suddenly alert.

Music, food, wine instantly forgotten.

What he was in his essence—an animal under constant threat—came instantly to the fore.

He looked carefully around the restaurant, no longer happy, no longer relaxed. If he'd been a submarine, the torpedo signal would be going off. He scanned the restaurant as a sniper would—in quadrants, careful to take in every single element.

Happy diners, innocuous-looking serving staff. A fat Santa Claus wishing everyone Merry Christmas.

What was wrong?

The frowning maître d' was conferring with the head waiter, heads together.

Drake started slowly hyperventilating. Whatever was wrong, his body knew it needed extra oxygen to deal with it.

He'd had his hand over Grace's and now removed it. He would need both hands.

Fuck. He was without weapons. He was a

superb shot but he was without any firepower whatsoever. It had been an executive decision. His jet had a disassembled long gun and a Beretta in a lockbox camouflaged as a first aid kit, but he'd decided to enter Australia clean. If he bought an apartment here, he'd stock it with weapons. Just in case.

A woman laughed and clinked glasses with another woman at a table ten meters away. They were obviously celebrating something.

His stomach twisted, muscles readying themselves for action.

What was wrong?

"Ho ho ho! Merry Christmas!" the Santa Claus cried, edging his way through the tables along the wall.

The maître d' was talking into a cell phone.

"Ho ho ho! Merry Christmas!"

It was delivered in the exact tone and cadence as before.

Drake looked at the Santa Claus more closely. There was something about the tone of the voice . . . at the next *ho ho ho* he got it.

It was a recording, the words on a loop every two minutes or so. He was wearing an excellent Santa Claus outfit. Even Drake, who'd never celebrated Christmas, could see that. The suit excellently tailored, made of expensive material. Snow white, blood red. Big black belt around a huge belly.

Santa Claus was making his way around the perimeter of the room, waving his hands covered in white gloves, wishing everyone a Merry Christmas in a recorded voice on a loop.

He was coming closer to Drake's table now. Drake could observe him more clearly.

All Drake's senses went on overdrive. The smells and sounds became acute. His vision sharpened. He'd swiftly eliminated all the diners as the source of his sharp sense of danger and now focused on Santa.

The suit, the felt cap, the fake beard—they all looked very hot on this warm evening. Sweat fell down Santa's face. Taking with it pale makeup. Beneath the makeup, Santa's skin was very brown.

The sweat was removing the pale makeup entirely, falling to the red jacket in pale streaks.

Santa's belly looked lumpy, as if full of hard things and not soft stuffing.

The maître d' finished his phone call, closing the cell with a snap, and headed Santa's way.

Santa saw him coming. His dark brown eyes opened so wide the whites showed and Drake's highly evolved danger signals overloaded.

Time slowed down almost to a stop.

Santa pulled at his jacket, closed with Velcro, the ripping sound preternaturally loud to his ears.

The maître d' was twenty meters away, raising his hand to Santa, palm out. The universal stop sign.

The panels of the red Santa suit were slowly pulled apart by Santa's white-gloved hands and instead of cotton stuffing there was a vest with black cylinders attached, a string with a round pull hanging from the cylinders.

In this time out of time, Santa's hand slowly moved up to tug at the dangling string while the maître d' shouted and Drake picked up the silver charger from his table with one hand and a sharp filet knife from a nearby serving tray with the other and hurled both at Santa with all his strength.

The charger and knife slowly, slowly made their way to Santa's throat just as Santa's hand closed around the string.

"Allahu akhbar!" Santa screamed.

Again, in that slow-motion state of time during combat, as soon as the charger and knife left Drake's hands, he slashed upward, knocking over the heavy wooden table so it was between him and Santa and pulled Grace to the ground, covering as much of her as he could, while Santa fell into the infinity pool.

Then time came roaring back.

There was a huge explosion, the sound making his diaphragm vibrate. Drake hunched over Grace, wishing he could punch her into the ground to give her more protection, his arms around her head.

A red rain fell while screams started up all around them. Horribly, a severed white-gloved hand thumped to the floor an inch away from him, bouncing once then rolling away.

"Grace," he shouted above the screams, still slightly deaf from the explosion. He lifted slightly and touched her frantically all over, face, torso, legs. "Are you all right?"

She was in shock, eyes wide in a completely white face. She nodded and swallowed heavily.

He chanced a look around, taking his attention away from Grace for just a second.

The diners, so happy and content only seconds ago, were screaming and scrambling for the door, tables and chairs overturned, slipping and sliding on the platters of food that had been dashed to the floor.

The infinity pool was red, bits and pieces of human being floating to the surface.

Drake took in the situation in a flash. There was confusion and a number of people were bleeding, one woman stared at her red hand and started screaming. Several people walked around, dazed.

But there was no one on the ground in the unmistakable sprawl of death. Everything Drake saw was minor—cuts and contusions and shock. The water had absorbed most of the blast.

The only dead man was the fucker in the suicide vest and he was now safely in that special hell reserved for people who killed in the name of God.

A siren started up outside, then two.

"My darling!" Drake kissed Grace, held her tightly. He could have lost her but he hadn't. His miracle of a wife, safe.

He was trembling. Drake had spent his entire life in combat, he had learned to keep his head in combat, otherwise he'd have been long dead.

But now he trembled as he embraced his wife.

Under him, Grace stirred, her arms snaked around his neck, hanging on to him as tightly as he clung to her.

Her rapid breaths of shock sounded loud in his ear, her heart hammered against his chest.

All wonderful signs that she was alive.

She gasped, as if she'd stopped breathing, took in a huge breath that sounded like a sob.

"Drake," she whispered, and he knew how shocked she was to use the name she'd forbidden herself to ever pass her lips.

"Right here," he answered back. He kissed her temple. "It's over now. It's all right. We're fine."

Her arms tightened even more, then relaxed slightly. "Drake?"

He lifted his head, able now to smile into his wife's eyes. "Hmm?"

She drew in another breath, and let it out shakily.

"Your pickle?" Grace lifted her head and kissed him. "Best. Gift. Ever."

Hot Secrets

A Dangerous Lover Novella

Summerville, Washington
Early morning, December 24

Jack Prescott kissed his wife's shoulder and watched as she smiled in her sleep. That smile came from the deepest part of her and was just for him.

It still dazzled him, a year into marriage. *She* still dazzled him.

Caroline. His wife. Caroline Lake, now Caroline Prescott. The woman who'd been in his head more than half his life and now was his.

He'd showed up exactly a year ago—in her bookstore in the middle of a snowstorm—after flying nonstop for forty-eight hours from Sierra Leone. Sierra Leone had been his last mission, an homage to his dead adoptive father.

On a pirogue from Abuja to Freetown, from

Lungi Airport to Paris, Paris to Atlanta, Atlanta to Seattle—and onto a tiny puddle jumper that barely made it through the wild weather, straight to Summerville. Thinking of Caroline every second of the way, the woman he'd never been able to get out of his head. While he joined the army, earned his Ranger tab, fought in innumerable hellholes throughout the world—there she'd been. Beautiful, kind, smart. The woman of any man's dreams and out of his reach throughout his twelve long, lonely years in hard and violent places.

She'd been in his head since he was a boy in a homeless shelter, bringing him books and food and a sense of the outside world, a world that didn't mean living with filthy crazies and violent drunks.

She'd been there in his head when he'd run away, was adopted by his father of the heart, Colonel Eugene Prescott. She'd been there through his deployments to bad places, trying to lend some order to a violent world. She'd been there over long, lonely nights in faraway hellholes, reminding him there was something in the world worth fighting for.

She'd been there so long, was so deeply embedded in his very soul, that when his adoptive father died and he inherited a fortune, he went back to where he'd been a lost boy and expected to find a married woman with kids—because what sane man wouldn't marry someone as beautiful and smart as Caroline?

But the world was made of wusses. Caroline had lost her parents, lost all her family money, and had looked after a badly injured younger brother for the better part of a decade—and not many men would put up with that.

He would have, no question. For Caroline he'd walk across lakes of fire, climb mountains of thorns, slay every dragon there was. Gladly. A sick brother was nothing. Plus, he had plenty of money of his own.

When he showed up on her doorstep, expecting to find a married Caroline and just wanting to see her one last time before starting the next stage of his life, it turned out she wasn't married after all and she *was* the next stage.

And he—the man who'd never had a family, the man who had known in his bones he'd never have a family because families were for other people— well, now he had a family of his own. Caroline. And the children they'd make.

At the thought of Caroline pregnant, his cock— already hard—turned to stone. A wave of heat washed over him and his breathing sped up.

It was the hardest thing about being married to Caroline. Everything else about marriage to her was incredibly easy. Intensely pleasurable. Around-the-clock delight.

She was even-tempered, without those mood swings that drove him crazy with other women. She was wicked-smart, with a sharp sense of humor. She was kind-hearted. Their home was beautiful, she was a fantastic cook. He'd never been as physically comfortable as he was being her husband. Everything was absolutely perfect, except—

Except he desired her so very much. All the time. It never seemed to switch off, and Jack had to restrain himself—otherwise he'd have Caroline on her back, fucking her hard, more or less all the time—day and night—and that wasn't good.

The desire was sometimes like a low-level ache, sometimes as sharp as a snakebite, but there, always.

Still . . . it was early morning. They'd last made love the previous night, before midnight. Technically, it was another day, wasn't it?

And if he didn't have her right now he'd die.

There would be a point in their marriage when he'd cool off, he knew there would be—he just didn't know when.

She was wearing one of those silky nightgowns he loved. When he slid his hand under the gown, he could feel the silk of her skin along his palms and the silk of the gown against the back of his hand.

He was spooned around her, a position both of them loved. He felt her smooth warmth all along his front, and even in sleep it felt like he could protect her. Surround her with his body, arms tucked around her middle. He felt like the dragon protecting the princess. During the day he had to let her go out into the world, of course. And he couldn't be there all day by her side, armed and ready. Even he understood that. So all day as he went about his business, he had a low-level hum of worry about her. In the very beginning of their marriage he'd call a billion times a day just to hear her voice.

He'd almost lost her to a violent man from his own violent past, and the image of those last moments . . . the raging snowstorm, a soldier rising from cover with Caroline in his sights, finger tightening on the trigger . . . he shuddered at the memory and Caroline stirred.

She'd gently taught him that she was okay, that he didn't have to worry about her and he didn't have to call a hundred times a day. Violence in

Summerville was rare. What were the odds of violent lightning striking twice?

Still, he insisted on giving her self-defense lessons, which she accepted and treated as gym classes. He was on a campaign to teach her firearms use but so far she'd refused with a shudder.

The imperative to keep Caroline safe while accepting that she had a life was a constant struggle.

But, by God, at night and in bed, that was when she was completely safe and all his.

His left hand cupped her thigh, relishing the silky smooth feel of her.

They liked to sleep with the curtains open. There was a full moon framed by the window, bathing the room with silvery light.

Caroline was so beautiful in daylight. Her colors came out in sunlight—the bright red-gold of her hair, that ivory skin with a faint blush underneath—but in moonlight she turned to marble perfection. Like now.

Jack watched, fascinated, as his hand slowly smoothed up her thigh, taking the silky nightgown with it. His hand was large and dark and rough, an erotic contrast to the pale smoothness of the skin of her thigh.

She was awake now, he could tell. And getting ready. The faint smell of roses drifted up. She didn't use perfume but her soap and body lotions and shampoo were all rose-scented. When she was aroused her skin heated up, and it was like having sex in a rose garden.

His hand smoothed over her hip. Caroline gave up wearing panties to bed in the first week of their marriage, honeymooning in Hawaii. Looking back on it, Jack realized he overdid it. On their honeymoon it was as if he'd never had sex in his entire life and was making up for it now that he was married.

He'd had sex, of course. Tons of it. Just not sex with Caroline, which was something so different there should be another word for it. Caro-sex, maybe.

Looking back on that first week of their honeymoon in Hawaii, his main memories were of their eating and swimming and of his cock in her.

One night they'd fallen asleep together while he was still erect and inside her. He'd been wiped out from nonstop lovemaking. He'd just gone out like a light inside her and woke himself up when his body took over in the morning and started moving.

Now Caroline sighed when his hand smoothed over her belly, shifting her hips closer to his. The hairs on the back of his neck stood up. He put his lips to the soft skin behind her ear and breathed in, trying not to sniff her like a dog. God, she always smelled so wonderful. And her arousal—ah, yes.

His hand drifted down, cupped her. She was warm and soft and starting to get excited. Jack had a keen sense of smell and could tell what stage she'd reached by smell alone sometimes.

She was starting to get ready and he was already at the starting gate, frantically revving the pedal.

Ah well, getting her to where he could enter her was always a pleasure. *Concentrate on that*, he told himself, ignoring his swollen dick.

Another small sigh as he outlined the lips of her sex with his fingers. "Good morning," he whispered in her ear, then bit her earlobe lightly.

She shuddered, her entire body moving against him. "It's not morning," she whispered. Her eyes opened, looked outside the window where the full moon was disappearing under the sill. "It's still night."

"Well, I'm feeling really, really awake," Jack said, and pressed himself against her backside.

Her smile was in her voice. "Yes, love. I can tell."

She lifted so he could pull her nightgown up and off, flinging it high so he could watch it billow down like a parachute made of pale pink silk. He didn't want her to wear panties because it was a barrier, but that moment in which he took off her nightgown and watched it float in the air—man. Pure sex.

"We won't need that," he growled in her ear, lifting her thigh with his.

"No, we won't need it," she whispered, taking in a deep breath. He could see her narrow rib cage rise and fall, breasts free for his hands. This was when he wished he had four of them. One to slide along her thighs, one to enter her, one to caress her breasts, one to let her soft hair run through his fingers.

Sex with Caroline was such a feast, a riot of colors and tastes and textures and scents. Each one delightful, each something to linger over if he didn't have the drum beat of fierce desire spurring him on.

Like now.

He wanted to rush things, wanted to get in her fast. Luckily, he knew some short cuts. This past year he'd studied Caroline like a medical student studies physiology. He knew her down to the bone.

For instance, he knew she went crazy when he kissed her neck. Caroline's neck was Pleasure Central, right after the soft, sensitive region between her thighs. But the neck was a close second.

His lips ran softly along a tendon, up and down

that long, slender neck. By the second run, her sighs were starting to sound like moans. He bit her lightly, then licked her skin. She jumped and her body seemed to pulse with heat. The smell of roses intensified. He closed his eyes as he kissed her neck so he could concentrate on her soft skin and the smell of roses mixed with the scent of her arousal, a combination he was addicted to.

God, how had he not understood how much he'd been missing before? Maybe because all of this was possible only with Caroline. She was the missing link.

Soft, biting kisses as he pulled her closer, nudging the head of his cock against her softness. God, that felt good—so good he moaned in her ear and felt her contract around him, soft and wet now.

"Put me in you," he whispered in her ear, so close his breath must have been like a caress because she shivered.

"Okay," she whispered back.

Oh yeah.

Jack slid his hand up to cover her belly, right over where a child of theirs would grow . . .

Caroline was holding him while opening herself up and she jerked a little as she felt him suddenly swell even larger. "Wow. Whatever that thought was, hold it."

"You bet." Oh yeah. Caroline, growing larger and larger every day. They'd hear the baby's heart beat at one point; she'd feel it move inside her.

Jack hoped with all his heart that they'd have a little girl who looked just like Caroline. Whatever they had, their child—or, even better, children—would for each of them be their only blood relation in this world.

He lifted her leg higher and she was completely exposed. Looking down over her shoulder, he could see two small, pale, perfect breasts; a tiny waist; flat belly; and—whoa—paradise. Puffy pink lips peeping out through ash-brown hair, her pretty hands holding him and holding herself open.

Clutching her tightly, he moved his hips forward, feeling her welcome every inch of the way. Her entire body opened to him. Her cunt, her legs, an arm reaching back. He loved this moment, when his body entered hers, when they were one, when he was home.

He always stopped at this moment simply to savor it. Inside the love of his life, part of her, whole at last.

But then, of course, his body took over. He was a guy and this was the moment when rosy, fuzzy thoughts of togetherness fled his head and all he could think about was how warm she was, how tight she was . . . it blew his mind. His brain just . . . left. And he was merely the sum total of his senses, unable to think—just feel.

When he came, Jack gave a great shout muffled in her hair. He retained just enough consciousness to fall asleep by her side and not on top of her while the rich blackness took him away.

He must have slept for a couple of hours. When he opened his eyes again the sky outside the window was pearly white, the sun behind the clouds shedding a diffuse light. The forecast was for snow late in the afternoon.

His eyes had popped open and he lay grinning in bed for a moment. He felt *great*. Like he could conquer the world while running a marathon and playing the piano at the same time. His body twitched and danced with energy. He lifted his head to see Caroline's face, hoping she was awake or at least close to waking.

Nope. Out like a light.

He slid out of bed and stretched tall, King of the Mountain, then dropped for a fast fifty push-ups. Which was nothing, considering in the Rangers they'd done a hundred and fifty before breakfast and another hundred before lunch. He knew he'd give himself a good workout at his gym today;

this was just to get the blood moving. Not that he needed it—his blood was flowing just fine.

A quick shower and he was by the bedside, watching Caroline sleep.

He clapped his hands, which usually worked to wake her instantly. This time she didn't even open her eyes, just flapped one hand as she snuggled deeper into the pillow.

"Go away," she mumbled.

Nope.

Jack shook her shoulder gently. "We have to train. There are a few new moves I want to show you, honey."

When he'd almost lost her to violence a year ago, he'd vowed to teach her self-defense, and he had. She didn't take the lessons too seriously but by sheer dint of repetition, she had some moves in her. He wanted to deepen that knowledge, drill it into her muscle memory so that when she needed it, if she was ever in trouble, it would come automatically.

As a soldier, Jack had trained endlessly and it had saved his life countless times. Sweat in training saves blood in battle. That had been drummed into him incessantly, and it was true.

Trouble could come from anywhere, at any time. Caroline had been born wealthy into a loving family, so her formative years had been spent far from trouble. Jack had been born into trouble. His entire life had been spent at risk and he reacted accordingly.

If this were a kind world, a just world, trouble would never find Caroline again. She'd had her fill, paid her dues—that side of the slate was in balance. But of course, life wasn't like that. Violence and danger were everywhere and didn't discriminate.

Twice Caroline had been in danger and had had no tools at all in her head or in her body to help herself. All the beauty and kindness and smarts in the world don't help when you're dealing with scum, and the world was full of scumbags.

It drove Jack a little crazy to think of trouble finding Caroline again. Because much as he tried to protect her—their home had been so revamped from a security point of view it could have been featured in *Beautiful Secure Homes & Fortress Gardens*—he couldn't be there 24/7. So the only way he could keep sane was to try to drill her in self-defense.

He was a little OCD about it, that was true. And Caroline wasn't too motivated. That was true, too. But it was the only thing he absolutely insisted on in their marriage. Everything else was her call. The house was decorated the way she wanted it, and they ate what she cooked, they travelled where she wanted to go, they saw the movies she wanted to see. Jack was fine with it all, as long as he was indulged in this.

"Come on, honey," he said when she didn't move.

"It's Christmas Eve, Jack." There was a little whine in there, which made him grin.

"Yeah? Training stops for no man."

"How about for women?"

"For no woman, either."

As an answer she burrowed deeper into the nest of blankets.

Stalemate.

Nothing left to do but use the atom bomb.

"I'll let you throw me," Jack said slyly.

Both eyes opened, focused on him.

"Yeah?" she said, interested.

He knew enough not to smile. "Yeah."

It was fairly painful, throwing himself to the mat, but he did it for her from time to time so she could have the feel of it in her hands and muscles.

"Twice." She made it a statement.

He frowned.

"Twice. You'll let me throw you twice."

Lisa Marie Rice

Ouch. "Okay," he said on a sigh. "Twice."

She gave a sunny smile and threw the blankets back.

First Page Bookstore
Late afternoon, Christmas Eve

"And here I have lamely related to you the un-eventful chronicle of two foolish children in a flat who most unwisely sacrificed for each other the greatest treasures of their house. But in a last word to the wise of these days, let it be said that of all who give gifts, these two were the wisest."

Caroline closed the book and smiled at her audience—twenty kids who lived in homeless shelters and foster homes in Summerville and Mona, ten miles away.

She'd deliberately chosen *The Gift of The Magi*.

An old-fashioned tale of old-fashioned feel-ings—love, tenderness, sacrifice.

Feelings utterly foreign to the kids gathered in front of her. Their lives were dark and danger-ous. Many of them had been betrayed by the very people who were supposed to protect them.

At first, they'd squirmed as they started to understand that the story wouldn't be slam-bang fast like video games and the few TV shows they watched on ancient donated sets in the shelters. There were words they clearly didn't understand and which she carefully explained. *Pier glass, fob, meretricious.*

She skirted around O. Henry's meaning of "chorus girls," painfully aware that several of the kids had moms who gave blow jobs in back seats for twenty-five bucks apiece. The language was archaic and slow and foreign to them. The emotions, too.

But they got there. Because, although the type of love that existed in the story wasn't one they'd seen firsthand, it was something every human aspired to. Something everyone instinctively understood.

They were baffled at first, looking around at each other, rolling their eyes as the story unfolded. But, as she suspected they would be, they were slowly drawn in, helplessly attracted by the kind of experiences they'd likely never encountered. Generosity and true love.

Her husband, Jack, had grown up as they had.

Worse, even. Some of these kids, like little Manuel sitting quietly at the outer edges of the group, had mothers who loved them. His stepfather was a drug addict who was so violent there was a restraining order against him. But Manuel's mother cared for Manuel. Caroline sometimes did readings in his shelter and he always nestled at her side like a small brown bird. Clothes old but carefully mended and clean.

Jack had never had a mother's love. He had never known his mother. All he'd known was shelter after shelter in the grip of a violent drunk for a father.

Utterly unlike her own early experience of life in the embrace of a solid, loving family. She'd lost her family to tragedy at twenty, but nothing could ever erase two decades of love.

Jack had turned into the finest man she knew, thanks to his rock-solid character and a few lucky breaks. These kids, too—born and raised in degradation—could turn their lives around. All they needed was to know that it was possible.

If you believed something was possible, you could make it come true. Caroline believed that from the bottom of her heart.

At the end, there was utter silence in the room, so different from the squirming and punching and shouting at the beginning. It had started to snow and in the silence you could hear the odd needle of sleet embedded in the snow as it hit the windows. Though the kids suffered in the cold, with frayed clothes and inadequate shoes, the few heads that turned to the window smiled at the snow falling like clouds, making the lit store windows along State Street glow with an unearthly light.

Caroline was glad that a sense of beauty hadn't been beaten out of them yet.

"So, kids." She put the book away carefully and leaned forward, looking each child in the eye. Unconsciously they leaned forward, too, watching her. Realizing that she *saw* them. Was listening to them.

I was invisible, her husband had said of his early life in shelters. *Nobody saw me except you.*

"What happened? How did Jim show his love for his wife?"

It had been a suggestion of her father, to volunteer at the shelter—she who had grown up with so much. Her eyes had been opened and she'd discovered an entire new layer of reality. Including befriending a tall, gangly boy who'd been hungrier for learning than he'd been for food. She'd brought him books he devoured until she realized he was also literally hungry, and started bringing sandwiches together with books.

He'd disappeared one Christmas and she hadn't seen him again until he showed up twelve years later—a man so completely changed she hadn't recognized him.

These kids felt as invisible as Jack had felt. There were more and more of them in this recession—women and children falling through the cracks. Unseen, unwanted, unloved.

Small arms were waving, like branches in the wind in a tiny forest. "Me, me, me!" they cried.

Caroline smiled. She was determined to let every kid speak, be heard. Then they would troop across the street to Sylvie's tea shop, where hot chocolate and muffins and a gift book for every child awaited. *The Hunger Games.* Because Jim and Della were the ideal, but Katniss . . . Katniss showed that you could grow up in terrible circumstances and you could still fight back—and prevail.

"Okay, Jamal." She pointed to a kid in the front row, whose eyes had grown larger and larger as the story progressed. She knew each kid's story—she'd insisted on it. She wanted to know who they were, what their lives were about. Jamal had no father and five half-siblings, all from different men. "How did Jim show his love for Della?"

"He sold his watch so he could buy a comb for her."

Yes, indeed. She'd read *The Gift of the Magi* a million times but it still made her smile.

"That's right. And why did he have to sell the watch?"

Silence. The reason was so very close to their lives. "Because he was poor," one girl whispered finally. "They were both poor." Shawna, who was twelve but so thin she looked eight.

"He could have stolen the comb and kept his watch," Caroline gently suggested. Twenty small heads nodded. Yes indeed, he could have. "Why didn't he?"

Silence once more. Why Jim hadn't stolen the comb was not very clear to them. In their world, a lot of people stole. It was just a question of not getting caught.

"Because . . ." a shy voice said, a slight lisp on the *s*. He couldn't be seen because he was behind Mack, who was huge for his age, but Caroline knew who it was. Manuel. Manuel, whose mother had been put in the hospital five times in the past year by his stepfather and was in the hospital right now.

"Because?" Caroline said.

"Because it showed how much he loved her."

"That's right, Manuel. Not stealing the comb—but rather, sacrificing something he cared about to buy something for her—showed how much he loved his wife. And she made a sacrifice too, didn't she? Who can tell me what she sacrificed?" Another forest of small arms. "Lucy?"

"Her hair. She sold her hair for him," Lucy sighed. Her mother was an addict who sold herself to buy drugs. Lucy'd been a ward of the state several times while her mother went to rehab. True love wasn't a big part of her world.

"That's right. So, kids, if you could buy anything at all for your mom or your dad or a sister or brother—what would it be?"

"Anything at all?" Jamal asked, scrunching his face up in puzzlement.

"Go wild," Caroline smiled. "Anything at all."

"PlayStation 4, for my mom," Jamal said decisively, and the room erupted in laughter.

It was an interesting exercise. It was probably the first time they'd ever thought about being able to get anything themselves without stealing it. And, for many, the first time they'd thought of sharing. Their lives were impoverished in every way there was. The gift ideas were all over the place—a house, a job, a dad out of prison, a trip to Disneyland, a pair of red shoes, a new car. Everyone spoke but Manuel.

Caroline watched him, sitting small and quiet. Trying very hard not to be noticed.

Jack had told her about his early childhood,

when he'd been small and weak. Perfecting the art of sliding by without attracting attention because attention was, more often than not, painful. Hiding in the shadows, never speaking, because anything could set his father off. And even when not speaking, his father could fill himself with rage all by himself.

Then Jack had grown big and strong and no one bothered him after the age of fourteen.

But before then, before filling out, he'd been prey. He'd taken care of that by joining the army and then the super elite soldiers, the Rangers. Jack was definitely not prey any more. And Jack had made it his life's work to teach the weak to defend themselves.

He was a security consultant, a very successful one. If you were a bank or a corporation and you wanted his expert help, he was happy to give it, at a premium price. He also ran a dojo school and fitness center, and if you were a lawyer or an executive hoping to firm up your abs and glutes, why, Jack was your man—at two hundred dollars an hour, when you could get him.

But if you were young and poor—and above all, if you were female—you got the best help in the world and the bill was torn up.

While the kids proposed wild presents, she

glanced out the window at the Cup of Tea. Across the street her friend Sylvie waved. A big table with a red tablecloth, plastic cups and a huge thermos, and festive red plates had been set out in the center of the tea shop. Along the counter were enough muffins to feed a brigade of soldiers—just waiting for the kids. Time to wrap this up.

One more kid.

"Manuel? What do you think your mom would like as a present?"

He was silent a long moment, long enough for the chattering of the kids to die down. He swallowed, small Adam's apple bobbing. "For my step-dad to die," he whispered.

Caroline actually felt her heart contract—with pity, with sorrow, with the heaviness of painful truth. Because it *was* true. Manuel's life and his mother's life would be infinitely better without that violent monster in it.

It wasn't until she'd worked in the shelter that she'd even known there was such a thing as bad fathers in the world. Her own father had been wonderful—loving and generous and fun. A larger-than-life figure whose love for his wife and children was manifested a thousand times a day.

Caroline was pregnant. She'd taken the test first thing this morning in the bookshop. She knew how much Jack wanted a child, so she didn't run the test at home. No sense disappointing him. Somehow, though, even before the strip had turned red, she knew.

Just as she knew, beyond a shadow of a doubt, that Jack would be a marvelous father. He'd probably be wildly overprotective, as he was with her, but he'd be there for his children in every way there was. She also had no doubt that he'd give his life for her without question. As he would for any children they might have.

Jack had come late to love, but he cherished it. Caroline hoped with all her heart that the young souls in front of her would one day experience the precious gift of love for themselves.

She thought of all she had in her own life—a loving husband, the beautiful home she'd grown up in, the prospect of a child to love—with enormous gratitude, because between the death of her family when she was twenty and the sudden, mysterious reappearance of Jack in her life, there had been hard, barren years. Years in which she'd cared for a sick brother, had watched her friends disappear one by one as her life grew harder and money grew scarcer. Years of working hard and watching her brother die, inch by slow inch. Years in which she couldn't allow herself to cry at night because Toby would have noticed her swollen eyes and blamed himself. Years of hardship and sorrow.

She knew firsthand how hard it was to hope when all around you is bleakness and despair.

But on this Christmas Eve, at least there'd be hot chocolate and muffins and a book for these children.

She clapped her hands. "Kids! Let's get ready! Put on your coats because we're going across the street for a treat."

The artificial lull created by the storytelling was over. The noise level rose and the twenty kids seemed to become a hundred and fifty as they pulled on ragged coats and dirty scarves.

The noise level was so loud she didn't hear the bell over the shop door ring, and only understood that someone had entered because within a minute, all the kids fell silent.

She looked behind her and froze.

Oh shit, was her first thought. She was instantly ashamed of it. The man who entered looked like a thug, but she knew better than to judge solely on appearance. One of Jack's best friends looked like an extra out of *Resident Evil*—rode a big black bike and spoke in a low growl—and was a sweetheart.

This man had the *Resident Evil* vibe down pat, but he didn't look like a sweetheart at all.

While her head was running through all this, her body went right ahead into overdrive. Sweat broke out all over and her heart kicked into a thumping beat guaranteed to pulse blood to her extremities simply because her body recognized that she was going to need it.

Nonetheless, ten thousand years of civilization and her mother's strict upbringing had her asking in a perfectly normal tone, "May I help you?"

The man had been scanning the room but at her voice he turned slowly toward her, and her involuntary danger signals started booming.

He was truly huge—taller even than Jack, and seemingly twice as broad. But where Jack was all tight muscle, this man looked like vats of lard had been thrown onto his frame before he'd been shoehorned into clothes. Underneath the fat, though, there had once been muscle. He must have weighed three hundred pounds, every ounce mean and stinking.

The stench reached across the room. Booze, unwashed clothes, unwashed man, and that awful something some humans emanated that was like a dog whistle to normal people. *This man is crazy.* She'd seldom come across it, but it was unmistakable.

There was absolute silence. The kids all had an

instinctive understanding that danger had just walked into the room. They'd lived shoulder to shoulder with danger. Several of the kids were hunched in on themselves as if to make themselves smaller. Some had hidden under her desk, in corners; some stood frozen, white-faced.

The man was dressed in filthy leather pants and a leather vest with no shirt, as if impervious to the cold outside. He shook the snow off himself like a polar bear and took a step forward.

God, he was *big*.

Jack had taught Caroline a lot of martial arts moves but there was nothing she could do against someone this massive. She simply didn't have the weight or muscle mass.

And anyway, the guy was flying higher than a kite.

Looking closer, it was clear. The pupils were dilated and his eyes were slightly unfocused. He swayed a little where he stood as if he were in a strong wind, though there was no wind in her bookstore. Just twenty little kids and a very frightened bookshop owner.

"Can I help you?" she repeated, keeping her voice neutral and soft, exactly as if she were trying to calm a wild beast.

"Help me?" he repeated. "Can you fucking help

me? Yeah, lady. Yeah, you can help me." His eyes narrowed. "Looking for my boy. Manuel."

Oh God, oh God. This man didn't only look dangerous, he *was* dangerous. He'd nearly killed his wife. He was like a walking bomb in her bookshop—a bookshop filled with twenty young kids. Her breath clogged in her lungs. She didn't dare look around, but from what she could see in her peripheral vision, Manuel had disappeared.

"So." The man swayed. For a second she hoped that he'd simply collapse to the ground, stoned, but he stayed on his feet. "Where the fuck's my boy?"

Caroline swallowed heavily. She heard Jack's voice in her head. *What do you do if you sense trouble, honey?*

They'd gone over it a million times, and each and every time they talked about it, he tried to convince her to carry a weapon. He'd lived in a dangerous world all his life and he was always armed in some way.

Not to mention the fact that, to a certain extent, Jack's entire body was a weapon.

"Where is he?" the man bellowed, voice hoarse and cracking. "Where the fuck is my boy? Where's that little shit?" Her heart nearly stopped when he reached behind him and a big black knife appeared in his hand.

In that instant, Caroline regretted bitterly not taking Jack up on his constant offers to teach her how to shoot. Oh man, if she had a gun and knew how to use it, she'd drill him right between the eyes—without any compunction at all, because it was clear he was here to hurt.

His black, piggy eyes scanned the room with a narrow focus and he moved toward the kids. One girl screamed, the sound abruptly cut off by her own hand. The kids were like small animals, hoping to avoid the gaze of the predator in their midst.

The man growled at the girl, moving forward unsteadily.

Caroline stepped in front of him. He swatted her away backhanded like a bothersome fly.

His blow took her by surprise. She landed against the corner of the bookshelf, the breath knocked out of her, and nearly passed out from the pain. She hung onto consciousness ferociously, understanding that she was the only thing between those kids and tragedy.

"Manuel!" the crazy guy screamed, the booming voice echoing in the room. He brandished the knife. "Come out, you little shithead! You're a worm, just like your fucking mom! Don't have the courage to come out, eh? Then I'm coming after you!"

He lurched forward and Caroline watched, horrified, as he plowed into the kids. Those who weren't quick enough to scramble out of the way were swatted away, as she had been.

She'd nearly been knocked unconscious by those huge ham hands. He could do real damage to a thin eight-year-old.

Though her head was still spinning, she rolled to her knees, waited for some strength in her limbs. The kids were crying, screaming, two lying in little heaps on the ground.

Caroline gritted her teeth and rose unsteadily to her feet. As she rose, she glanced across the street and saw Sylvie staring, wide-eyed. The man's back was to her so Caroline pantomimed a phone to her ear. Sylvia grabbed a cell from the counter and punched three numbers in.

9-1-1. Good girl.

Sylvie spoke into the phone, clearly reporting what was happening in First Page. A huge man armed with a knife, a roomful of kids, and a potential hostage situation. They'd want to know numbers and positions and Sylvie spoke for a full minute.

Sylvie gave a thumbs up and Caroline motioned for her to get down, since she was highlighted in the huge picture window. Sylvie dropped from sight.

"Come out, you little fucker!" the monster was screaming. Except for the two small heaps, all the kids had scrambled out of his way. He didn't pay them any attention, focusing on his specific prey.

Please, Manuel, run out the back door, she prayed. Maybe he had, because he was nowhere to be found. Monster Man was roaring with rage, up-ending bookcases, scattering books and magazines, shattering a lamp.

Caroline's mind cleared. The first thing to do was get as many kids out of here as possible. While the monster was bellowing, wallowing in his rage, she quietly went behind a waist-high counter and opened the back door. Holding a finger to her lips, she ushered out ten of the kids while the man's back was turned. When he turned around, all he saw was Caroline, who'd moved ten feet from the door. The counter hid the kids slipping out, one by one.

Now for help.

Sylvie had called for official help, but Caroline had a husband who was way more dangerous than Monster Man. She had on a sweater and a long wool jacket over it. Out of habit, she always kept her cell on her at all times. Jack had insisted early in their marriage and it was second nature by now.

Jack's cell number was the first on speed dial. "Honey, hi." His deep voice was unmistakable.

Oh God, she'd forgotten to take it off speaker!

She pressed the button to disengage speaker-phone and took a chance, knocking over an earthenware bowl of apples to catch the monster's attention. He turned his head briefly. It was almost painful to watch his reflexes. He was so drugged up they were slow, stimuli penetrating with difficulty.

"Put down that knife!" she screamed, knowing Jack was listening. "There are kids here in the bookstore!"

That would be enough.

Wherever he was, Jack was coming for her now. She knew that like she knew the sun rose in the East. Monster Man paused in trashing her store to look back at her, narrow-eyed. He looked her up and down and, horribly, licked his lips, opening his mouth in a grotesque smile. His teeth were ground down and brown. "Pretty lady," he growled, and pointed the knife at her. "You're next. After the brat." Then he turned back around, looking for Manuel.

Caroline beckoned, and the kids who had been trapped behind Monster Man ran to her. She herded them behind her, pointing to the back door. Five kids were left. Jamal was by her side, trembling with fear. "Where's Manuel?" she whispered. "Did he get out?"

Jamal shook his head. "He's holed up in your office," he whispered. Oh God. The door to her office could be locked from the inside, but it was only a pine door. Monster Man could shove it in with one kick from his boots.

The five kids left were crouching behind the counter. There were none left in the shop. She had to hope that screaming Monster Man, who seemed to have the intelligence of a slug, had the attention span of one, too.

Quietly, Caroline signaled to the kids around her to scuttle to the back door. She shepherded them out as fast as she could while the man bellowed and crashed into chairs and shelves, screaming for Manuel.

Across the street, Sylvie's head peeped up over the counter and she made the OK sign, then the gun sign. Caroline nodded, then signaled for her to duck back down.

Okay. The police were here, hopefully with SWAT snipers.

She jolted at the sound of wood crashing, but what terrified her even more than that were the animal sounds Monster Man was making as he dragged little Manuel out by the hair. High-pitched, unholy screams of rage that raised the hairs on the back of her neck and along her fore-arms.

To her dying day, Caroline would never forget those bestial sounds coming out of a human be-ing's mouth. It was terrifying, like being in the room with a wild animal.

Heart in her mouth, she watched as he dragged little Manuel out by the hair to the middle of the room, stood him up, and held the knife to his throat.

What horrified her most was that the little boy didn't make a sound. White-faced and trembling, he stood as still as a soldier—even when that meaty fist pulled his hair so hard the scalp raised a little.

And Caroline knew with a sudden swift cer-tainty that this was not the first time this had happened to Manuel. Not the first time he was terrorized and tormented by this human beast.

But by God it would be the last.

A deep calmness settled in her. That child was not leaving these premises with that monster. She'd die first.

"Where's that worthless bitch?" Manuel's step-father screamed. He was purple-faced, sweat streaming from his temples, dripping off his cheeks. The animal smell intensified, a sickening stench. "Where's your fucking mom?"

Little Manuel's eyes were closed and his lips were moving. He was praying.

"Huh?" The man shook his stepson like a rag doll. "Where the fuck is she?"

"In the hospital," Manuel whispered.

"You fucking *liar!* You lie, just like she lies. There's nothing wrong with the bitch! All she does is lie about me!" He whipped that big black knife back up, held it to Manuel's slender throat.

Jack had put her through drills in her training. One of the drills had been observation. He'd suddenly ask her in a restaurant how many waiters there were in a room. How many lamps in a hotel room. Where the back exit was in a coffee shop. How many chairs in the bank lobby.

For a period he drilled her so hard she started observing and memorizing in exasperation, even when he wasn't there, because he was there in her head.

And now it paid off, because out of the corner of her eye she saw a slender black rod slide over the counter across the street at Sylvie's. A rifle barrel! And another rod slid over the balustrade of the rooftop of Sylvie's building. Another sniper.

The cavalry had truly arrived.

She'd learned enough of shooting from Jack to know that the expert marksmen that were behind those rifles wouldn't miss across twenty yards of street. They couldn't shoot what they couldn't see, though, and the monster was in the short side of her L-shaped shop, hidden by a wall. They could hear his bellows but they couldn't see him.

She could wait it out. Sooner or later, the snipers would get him. But if it was later, he could harm Manuel. Kill him with a flick of that meaty wrist.

Already he was working himself up into a greater state of rage, spittle at the edges of his mouth. He jerked in his agitation and a thin line of red appeared on Manuel's neck, slowly starting to drip blood.

It was terrifying to see little Manuel's calm expression. He'd seen this man beat up his mother countless times. His brown eyes lifted to the roof—to heaven—and his white lips moved more quickly.

He was preparing to die. This small, innocent child expected to die at the hands of this monster.

"Hey!" Caroline stood up, waved her hands. Across the street, through a break in the snow, she saw Sylvie's head above the counter. Sylvie's eyes opened wide in shock.

But Caroline knew what she was doing. She had a plan and it all depended on the skill and nerve of the police snipers. She trusted them. Jack was friends with more or less everyone on the force and he said they were all good guys and good cops.

They'd better be, because she was just about to put her life in their hands.

"Hey!" she yelled again. "Let that boy go, you son of a bitch!"

His eyes widened. Clearly, no one talked to him like that. At least, no woman.

There was utter silence in her bookstore while Caroline walked over to the man She stopped halfway across the room. He was a bully. He used his bulk to intimidate. He'd want to come to her, loom over her. Make her scared.

If she hadn't been so incandescent with rage, maybe she would have been scared, because as he walked to her—Manuel stumbling in front of him, blood staining his beige t-shirt—she realized all over again just how huge he was. At least six-five, maybe three hundred pounds. Most of it fat, but some of it muscle. Certainly enough to hurt her. Maybe kill her.

"What do you want with M—" She almost said Manuel's name and stopped herself just in time. If

Monster Man felt she had a connection to the boy, he'd use it. "With the boy?"

"This worthless piece of trash? This fag? He snivels every time I teach him what's right and wrong. Ain't that right, boy?" He gave Manuel a vicious shake. Manuel remained utterly and completely still. Only his lips moved. *"Ain't that right, boy?"*

Sweat broke out all over her body when he pulled Manuel's head back more forcefully, exposing the throat like a lamb's at slaughter time.

"Little fucker's gonna make her come back to me. She left me. My wife fucking *left me!* Police told me I can't go near her or the boy. Well, how about this? I've got the boy and now I'll get her."

They were fully in the center of the room now, lit up like actors on a stage. Everyone outside could see exactly what the situation was. She understood completely that they didn't dare take a shot because the man was so huge he could fall on Manuel, or slit the boy's throat as he dropped.

He was also close enough to Caroline to take another swipe at her.

It was too dangerous to take a shot now. They would be watching carefully through their scopes. If matters precipitated, if he pressed the knife more closely, they just might take the shot. And it might kill Manuel.

Caroline made sure she was off to the side, affording the snipers a clear shot. "Do you want me to call her?" she asked.

"Huh?"

He frowned, the words slowly making their way through the rot and pus in his drug-addled head.

She pulled her smart-phone from her pocket, finger hovering over the screen. "Do you want me to call your wife? Tell her to come?"

Unseen by the monster, Manuel went even whiter, trying to shake his head no, though his head was held in an iron grip.

The idea had made its way through what passed for the man's brains. A wide smile broke through. "Yeah. Fuck yeah. Tell that bitch to get here pronto. I have things to say to her."

"Where is she?"

"Hospital," he said sullenly. "Faking it."

There was only one hospital in town. Caroline nodded. "I happen to have the hospital right on speed dial," she lied. "So . . . what's her name?"

"*Bitch!*" he screamed. "Her name is Bitch! Because she is one!"

"I'm sure she is," Caroline said smoothly. "But I still need a name."

"Anna." The word was dragged out of him in

a snarl. "Anna Ramirez Pedersen. Sometimes she drops my name, the cunt. Just calls herself Ramirez."

"Okay. I'm calling now." She pretended to punch in a number and brought the phone to her ear. "Yes," she said brightly, as if to a receptionist. "This is Caroline Prescott at First Page. I'd like to speak with Anna Ramirez Pedersen, please."

"Honey." Jack's voice came on, deep and low. "I'm right outside. We've got rifles on the guy. The instant you and the boy drop to the floor they'll take the shot."

Oh God. Her knees nearly buckled with relief at hearing Jack's voice, a lifeline to sanity.

"Okay, yes," she answered, as if in response to someone at the hospital. "I understand. I'll wait."

"Try to get away from the window, there'll be glass everywhere," Jack said.

"Uh huh." She looked over at Monster Man. "Yes, I'll hold."

Jack was in her head now. All the thousands of hours of lessons she'd absorbed.

Combat time is in slow motion. Everything slows, including your heart rate. Don't get tunnel vision. Keep all your senses open. Observe before acting.

And damned if time didn't slow down. She

took in everything—the man's stance, the angle at which he held the knife to Manuel's throat, their distance to the window.

She started hyperventilating, dragging in oxygen, and in her head calculated the three elements forming a triangle—herself, the monster holding Manuel, and the snipers outside.

She ran through her head the things that had to happen to free the little boy from his lunatic stepfather—visualized it—and acted.

Caroline had never been particularly athletic in her childhood but she had loved softball and had been an excellent pitcher.

"Yes," she said, straightening suddenly as if a new voice were on the line. "Mrs. Pedersen? Yes, there's someone who wants to talk to you."

Monster Man's eyes gleamed. Finally. The woman he was hard-wired to torment. On the phone, and with their son under threat, so she'd be guaranteed to obey and to suffer. He was in monster heaven. With his free hand he curled his meaty fingers upwards in the universal *gimme* gesture.

Oh, yeah.

Everything slowed down even more, her movements became calculated and precise.

She pitched the phone to the man, ensuring it

fell short, so he'd have to lunge to pick it up. He loosened his hold on Manuel, the knife hand moving away. While the phone was still in the air, Caroline launched herself at Manuel, taking him to the ground and rolling with him, coming to a stop with her body covering his, shielding his little head with her arms.

The world exploded.

Glass flew in bright shiny shards almost indistinguishable from the gusts of snow blowing into the shop. She looked up in horror at the red mist in the midst of the white glass and snow, then down at the man who'd fallen like a sack of meat.

Deader'n shit, as Jack said.

Good! she thought viciously.

And then she didn't have time to think anything at all because a billion men dressed in black and wielding big black guns flooded the bookstore shouting, and a white-faced Jack had pulled her up and into an embrace so tight she couldn't breathe.

He was trembling.

Her husband, tough-as-nails Jack Prescott, was trembling, and his cheeks were wet.

"God," he groaned and gave a huge shudder. "I think I lost about fifty years off my life."

Caroline reached up to kiss him, then fought free.

Four men were crouched on their haunches around the massive corpse, holding on to their rifle barrels. Blood seeped from the back of the monster's head. Caroline looked down at him, rage and hatred in her heart, a mix of emotions she'd never had before. Didn't even know she was capable of having.

He was dead and she was glad he was dead. Maybe, just maybe, Manuel and his mother could put this behind them and make a life for themselves.

An image blossomed in her head—of tiny, trembling Manuel, holding still, frozen with terror, because he knew his stepfather was perfectly capable of slitting his throat—and she hauled off and kicked the corpse in the side as hard as she could.

Four hard male faces turned to her in surprise.

"Sorry," she gritted. "Tell the coroner he fell on something."

One guy, who looked like he ate nails for breakfast, snapped off a two-fingered salute. "Yes, ma'am."

Caroline dropped to her knees next to Manuel, who was still curled up in a little ball. Her heart squeezed tightly. He looked so slight, so vulnerable. How could anyone do this to a child?

She touched the back of his head, cupping it lightly, not knowing if he wanted to be touched at all. Abused children often couldn't bear to be touched by an adult.

"It's okay," she whispered. "It's all over."

His head whipped up and he tried to turn to look back at the corpse of his stepfather, but she gently turned his face back to hers. The sadness in his gaze wrenched her heart. He wasn't crying, though. His eyes were dry. He was a tough little soldier. "I want Mama," he whispered.

The tough-looking police officer rose and crossed to them, holding out a huge hand. Caroline rose, too, with the help of Jack's strong hand because her legs felt light. She was feeling light all over, particularly her head. It was like a helium-filled balloon that would float away if it weren't attached to her neck.

The big officer kept his hand out to Manuel, waiting patiently. "We'll take you to your mama," he said gently. "She's waiting for you." His big hand didn't move. Finally, Manuel put his tiny hand in his.

Caroline let out a pent-up breath.

The police officer's eyes met hers. For such a big bruiser, he had kind eyes. "Social services is on the way over, ma'am." He waved his free hand.

"For everyone else, too. All the other kids are safe out back."

Caroline shivered. The temperature in her bookshop was the same as outside. "Can the kids wait across the street, where there's hot chocolate and muffins?" she asked. "There'd be plenty of hot chocolate and muffins for your men, too."

She shivered again. It wasn't the cold, or just the cold. It was aftershock.

"Yes, ma'am. Thank you. We'll be taking your statement—"

"Tomorrow," Jack said in a hard voice. "She'll be giving her statement tomorrow. She's been through hell and I'm taking her home. Right now."

The two men stared at each other, two alpha males with two different agendas. Caroline could almost see the waves of male will battling back and forth, and the officer broke first. He looked away, then back at Jack with a huff of breath. "Okay, Prescott. Tomorrow. I'll be expecting her no later than eleven."

"Noon," her husband responded. He gestured to her ruined bookshop. "I'm sending people in to board up the windows and clean up. We'll be spending tomorrow morning here."

The cop rolled his eyes. "Okay. Noon. The hot chocolate and those muffins better be good."

"The best," Caroline promised, then sagged against Jack, the voices around her growing distant, the room turning black.

Jack scooped up his wife and walked out with her in his arms, meeting the eyes of all the cops filling the room. He was awash in fear and anxiety and would have welcomed someone trying to stop him.

He was itching for a fight, since the motherfucker with the knife was already dead.

But no one said anything—just silently shifted and made way for him in the swirling snow coming in through the shattered picture window.

It was a miracle his heart hadn't stopped when he answered his cell, only to hear the screams of children and Caroline yelling *put down that knife!*

He'd been coming back from consulting with the Chief Financial Officer of a bank about banking security. Every hair on his head had stood on end and sweat had broken out all over his body. He'd been in battle countless times, survived dozens of firefights and kept his cool. Right then, though, his entire system had gone haywire.

He was perfectly equipped, by nature and by training, to deal with threats to himself. He had no defenses against threats to Caroline—none. There was nothing in his system that could handle this.

It had begun to snow, but he'd gunned the engine, running through red lights, taking corners so tightly he'd have tipped over if he hadn't been a combat driving instructor.

Smart Caroline. She'd managed to alert him to the threat and to where she was. He'd made a beeline to the bookstore while listening to what was happening inside First Page. He'd parked half a block away and pulled out the loaded Glock he kept in a concealed holder under the driver's seat, leaping out of the Explorer before it stopped rocking on its chassis.

He was tackled before he'd taken ten steps, and did some serious damage before he realized he was fighting a SWAT officer.

Even then, the drumbeat of Caroline in danger pounded in his head.

"Sitrep!" he'd barked at the first face he recognized. Sgt. Glenn Baker. Good guy with a gun, good guy to have on your side, good guy all around. Except right now he was keeping him from Caroline.

"Arne Pedersen, thirty-four, rap sheet as long as my dick. Likes beating up on his wife, Anna, who is currently in the county hospital. There's a restraining order against him—which he has just broken—so with that and endangerment, he's going away for a long time, no matter what. He's holding his stepson hostage. Wants his wife. Who is still in a coma. Our medic says he's hopped up. Here, get a look."

Baker put a restraining hand on Jack's shoulder, then showed him a video feed off his cell, and Jack froze. Huge guy, holding a Ka-Bar to a little boy's throat. The knife was already biting into the skin, blood seeping from a cut.

It would take nothing for the bruiser to slice the boy open.

And there was Caroline, several feet off. White-faced, staring at the man in anger.

"Here." Jack handed over his cell to Baker. "It's an open line."

They put the two feeds together—video and audio—and followed what was happening. Baker was talking quietly to his team through his boom mic.

He suddenly heard Caroline's voice clearly, talking into the cell. "This is Caroline Prescott at First Page. I'd like to speak with Anna Ramirez Pedersen, please."

"Honey," Jack said in a low voice, meeting Baker's eyes. "I'm right outside. We've got rifles on the guy. The instant you and the boy get down, they'll take the shot."

Baker notified the team and Jack stood away from the line of sight, heart pounding, listening to Caroline orchestrate the takedown. Admiring her courage, wishing for his sake she was more of a wimp, understanding very well that she was saving that little boy's life.

At risk to her own.

But now he was holding her. At the thought he might have lost her, he shuddered again.

A warm hand against his face. "Jack." Caroline smiled at him. "Don't look like that. I'm fine."

"I'm not," he answered, shifting her in his arms so he could open the passenger-side door.

They'd reached his SUV, the driver-side door still open, snow collecting in the footwell.

He placed her in the passenger seat—which was dry, thank God—and rounded the vehicle. Once she was belted in with a blanket from the back over her, he took off, trying to make it home as fast as he could before his nerves gave out.

"Well," Caroline said, picking at the blanket, looking at him out of the corner of her eye. "That was interesting."

He ground his teeth so hard the sound was audible.

"What's the matter, Jack?" She placed her pretty

hand on his forearm, as she'd done a thousand times before. She often touched him while talking to him—as if judging his reactions through his skin—and he loved it.

He loved everything she did. He loved everything she said. He loved her.

"I almost lost you," he said through gritted teeth.

Caroline sighed. "Yes, but you didn't. 'Almost' only counts in horseshoes."

"And hand grenades," he answered without thinking, watching her.

"What?"

"The whole quote is ' "Almost" only counts in horseshoes and hand grenades.' "

"Oh. Makes sense." She reached out to turn his face back to the road. "Pay attention. Just because I tricked death once today doesn't mean we can't still die."

She was right, damn it. He kept his face turned to the road, though all his attention was on the pale, fragile woman by his side.

"I thought I was going to lose you," Jack said, his voice tight. "I don't think I could live without you."

"You're not going to have to." Her voice was

gentle and soothing, as if he'd been in danger and not she. Except she seemed to be calm and he was all over the place. Skin too tight, nerves twitching, heart racing.

Mr. Cool, losing it.

He'd almost lost her. The thought was there, like a burr biting into his skin—making him sweat, making him bleed. He'd almost lost her.

Jack couldn't even contemplate living his life without Caroline by his side. This past year had been the happiest of his life. Going back to the bleak emptiness of Before Caroline was unthinkable. He couldn't do it, simply couldn't.

His hands were slick on the steering wheel by the time he drove into the garage.

Something was happening to him, something big. He felt like he was about to explode if he didn't do something, something . . . right . . . *now*.

But what?

The answer came when he gave Caroline his hand to help her out of the vehicle, and her skin burned against his.

What to do?

Fuck her.

Get in her and stay in her as long as was possible, because while he was in her nothing bad could ever happen to her. He could keep her safe, keep her his. Nothing else would do.

He was as hard as a rock, every nerve ending sparking like torn electric wires.

"Jack?" Caroline's voice rose, startled, as he headed through the house with her in tow. Nearly running up the stairs, striding fast down the hallway to their bedroom, where he slammed the door behind them with his boot and stood in the middle of the room, breathing hard, holding both her hands in his. "Jack, darling. What's wrong?"

Caroline kept her voice low and soothing as if he were a wild animal—and that's exactly how he felt. He was sure his eyes showed the whites all around like a panicked pony.

Jack looked at her, at his miracle of a wife. Grace, goodness, and beauty. A woman in a million, and he'd nearly lost her.

He told her his deepest truth. "I need you," he whispered hoarsely. "Right now. If I don't have you right now, I think I'll die."

She stepped closer to him, closer still, until her breasts touched his jacket, watching his eyes all the time. "My darling Jack." She lifted herself up on tiptoe and awkwardly kissed the side of his mouth. "I'm yours. You know that."

His control broke. His hands fisted in her hair and he kissed her hard, almost savagely. He knew he was bruising her mouth but he couldn't stop himself. It was as if her mouth were giving him life. He would stay alive as long as he was kissing her.

He picked her up and carried her to the bed, landing on top of her, still kissing her. Somehow he got them both naked, ripping her underwear, but it didn't matter because then he was touching her silky-soft skin all over—particularly the silky-soft *wet* skin between her legs—and it blew all his circuits.

He couldn't wait—not one second more—and entered her with one long hard thrust. He was so careful with her, always, but this time he couldn't be careful, couldn't be gentle; he needed to possess her the way he needed to breathe.

He pumped in her—hard, fast thrusts that made the headboard beat against the wall—and watched her face move up and down under him, breasts swaying to his beat. Her head was arched back, eyes closed, breathing heavy. Her arms and legs were wrapped around him, holding him tightly. She, too, was celebrating the escape from danger with sex.

Jack groaned, cupping her buttocks, moving

his hands down to her thighs, lifting the backs of them higher. The fit became deeper, tighter.

He fucked her with the full strength of his body, mindless heat filling his head. He couldn't slow down, couldn't do anything but ride her as hard and as fast as he was able.

Caroline groaned and she tightened around him, one strong pulse. It lit him up and he moved even faster and harder, in an almost brutal rhythm that would shame him later but which now seemed as inevitable as the tides. Simply the way it had to be.

Another sharp pulse and another. Caroline cried out and he swelled inside her and then exploded, his entire body electrified by something that was more than sex, more than an orgasm.

This was something he'd never felt before, as if the universe itself were moving through him. He moved his face to the pillow and shouted into it as he came and came endlessly in the strongest orgasm he'd ever had.

When it was over, he realized he was plastered to his love with his own sweat. He was panting, completely drained. He turned his head to see if she was all right, but he never completed the move because he fell into a sleep so deep it could have been a coma.

Christmas Day

"Get up, sleepyhead! We've got some training to do. Today you're going to start teaching me how to shoot. I want to be Annie Oakley!"

The words came from several universes away and barely made sense to him.

Someone shook his shoulder.

Jack didn't even have the strength to open his eyes. He was under some kind of boulder that wouldn't let him move his muscles.

"Jack, wake up!"

A finger pulled up one eyelid and he saw a sideways Caroline, watching him with bright eyes.

How could she be bright-eyed when he felt like he'd been hit by a train?

"Open both those baby browns," she crooned. "That's right. Good boy."

He could open his eyes, barely, but nothing else could move. He was utterly and completely wiped out.

His eyes tracked around the room. It was morning, the pale pearly light of a snowy morning filtering in through the windows. How could it be morning when two seconds ago he'd fallen asleep?

"Get up, get up! We've got work to do!" his wife cried. "Training, cleaning up the bookstore, celebrating Christmas . . . and celebrating something even more important. But first—Rambette!"

She was grinning. He blinked. Her eyes were bright and her color was high. She was dressed for the outdoors, mittens hanging from her parka by their strings. She danced in place like a boxer.

Jack licked dry lips. "Work?" he croaked. How could she have all this energy when he felt like he'd died a week ago?

"I'm going to start training seriously, and by God, you were right!"

Jack blinked, his thought processes fuzzy and slow. "I was?"

"Absolutely! I need to train harder and I need to know how to shoot. And I'm going to *pack heat!* I'm going to get myself a pink shoulder holster and no one is ever going to mess with me again. Ever!"

He smiled. She was so amazingly beautiful right now. "Yeah?"

"Yup." She nodded sharply. "And today—I'm going to throw you. For real."

And she did.

If you enjoyed
RECKLESS NIGHT
and
HOT SECRETS,
read on to see where the stories began in
Lisa Marie Rice's Dangerous series

Dangerous Lover

Dangerous Secrets

Dangerous Passion

Available Now

Dangerous Lover

Prologue

Summerville, Washington
St. Jude Homeless Shelter
Christmas Eve

He needed Caroline like he needed light and air.
More.

The tall, emaciated boy dressed in rags rose
from his father's lifeless body sprawled bonelessly
on the icy, concrete floor of the shelter.

His father had been dying for a long time—
most of his life, in fact. There had always been
something in him that didn't want to live. The
boy couldn't remember the last time he'd seen his
father clean and sober. He had no mother. All his
life, it had been just the two of them, father and

son, drifting from shelter to shelter, staying until they were kicked out.

The boy stood for a moment, looking down at his only blood relation in this world, dead in a pool of vomit and shit. Nobody had noticed his father's dead body yet. Nobody ever noticed them or even looked their way if they could help it. Even the other lost, hopeless souls in the shelter recognized someone worse off than they were and shunned them.

The boy looked around at the averted faces, eyes cast to the floor.

Nobody cared that the drunk wasn't getting up again. Nobody cared what happened to his son.

There was nothing for the boy here. Nothing.

He had to get to Caroline.

He had to move fast before they discovered that his father was dead. If they found the body here, the police and social workers and administrators would come for him. He was eighteen, but he couldn't prove it. And he knew enough about the way things worked to know that he'd become a ward of the state. He'd be locked up in some pris-onlike orphanage.

No. No way. He'd rather die.

The boy moved toward the stairs that would take him up out of the shelter into the gelid, sleety afternoon.

An old woman looked up as he passed by, cloudy eyes flickering with recognition. Susie. Ancient, toothless Susie. She wasn't lost in alcohol like his father. She was lost in the smoky depths of her own mind.

"Ben, chocolate chocolate?" she cackled and smacked her wrinkled, rubbery lips. He'd once shared a chocolate bar Caroline had brought him, and Susie had looked to him for sweets ever since.

Here he was known as Ben. In the last shelter—Portland, was it?—his father had called him Dick. Naming him after the manager of the shelter always bought them some time. Not enough. Eventually, the shelters got sick of his father's drunken rages and found a way to kick them out.

Susie's hands, with their long, black, ragged nails, grasped at him. Ben stopped and held her hand a moment. "No chocolate, Susie," he said gently.

Like a child, her eyes filled with tears. Ben stooped to give her grimy wrinkled cheek a kiss, then rushed up the stairs and out into the open air.

No hesitation as he turned into Morrison Street. He knew exactly where he was going. To Greenbriars. To Caroline.

To the one person on the face of the earth who cared about him. To the only person who treated him as a human being and not some half-wild animal who smelled of dirty clothes and rotting food.

Ben hadn't eaten in two days, and he had only a too-short cotton jacket on to keep the cold away. His big, bony wrists stuck out of the jacket's sleeves, and he had to tuck his hands into his armpits to keep them warm.

No matter. He'd been cold and hungry before.

The only warm thing he wanted right now was Caroline's smile.

Like the arrow of a compass to a lodestar, he leaned into the wind to walk the mile and a half to Greenbriars.

No one looked his way as he trudged by. He was invisible, a lone, tall figure dressed in rags. It didn't bother him. He'd always been invisible. Being invisible had helped him survive.

The weather worsened. The wind blew icy needles of sleet directly into his eyes until he had to close them into slits.

Didn't matter. He had an excellent sense of direction and could make his way to Greenbriars blindfolded.

Head down, arms wrapped around himself to conserve what little warmth he'd been able to absorb at the shelter, Ben slowly left behind the dark, sullen buildings of the part of the city that housed the shelter. Soon the roads opened up into tree-lined avenues. Ancient brick buildings gave way to graceful, modern buildings of glass and steel.

No cars passed—the weather was too severe for that. There was nobody on the streets. Under his feet, the icy buildup crackled.

He was almost there. The houses were big here, in this wealthy part of town. Large, well built, with sloping green lawns that were now covered in ice and snow.

He usually made his way through the back streets, invisible as always. Someone like him in this place of rich and powerful people would be immediately stopped by the police, so he always took the back streets on a normal day. But today the streets were deserted, and he walked openly on the broad sidewalks.

It usually took him half an hour to walk to Greenbriars but today the ice-slick sidewalks and hard wind dragged at him. An hour after leaving the shelter, he was still walking. He was strong, but hunger and cold started to wear him down. His feet, in their cracked shoes, were numb.

Music sounded, so lightly at first that he wondered whether he was hallucinating from cold and hunger. Notes floated in the air, as if borne by the snow.

He rounded a corner and there it was—Greenbriars. Caroline's home. His heart pounded as it loomed out of the sleety mist. It always pounded when he came here, just as it pounded whenever she was near.

He usually came in through the back entrance, when her parents were at work and Caroline and her brother in school. The maid left at noon and from noon to one the house was his to explore. He could move in and out like a ghost. The back door lock was flimsy, and he'd been picking locks since he was five.

He'd wander from room to room, soaking up the rich, scented atmosphere of Caroline's home.

The shelter rarely had hot water, but still he took care to wash as well as he could whenever he headed out to Greenbriars. The stench of the shelter had no place in Caroline's home.

Greenbriars was so far beyond what he could ever hope to have that there was no jealousy, no envy in him as he touched the backs of the thousands of books in the library, walked into sweet-smelling closets full of new clothes, opened the huge refrigerator to see fresh fruits and vegetables. Caroline's family was rich in a way he couldn't comprehend, as if they belonged to a different species living on another planet.

To him, it was simply Caroline's world. And living in it for an hour a day was like touching the sky.

Today nobody could see him approach in the storm. He walked right up the driveway, feeling the gravel through the thin soles of his shoes. The snow intensified, the wind whipping painful icy particles through the air. Ben knew how to move quietly, stealthily when he had to. But it wasn't necessary now. There was no one to see him or hear him as he crunched his way to the window.

The music was louder now, the source a yellow glow. It wasn't until he had reached the end of the driveway that Ben realized that the yellow glow was the big twelve-pane window of the living room, and the music was someone playing the piano.

He knew that living room well, as he knew all the rooms of the big mansion. He'd wandered them all, for hours. He knew that the huge living room always smelled faintly of woodsmoke from the big fireplace. He knew that the couches were deep and comfortable and the rugs soft and thick.

He walked straight up to the window. The snow was already filling in the tracks his shoes made. No one could see him, no one could hear him.

He was tall, and could see over the windowsill if he stood on tiptoe. Light had drained from the sky, and he knew no one in the room could see him outside.

The living room was like something out of a painting. Hundreds of candles flickered everywhere—on the mantelpiece, on all the tables. The coffee table held the remains of a feast—half a ham on a carving board, a huge loaf of bread, a big platter of cheeses, several cakes, and two pies. A teapot, cups, glasses, an open bottle of wine, a bottle of whiskey.

Water pooled in his mouth. He hadn't eaten for two days. His empty stomach ached. He could almost smell the food in the room through the windowpane.

Then food completely disappeared from his mind.

A lovely voice rang out, clear and pure, singing a Christmas carol he'd heard in a shopping mall once while he helped his dad panhandle. Something about a shepherd boy.

It was Caroline's voice. He'd recognize it anywhere.

A frigid gust of wind buffeted the garden, raking his face with sleet. He didn't even feel it as he edged his head farther up over the windowsill.

There she was! As always, his breath caught when he saw her.

She was so beautiful, it sometimes hurt him to look at her. When she visited him in the shelter, he'd refuse to look at her for the first few minutes. It was like looking into the sun.

He watched her hungrily, committing each second to memory. He remembered every word she'd ever spoken to him, he'd read and reread every book she'd ever brought him, he remembered every item of clothing he'd ever seen her in.

She was at the piano, playing. He'd never seen anyone actually play the piano, and it seemed like magic to him. Her fingers moved gracefully over the black and white keys, and music poured out like water in a stream. His head filled with the wonder of it.

She was in profile. Her eyes were closed as she played, a slight smile on her face, as if she and the music shared a secret understanding. She was singing another song even he recognized. "Silent Night." Her voice rose, pure and light.

The piano was tall and black, with lit candles held in shiny brass holders along the sides.

Though the entire room was filled with candles, Caroline glowed more brightly than any of them. She was lit with light, her pale skin gleaming in the glowing candlelight as she sang and played.

The song came to an end, and her hands dropped to her lap. She looked up, smiling, at the applause, then started another carol, her voice rising pure and high.

The whole family was there. Mr. Lake, a big-shot businessman, tall, blond, looking like the king of the world. Mrs. Lake, impossibly beautiful and elegant. Toby, Caroline's seven-year-old brother. There was another person in the room, a handsome young man. He was elegantly dressed, his dark blond hair combed straight back. His fingers were beating time with the carol on the piano top. When Caroline stopped playing, he leaned down and gave her a kiss on the mouth.

Caroline's parents laughed, and Toby did a somersault on the big rug.

Caroline smiled up at the handsome young man and said something that made him laugh. He bent to kiss her hair.

Ben watched, his heart nearly stopping.

This was Caroline's boyfriend. Of course. They shared a look—blond, poised, privileged. Good-looking, rich, educated. They belonged to the same species. They were meant to be together, it was so clear.

His heart slowed in his chest. For the first time, he felt the danger from the cold. He felt its icy fingers reaching out to him to drag him down to where his father had gone.

Maybe he should just let it take him.

There was nothing for him here, in this lovely candlelit room. He would never be a part of this world. He belonged to the darkness and the cold.

Ben dropped back down on his heels, backing slowly away from the house until the yellow light of the window was lost in the sleet and mist. He was shaking with the cold as he trudged back down the driveway, the wet snow seeping through the holes in his shoes to soak his feet.

Half an hour later, he came to the interstate junction and stopped, swaying on his feet.

The human in him wanted to sink to the ground, curl up in a ball, and wait for despair and then death to take him, as they had taken his father. It wouldn't take long.

But the animal in him was strong and wanted, fiercely, to live.

To the right, the road stretched northward, right up into Canada. To the left, it went south.

If he went north, he would die. It was as simple as that.

Turning left, Ben shuffled forward, head low, into the icy wind.

Dangerous Secrets

Chapter One

Parker's Ridge

"Read any good books lately?"

The pretty young woman stacking books and sorting papers in the Parker's Ridge County Library turned around in surprise. It was closing time and the library wasn't overwhelmed with people at the best of times. By closing time it was always deserted. Nick Ireland should know. He'd been staking it out for a week.

"Oh! Hello, Mr. Ames." Her cheeks pinked with pleasure at seeing him. "Did you need something else?" She checked the big old-fashioned clock on the wall. "We're closing up, but I can stay on for another quarter of an hour if you need anything."

He'd been in that morning and she'd been charmingly helpful to him. Or, rather, to Nicholas Ames, stockbroker, retired from the Wall Street rat race after several years of very lucky investments paid off big, now looking to start his own investment firm. Son of Keith and Amanda Ames, investment banker and family lawyer, respectively, both tragically dead at a young age. Nicholas Ames was thirty-four years old, a Capricorn, divorced after a short-lived starter marriage in his twenties, collector of vintage wines, affable, harmless, all-round good guy.

Not a word of that was true. Not one word.

They were alone in the library, which pleased him and annoyed him at the same time. It pleased him because he'd have Charity Prewitt's undivided attention. It annoyed him because . . . because.

Because through the huge library windows she looked like a lovely little lamb staked out for the predators. It had been dark for an hour up here in this frozen northern state. In the well-lit library, Charity Prewitt had been showcased against the darkness of the evening. One very pretty young woman all alone in an enclosed space. It screamed out to any passing scumbag—*come and get me!*

Nothing scumbags liked better than to eat up lovely young women. If there was one thing Nick knew with every fiber of his being, it was that the world was full of scumbags. He'd been fighting them all his life.

She was smiling up at him, much, *much* prettier than the photographs in the file he'd studied.

"No, thank you, Miss Prewitt," he answered, keeping his deep, naturally rough voice gentle. "I don't need to do any more research. You were very helpful this morning."

Her head tilted, the soft dark-blond hair brushing her right shoulder. "Did you have a good day, then?"

"Yes, I did, a very good day. Thank you for asking. I saw three factories, a promising new Web design start-up, and an old-economy sawmill that has some very innovative ideas about using recycled wood chips. All in all, very satisfactory."

Actually, it had been a shitty day, just one of many shitty days on this mission. A total waste of time spent in the surveillance van with two smelly men and jack shit to show for it except for one cryptic call to Worontzoff about a friend staying safe.

Nick smiled the satisfaction he didn't feel. "So. It's closing time now, isn't it?"

She smiled back. "Why, yes. We close at six. But as I said, if you need something—"

"Well, to tell you the truth . . ." Nick looked down at his shoes shyly, as if working up the courage to ask. Man, he loved looking down at those shoes. They were three-hundred-dollar Italian imports, worlds away from his usual comfortable but battered combat boots that dated back to his army days.

Being Nicholas Ames, very successful businessman, was great because he got to dress the part and Uncle Sam had to foot the bill. He had an entire wardrobe to fit those magnificent shoes. Who knew if he'd get to keep any of it? Maybe the two Armanis that had been specially tailored for his broad shoulders.

And even better was dealing with this librarian, Charity Prewitt, one of the prettiest women he'd ever seen. Small, curvy, classy with large eyes the color of the sea at dawn.

Nick looked up from contemplating his black shiny wingtips and smiled into her beautiful gray eyes. "Actually, I was hoping that I could invite you out to dinner to thank you for your help. If I hadn't done this preliminary research here, with your able help, my day wouldn't have been half as productive. Asking you out to dinner is the least I can do to show you my appreciation."

She blinked. "Well . . . ," she began.

"You have nothing to fear from me," he said hastily. "I'm a solid citizen—just ask my accountant and my physician. And I'm perfectly harmless."

He wasn't, of course, he was dangerous as hell. Ten years a Delta operator before joining the Unit. He'd spent the past decade in black ops, perfecting the art of killing people.

He was sure harmless to *her*, though.

Charity Prewitt had the most delicious skin he'd ever seen on a woman—pale ivory with a touch of rose underneath—so delicate it looked like it would bruise if he so much as breathed on it. That was skin meant for touching and stroking, not hurting.

"Ms. Prewitt?" She hadn't answered his question about going out. She simply stood there, head tilted to one side, watching him as if he were some kind of problem to be sorted out, but she needed more information before she could solve it.

In a way, he liked that. She didn't jump at the invitation, which was a welcome relief from his last date—well, last fuck. Five minutes after "hello" in a bar, she'd had his dick in her hand. At least she hadn't been into pain like Consuelo. God.

Charity Prewitt was assessing him quietly and he let her do it, understanding that smooth words weren't going to do the trick. Stillness would, so he stood still. Special Forces soldiers have the gift of stillness. The ones who don't, die young and badly.

Nick was engaging in a little assessment himself. This morning he'd been bowled over by little Miss Charity Prewitt. Christ, with a name like that, with her job as chief librarian of the library of a one-traffic-light town, single at twenty-eight, he'd been expecting a dried-up prune.

The photographs of her in his file had been fuzzy, taken with a telescopic lens, and just showed the generics—hair and skin color, general size and shape. A perfectly normal woman. A little on the small side, but other than that, ordinary.

But up close and personal, Jesus, she'd turned out to be a knockout. A quiet knockout. You had to look twice for the full impact of large light-gray eyes, porcelain skin, shiny dark-blond hair and a curvy slender figure to make itself felt. Coupled with a natural elegance and a soft, attractive voice—well.

Nick was used to being undercover, but most of

his jobs involved scumbags, not beautiful young women.

Actually, this one did, too—a major scumbag called Vassily Worontzoff everyone on earth but the operatives in the Unit revered for being a great writer. Even nominated for the friggin' Nobel, though, as the Unit knew well but couldn't yet prove, the sick fuck was the head of a huge international OC syndicate. Nick was intent on bringing him down.

So on this op he was dealing with scumbags, yeah, but the mission also involved romancing this pretty woman—and on Uncle Sam's dime, to boot.

Didn't get much better than that.

"All right," Charity said suddenly. Whatever her doubts had been, apparently they were now cleared up. "What time do you want to pick me up?"

Yes! Nick felt a surge of energy that had nothing to do with the mission and everything to do with the woman in front of him.

"Well . . ." Nick smiled, all affable, utterly safe, utterly reliable businessman, "I was wondering whether you wouldn't mind going now. I found this fabulous Italian place near Rockville. It has a really nice bar area and I thought we might talk over a drink while waiting for our dinner."

"Da Emilio's," Charity said. "It's a very nice

place and the food is excellent." She looked down at herself, frowning. "But I'm not dressed for a dinner out. I should go home and change."

She was wearing a light blue-gray sweater that exactly matched the color of her eyes and hugged round breasts and a narrow waist, a slim black skirt, shiny black stockings, and pretty ankle boots. Pearl necklace and pearl earrings. She was the classiest-looking dame he'd seen in a long while, even in her work clothes.

"You look—" *Perfect. Sexy as hell.* He bit his jaws closed on the words. Ireland, roughneck soldier that he was, could say something like that, but Ames, sophisticated businessman, sure as hell couldn't. Even if it was God's own truth. "Fine. You look just fine. You could go to dinner at the White House dressed like that."

It made her smile, which was what he wanted. Her smile was like a secret weapon. She sighed. "Okay. I'll just need to lock up here."

Locking up entailed pulling the library door closed and turning a key once in the lock.

Nick waited. Charity looked up at him, a tiny frown between her brows when she saw his scowl. "Is something wrong?"

"That's it? That's locking up? Turning the key once in the lock?"

She smiled gently. "This isn't the big bad city, Mr. Ames."

"My friends call me Nick."

"Okay, Nick. I don't know if you've had a chance to walk around town. This isn't New York or even Burlington. The library, in case you haven't noticed, is full of books and not much else besides some scuffed tables. What would there be to steal? And anyway, I don't remember the last time a crime was committed in Parker's Ridge."

The elation Nick felt at the thought of an evening with Charity Prewitt dissipated.

Parker's Ridge housed one of the world's most dangerous criminals. An evil man. A man directly responsible for hundreds of lives lost, for untold misery and suffering.

And he was Charity Prewitt's best friend.

Dangerous Passion

Chapter One

Alleyway outside the Feinstein Art Gallery
Manhattan
November 17

Feelings kill faster than bullets, that old Russian army saying, raced through Viktor "Drake" Drakovich's mind when he heard the noise behind him. It was barely audible. The faint sound of metal against leather, fabric against fabric and the softest whisper of a metallic click.

The sound of a gun being pulled from its holster, the safety being switched off. He'd heard a variation of this sound thousands and thousands of times over the years.

He'd known for a year now that this moment would come. It was only a question of when, not if. He'd been barreling toward it, against every instinct in his body, completely out of control, for a full year.

From his boyhood living wild on the streets of Odessa, he'd survived the most brutal conditions possible, over and over again, by being cautious, by never exposing himself unnecessarily, by being security conscious, always.

What he'd been doing for the past year was the equivalent of suicide.

It didn't feel that way, though.

It felt like . . . like life itself.

He could remember to the second when his life changed. Utterly, completely, instantly.

He'd been in his limousine, separated from Mischa, his driver, by the soundproof partition. In the car he never talked, and used the time to catch up on paperwork. It had been years since he'd driven anywhere for pleasure. Cars were to get from A to B, when he couldn't fly.

The windows were heavily smoked. For security, of course. But also because it had been a long time since the outside world had interested him enough to glance out the windows at the passing scenery.

The heavy armor-plated Mercedes S600 was stopped in traffic. The overhead stoplight continued cycling through the colors, green-yellow-red, green-yellow-red, over and over again, but traffic was at a standstill. Something had happened up ahead. The blare of impatient horns filtered through the armored walls and bulletproof glass of his car, sounding as if coming from far away, like the buzzing of crazed insects in the distance.

A motorcycle eased past the cars like an eel in water. One driver was so enraged at the sight of the motorcyclist making headway, he leaned angrily on his horn, rolled down the window and stuck his middle finger up in the air. He shouted something out, red faced, spittle flying.

Drake closed his eyes in disgust. Even in America, where there was order and plenty and peace—even here there was aggression and envy. Humans never learned. They were like violent children, petulant and greedy and out of control.

It was an old feeling, dating from his childhood, as familiar to him as the feel of his hands and feet. Humans were flawed and rapacious and violent. You used that, profited from it and stayed as much out of their way as possible. It was the closest thing to a creed he had and it had served him well all his life.

Oddly enough, though, lately this kind of thinking had made him . . . impatient. Annoyed. Wanting to step away from it all. Go . . . somewhere else. Do something else. *Be* someone else.

If there were another world, he'd emigrate to it. But there was only this world, filled with greedy and violent people.

Whenever he found himself in this mood, which was more and more often lately, he tried to shake himself out of it. Moods were an excellent way to get killed.

Strangely out of sorts, he looked again at the spreadsheets on his lap. They tracked a 10-million-dollar contract to supply weapons to a Tajikistani warlord, the first of what Drake hoped would be several deals with the self-styled "general." There was newfound oil in the general's fiefdom, a god-damned lake of it right underneath the barren, hard-packed earth, and the general was in the mood to buy whatever was necessary to hold on to the power and the oil. When this deal went through smoothly, as it certainly would, Drake knew there would be many more down the line.

Years ago, if nothing else, the thought would have given him satisfaction. Now, he felt nothing at all. It was a business deal. He would put in the work; it would net him more money. Nothing he hadn't done thousands and thousands of times before.

He stared at the printouts until they blurred, trying to drum up interest in the deal. It wasn't there, which was alarming. What was even more alarming was the dull void in his chest as he reflected on his indifference. Not being able to care about not being able to care was frightening. Would have been frightening, if he could work up the energy to be frightened.

Restless, he glanced to his right. This section of Lexington was full of bookshops and art galleries, the shop windows more pleasing, less crass than the boutiques with their stupid, outlandish clothes a block uptown.

And that was when he saw them.

Paintings. A wall of them, together with a few watercolors and ink drawings. All heartbreakingly beautiful, all clearly by the same fine hand. A hand even he recognized was extraordinary.

Though the car windows were smoked, the gallery was well lit and each work of art had its own wall-mounted spotlight, so Drake got a good look at them all, stalled there in a mid-Manhattan traffic jam. And anyway, his eyesight was sniper grade.

He did something he'd never done before. He buzzed down his window. The driver's mouth fell open. Drake flicked his gaze to the rearview mirror. The driver's mouth snapped shut and his face assumed an impassive expression.

The car instantly filled with the smell of exhaust fumes and the loud cacophony of a Manhattan traffic jam.

Drake ignored it completely. The important thing was he had a better view of the paintings now.

The first painting he saw took his breath away. A simple image—a woman alone at sunset on a long, empty beach. The rendering of the sea, the colors of the sunset, the grainy beach—all those details were technically perfect. But what came off the surface of the painting like steam off an iron was the loneliness of the woman. It could have been the portrait of the last human on earth.

The Mercedes lurched forward a foot then stopped. He barely noticed.

The paintings were like little miracles on a wall. A glowing still life of wildflowers in a can and an open paperback on a table, as if someone had just come in from the garden. A pensive man reflecting himself in a shop window. Delicate female hands holding a book. The artwork was realistic, delicate, stunning. It pulled you in to the world of the picture and didn't let you go.

Drake had no way to judge the artwork in technical terms; all he knew was that each work was brilliant, perfect, and called to him in some way he'd never felt before.

The car rolled forward ten feet, bringing another section of the wall into view.

The last painting on the wall jolted him.

It was the left profile of a man rendered in earth tones. The man's face was hard, strong-jawed, unsmiling. His dark hair was cut so short the skull beneath was visible, which was exactly as Drake wore it in the field, particularly in Afghanistan. Far from even the faintest hope of running water, he shaved his head and his body hair, the only way to avoid lice. The face of the man didn't exactly look like him, but the portrait had the look of him—features harsh, grim, unyielding.

Running from the forehead over the high cheekbone and down to the jaw, brushing perilously close to the left eye, was a ragged white scar, like a lightning bolt etched in flesh.

Reflexively, Drake lifted a hand to his face, remembering.

He'd been a street rat on the streets of Odessa, sleeping in a doorway in the dead of winter. Some warmth seeped through the cracks in the door, allowing him to sleep without fear of freezing to death in the subzero temperatures.

Emaciated, dressed in rags, he was perfect prey for the sailors just ashore from months working brutal shifts at sea, reeling drunk through the streets. Sailors who hadn't had sex in months and didn't much care who they fucked—boy or girl— as long as whoever it was held still long enough. Most of the sailors didn't even care whether who they fucked stayed still because they were tied down or dead.

Drake came awake in a rush as the fetid breath of two Russian sailors washed over his face. One of the sailors held a knife to Drake's throat while the other dropped his pants, already hauling out a long, thin, beet-red cock.

Drake was a born street fighter and fought best when he was close to the ground. He was born with the ability and had honed it by observation and practice. He scissored his legs, bringing the man with the knife toppling to the ground, then hurled himself at the knees of the second man, hobbled by his pants. The man fell heavily to the ground, his head hitting the broken pavement with a sickening crack.

Drake turned to the first man, who'd scrambled to his feet and was holding the knife in front of him like an expert, edge down. The chances of surviving a knife fight barehanded were ludicrously low. Drake knew he had to even the odds fast, do something unexpected.

He flung himself forward, into the knife. The blade sliced the side of his face open, but the surprise move loosened the sailor's grip. Drake wrenched the knife out of his hand and jabbed it into the man's eye, to the hilt.

The sailor dropped like a stone.

Drake stood over him, panting, his blood dripping over the man's face, then pulled the knife out of his attacker's skull and wiped it down on the man's tattered jacket.

He took both men's knives. One was a *nozh razvedchika*, a scout's knife. The other was a Finnish Pukka, rare in those parts and very valuable. He bartered both along the Odessa waterfront for two guns, a Skorpion and an AK–47—including clips and shooting lessons—sold cheaply because they were stolen.

He was on his way.

Later, as soon as he could afford it, he had plastic surgery on the long, jagged white scar on the left side of his face. He was known for being able to blend into almost any environment, for turning himself invisible, but a very visible scar was like a flag, something no one forgot. It had to go.

The surgeon was good, one of the best. There

was nothing visible left of his scar. Besides himself, only the surgeon could remember the shape of the long-gone scar. But there it was, in a painting in a gallery in Manhattan, half a world away and two decades later. However crazy it sounded, the scar in the painting was the same scar the surgeon had eliminated, all those years ago.

Traffic suddenly cleared and the Mercedes rolled smoothly forward. Drake punched the button in the center console that allowed him to communicate with the driver.

"Sir?" Mischa sounded startled over the intercom. Drake rarely spoke while they were traveling.

"Turn right at the next intersection and let me off after two blocks."

"*Sir?*" This time the driver's voice sounded confused. Drake never left the car en route. He got into one of his many vehicles in his building's garage and got out at his destination. The driver caught himself. Drake never had to repeat himself with his men. "Yessir," the driver replied.

Once out of the limousine, Drake continued walking in the direction of the car until it disappeared into the traffic, then ducked into a nearby department store. Ten minutes later, satisfied that he wasn't being followed, he doubled back to the art gallery, having ditched his eight-hundred-dollar

Boss jacket, Brioni pants, Armani cashmere sweater and scarf and having bought a cheap parka, long-sleeved cotton tee, jeans, watch cap and sunglasses. He was as certain as he could be that no one was tailing him and that he was unrecognizable.

The art gallery was warm after the chill of the street. Drake stopped just inside the door, taking in the scent of tea brewing and that mixture of expensive perfumes and men's cologne typical of Manhattan haunts, mixed with the more down-to-earth smells of resin and solvents.

At the sound of the bell over the door, a man came out from a back room, smiling, holding a porcelain mug. Steam rose in white fingers from the mug.

"Hello and welcome." The man transferred the mug from his right hand to his left and offered his hand. "My name is Harold Feinstein. Welcome to the Feinstein Gallery."

The smile seemed genuine, not a salesman's smile. Drake had seen too many of those from people who knew who he was and knew what resources he could command. Everything that could possibly be sold—including humans—had been offered to him, with a smile.

But the man holding his hand out couldn't know who he was, and wasn't presuming he was rich. Not dressed the way he was.

Drake took the proffered hand gingerly, not remembering the last time he'd clasped another man's hand. He touched other people rarely, not even during sex. Usually, he employed his hands to keep his torso up and away from the woman.

Harold Feinstein's hand was soft, well-manicured, but the grip was surprisingly strong.

"Have a look around," he urged. "No need to buy. Art enriches us all, whether we own it or not."

Without seeming to study him, Feinstein had taken in the cheap clothes and pegged him as a window-shopper, but wasn't bothered by it. Unusual in a man of commerce.

Drake's eyes traversed the wall and Harold Feinstein turned amiably.

"Take my latest discovery," he said, waving his free hand. "Grace Larsen. Remarkable eye for detail, amazing technical expertise, perfect brush strokes. Command of chiaroscuro in the etchings. Quite remarkable."

The artist was a *woman*? Drake focused on the paintings. Man, woman, whoever the artist was, the work was extraordinary. And now that he was here, he could see that a side wall, invisible from the street, was covered with etchings and watercolors.

He stopped in front of an oil, a portrait of an old

woman. She was stooped, graying, hair pulled back in a bun, face weatherbeaten from the sun, large hands gnarled from physical labor, dressed in a cheap cotton print dress. She looked as if she were just about to step down from the painting, drop to her knees and start scrubbing the floor.

Yet she was beautiful, because the artist saw her as beautiful. A specific woman, the very epitome of a female workhorse, the kind that held the world together with her labor. Drake had seen that woman in the thousands, toiling in fields around the world, sweeping the streets of Moscow.

All the sorrow and strength of the human race was right there, in her sloping shoulders and tired eyes.

Amazing.

The door behind him chimed as someone entered the gallery.

Feinstein straightened, his smile broadened. "And here's the artist herself." He looked at Drake, dressed in his poor clothes. "Take your time and enjoy the paintings," he said gently.

Drake smelled her before he saw her. A fresh smell, like spring and sunshine, not a perfume. Completely out of place in the fumes of midtown Manhattan. His first thought was, *No woman can live up to that smell.*

"Hello, Harold," he heard a woman's voice say behind him. "I brought some india-ink drawings. I thought you might like to look at them. And I finished the waterfront. Stayed up all night to do it." The voice was soft, utterly female, with a smile in it.

His second thought was, *No woman can live up to that voice.* The voice was soft, melodic, seeming to hit him like a note on a tuning fork, reverberating through him so strongly he actually had to concentrate on the words.

Drake turned—and stared.

His entire body froze. He found himself completely incapable of moving for a heartbeat—two—until he managed to shake himself from his paralysis by sheer force of will.

Something—some atavistic survival instinct dwelling deep in his DNA—made him turn away so she wouldn't see him full face, but he had excellent peripheral vision and he watched intently as the woman—Grace—opened a big portfolio carrier and started laying out heavy sheets of paper, setting them out precisely on a huge glass table. Then she brought out what looked like a spool of 10-inch-wide paper from her purse.

Goddamn. The woman was . . . exquisite.

Can't get enough of Lisa Marie Rice?
Keep reading for a sneak peek from

I DREAM OF DANGER
A Ghost Ops Novel

Hard to kill, dangerous to love . . .
Coming Summer 2013!

Chapter One

Burial of Judge Oren Thomason
St. Mary's Cemetery
Lawrence, Kansas
January 10

He came.

She knew he'd come. Somehow she'd known.

She dreamed of him last night. She often dreamt of him, dreams so vivid she woke with tears on her face, aching for him.

Elle Thomason rose from where she'd thrown dirt onto her father's coffin before the two undertaker's assistants covered it with earth and he would finally, finally be at peace and that was when she saw him.

He was outlined against the chilly winter sun on the small hill where the chapel stood. He was only a dark figure against the dying sun but she would recognize him anywhere, any time.

Nick Ross. The boy she'd loved so much, now clearly a man. The dark outline against the pale winter sun was tall and broad-shouldered, with the heavy muscles of a strong man. He'd been lean as a boy, like a young panther. Now he was a lion.

He saw her. He didn't wave to her or nod. Neither did she. She simply watched as he walked down the small hill toward her, eyeing him hungrily. She'd waited five long years for this moment.

In all the dead years, the years of caring for her father as his mind died long before his body, she'd longed for this moment. As everything else fell from her life, as she lost everything, as her life was taken over by daily care of a man who no longer controlled anything about himself, the only thing left to her was her imagination. And in her mind, she went wild.

In her mind, she and Nick were together.

Her favorite daydream was meeting him in some sophisticated city. New York, Chicago, San Francisco. Even better, London or Paris. Of course, she was sophisticated herself. She'd had a number of love affairs that had taught her a lot. She was well-groomed, successful, utterly in control.

Turning around in an expensive restaurant, there he'd be.

In her fantasies she could figure out what she was—poised and successful and happy. But she could never figure out what Nick was. What he'd become. She only knew he'd be handsome and he'd love her. She couldn't get beyond that point. That he still loved her, after all these years.

She'd ask why he'd disappeared so suddenly. It was still unfathomable to her. One night she'd gone to bed teasing him that he'd grow up to be Commander Adama of Battlestar Galactica and the next morning he was gone. Completely disappeared. His things were in his room. The only articles missing were two pairs of jeans, some tee shirts, a winter jacket and his gym bag.

She'd been frantic. She wanted to call the cops, report him missing but her father had gently taken the phone from her hand and flipped it closed. He never answered her questions and soon, very soon, he became incapable of answering any questions at all.

Not a phone call, not a letter, not even a postcard. It was as if Nick had dropped off the face of the earth, taking with him her entire existence. From a carefree teenager, the beloved only daughter of a respected and wealthy judge, her life plunged into the pits of hell. Her father started losing his mind day by day, darkness descending, and Nick wasn't there.

How many evenings she stared out the window, pretending to read, her father having finally exhausted himself enough to nap in an armchair. Going out on a date was unthinkable. There wasn't enough money to pay a nurse for evening hours. She'd had to earn extra credits over the summers to graduate at seventeen because she could see the day coming when the money would run out and she'd have to stay home all day to nurse her father and she wanted at least a high school certificate.

Dating was out, going to movies with girlfriends was out, having friends over was definitely out. What she got was a nurse coming for a few hours a day in which she could rush to do the shopping and rush into the library to stock up on books. What she got was staring out the window, waiting for Nick.

Hoping for Nick.

Yearning for Nick.

Who never came.

So in her daydreams, when she finally did meet him, utterly by chance in a big city, she got to choose how it would be. He was either immensely rich and handsome or powerful and handsome. He was never a loser, a drunk or an addict. That wasn't Nick.

Hello, he'd say, stepping back in admiration. *Aren't you beautiful?*

Thank you, she'd answer. *I hope you're well. I'd love to stay and chat but I need to get back to my—*

Here Elle's imagination struggled a little. To what? Get back to what? What could possibly be more important than Nick?

But it didn't really matter because then he'd say—*Have a drink with me. Please. Just five minutes. I'm so glad to see you.*

And, well, this was *Nick*. And so she would. And then he'd say he loved her and would never leave her again.

It was a fine daydream and it had to be because it replaced more or less everything a young girl should have—school, friends, first love, dreams, plans . . .

The details wavered but the core of it was always the same, though. He found her whole and happy and successful. Beautiful and elegant and self-assured.

Not the miserable creature she was now. Pale and pinched from the last four nights of watching her father die when she hadn't slept at all. Wearing a too-thin jacket that didn't protect in any way against the cold because the only winter coat she had was ripped along the sleeve.

It wasn't supposed to be this way at all. But it was.

She simply watched as he walked toward her and everything about her was numb except her heart. Her treacherous, treacherous heart, which leaped in joy to see him.

He didn't hurry down to her, but his long legs seemed to carry him to her quickly. He had on a big down jacket that came down to mid-thigh, gloved hands hanging down by his side.

Elle was aware of her own hands, gloveless, almost blue with cold. Embarrassed, she stuck them behind her back.

And that was how they met, Nick towering over her, face in shadow, looking down at her. The sun was at his back, huge just before sunset, an enormous pale disk. They stood and looked at each other. Elle was struck dumb.

He was here, right in front of her.

How she'd longed for this moment and here it was, by the side of her father's coffin.

She should say something, she should—

"Miss?"

Elle turned. She'd completely forgotten the attendants. "Yes?"

"You're going to have to stand back, Miss. We're going to cover the coffin with dirt."

"Oh." She stepped back and Nick stepped with her. "Of course."

She and Nick watched as dirt covered the coffin of her only living relative. She didn't cry. She'd shed so many tears over the years. There were none left. Her father had gone long before this. What had been left behind was a shell of a person, human meat.

Her father had been witty, well-read, strongly opinionated, charming. That man had died years ago.

So she watched as they covered the coffin, quickly and efficiently. It was cold and they wanted the job over with as fast as possible. When they finished, they put away their tools and faced her.

There was a gash in the ground now, raw and red. Someday it would be covered with grass as the other graves were but for now, it was clear that the earth had recently claimed one of its own. A tombstone would come, eventually, when she could afford it.

The funeral home director had quoted figures that made no sense to her. The cheapest one cost over two thousand dollars. It might as well have cost a million. She didn't have it.

She didn't have anything.

One of the gravediggers pulled off his hat. "Real sorry about the Judge, ma'am. You have our condolences."

Elle dipped her head. "Thank you. Um . . ." She opened her purse and peered inside, though she didn't need to look to see what was in it. One bill. Not a big one, either. She pulled out the twenty and handed it to the man, well aware of the fact that it should have been a hundred dollar bill, fifty each.

He picked it up gingerly, looked at his mate in disgust, stuck it in his pants pocket and glared at her.

Elle understood completely. They had done a hard job. The ground was frozen and they'd toiled. The funeral director had let her know clearly that the cheap option she'd chosen didn't cover the diggers and that she would have to recompense them herself.

This was so *awful*. She felt so raw and exposed, reduced to ashes, to dust. All of this was playing out right in front of Nick, who was observing everything.

She remembered how observant he was. He always had been. He was seeing her humiliation in 3D HD, up close and personal.

Elle cleared her throat, reached out a hand

toward the gravedigger, then stuck it in her pocket. "I'm sorry it's not more," she said quietly. "Perhaps—"

"Here." Nick handed over two bills. Her eyes widened when she saw Benjamin Franklin's face twice. "Thanks for your help."

The cap came off again, both men thanked him, nodded to her and walked off.

Elle stared at the ground, breathing through her pain. Nick had left many years ago and for all those years, not a day, not a *minute* had gone by in which she hadn't missed him so fiercely she thought she might explode from it.

All this time she'd yearned for Nick.

And here he was. At her lowest point.

"He loved you very much," she said, looking at the ground.

"I know," he said quietly.

His voice, already deep as a boy, had become deeper, rougher. The voice of a man.

He was a man. He'd been mature beyond his years when he'd come into their life, a runaway her father found in their backyard one winter evening. He was lying in the snow with a broken, badly-infected wrist, dying, so emaciated her father was able to pick him up and carry him in his arms to the car to take him to the hospital.

343

From that moment on, Nick Ross belonged to them.

Until he left them, inexplicably, another cold winter night.

She looked up at him, hungry for the sight of him. How she'd dreamed of him over these past years! Her dreams had been so vivid, often unsettling. She'd seen him shooting, jumping out of planes, fighting.

She'd seen him with other women. That had been so hard because her dreams had the bite of reality. She'd seen him naked, making love to women, harsh and demanding, impossibly sexy.

The Nick standing next to her looked just as he had in her dreams—hard, tough, fully a man. Dark eyes that gave nothing away, close-cropped dark hair, broad shoulders, lean muscles. A formidable man in every way, even though the last time she'd seen him he'd been just on the verge of manhood.

"He was . . . sick?" Nick's voice was hesitant.

"Yes," she replied, looking down at the raw gash in the frozen earth. "For a long time."

Since you left, she thought to herself. *He was never the same, and then he started his fast decline.*

"I'm sorry." The deep voice was low, as if murmuring for her ears alone, though there was no one else on the cemetery grounds. There had been about thirty people at the funeral itself, but they left immediately, as soon as the service was over. Everyone had jobs, places to be, things to do. Nobody stayed for the interment. They'd paid their respects to the man her father had been and left. Her father had been dead to the town long before his body left this earth.

She nodded, throat tight.

"It's cold. You should have worn something warmer."

Elle huffed out a breath that would have been laughter in other circumstances. The cloud of steam rose quickly and dissipated into the frigid air. Yes, she should have worn something warmer. Of course.

"Yes," she murmured. "I, ahm, I forgot."

Why were they talking about coats? It seemed so surreal.

"Where's your car?" Nick asked, in his rough voice. "You should get home. You're freezing."

Elle looked back up at him in panic. *He was leaving already?* That couldn't be!

Her throat tightened even more. He couldn't leave, he couldn't. He couldn't be that cruel.

The words tumbled out without her thinking. "I don't have a car. The undertakers were supposed to give me a ride home." Nolan Cruise, the DA, had driven her to the edge of the cemetery and dropped her off, apologizing for not being able to stay.

She looked around, but they'd gone. The cemetery was utterly deserted. Obviously, the two men had thought she already had a ride home. With Nick.

Oh God. The first time she saw him in five years and she needed to beg a ride home from him. She straightened, pulled her lightweight jacket around her tightly, trying to wrap her dignity around her too.

"That's okay. I—" Her mind whirred uselessly. Saying she'd walk would be ridiculous. Nick knew perfectly well how far home was. At least a two-hour walk. She was trying to invent someone who could plausibly give her a ride home when he took her elbow in a firm grip and started walking toward the exit. "Let's go."

Elle scrambled to keep up. Nick, always tall, had grown another couple of inches. His long legs ate up the grassy terrain. In a few minutes they were outside the gates of the cemetery, walking under the arched stone sign with *Requiescat in Pacem* engraved on the front.

Yes, indeed. *Rest in peace, Daddy.*

His last years had not been peaceful as his mind went. They had been dark and despairing as he felt himself slip day by day. Even after his mind had gone, she'd sensed the lingering despair.

He's gone to a better place, the few people who'd come to the funeral had said. The old truism was right. Wherever he was now, it couldn't be worse than the life he had left behind.

She and Nick were walking along an empty driveway which was always full of cars on Memorial Day and was mainly empty the other 364 days a year. Nick pulled out a remote and a big black expensive-looking car lit up and the doors unlocked with a *whomp*.

"Nice car," she ventured. There was so much to be said, but his face was so forbidding, so remote, she could only make the blandest of comments.

"Rental," he said tersely and held open the passenger-side door for her.

A thousand questions jostled in her head but she simply sat, holding her jacket tightly around her while he got into the driver's seat and took off. A minute later, warm air was washing over her and the trembling she hadn't noticed eased off.

He knew exactly where to go, of course.

He might have forgotten her, he might have forgotten her father, but he wouldn't have forgotten where they had all lived together. That was another thing about Nick. His amazing sense of direction. The last few years, before he ran off, whenever they went on an outing together her father counted on Nick to guide them. And, the last two years, after he got his learner's license, to drive them all where they needed to go.

The judge had probably started dementing already though there were no signs of it then. He had been, as always, ramrod straight, iron gray hair brushed back, always elegant and collected. The opposite of the shambles of a man she'd buried.

It helped to think of Daddy and not concentrate on Nick, driving with careless expertise. He'd always been superb behind the wheel, right from the start. The instructor had told Daddy that he hadn't had to teach Nick anything. It was as if he'd been born knowing how to drive.

Elle stared straight ahead, doing her best not to take peeks at Nick. It was almost impossible. He was like a black hole, pulling in gravity toward him. Impossible to ignore, yet impossible to look at directly.

A thousand words were on the tip of her tongue. *How are you how have you been where do you live now do you like it there* . . . Empty words really. Because what she wanted to know, she couldn't say.

Why did you leave us? Why did you leave me?

The unspoken words choked her. She was afraid to open her mouth because they would come tumbling out. She had no filter, no defense mechanism. Plus, she'd lived alone so long with a father who could neither understand her nor respond to her she'd grown used to saying exactly what she thought.

She wasn't even fit company anymore.

But *something* should be said. They hadn't seen each other in five years. Five years, seven months and two days. Each minute of which she'd missed him. Even in her sleep.

She concentrated on practicing the words. If she said them slowly, one at a time, surely nothing else would escape her mouth. *How have you been?*

How. Have. You. Been?

There, she could say that. Four simple words. And he'd answer and she'd try really, really hard not to push. She could do this. She could—

"We're here," Nick said and swerved so that the vehicle was parked outside the garage.

She hadn't even noticed that they'd made it home.

She swallowed. The garage had been left open. Her mistake. She'd rushed in to get slippers for Daddy's last visit to the hospital and in her haste hadn't closed it. There were no cars. Daddy had always kept a Cadillac and a Toyota but both had been sold two years ago. She took the bus to the few places she had to go.

Nick didn't bother putting the rental inside the garage.

He wasn't staying.

Elle swallowed the pain and turned when he opened the passenger door. He held out a big hand. She didn't need help. But . . . this might be her only, her last chance to touch him.

She put her hand in his and in a second, he guided her down to the gravel, dropped her hand, then held it out again, palm up.

She looked at it blankly, then up at him. *He wanted to hold her hand?*

"Keys," he said tersely.

Oh.

Numb with cold and pain, she opened her purse and gave him the door keys. She didn't have to rummage. Her purse held a now-empty wallet, a cellphone with very few minutes left, an old lipstick, and the keys.

In a moment, Nick had the door open and was standing there, waiting for her.

He watched her walk the few short steps to

the porch and up to the portico. Lucky thing he wasn't looking around.

The grounds had always been a showpiece. When Nick disappeared, Rodrigo was still coming twice a week to take care of the extensive gardens. The drive had been flanked by seasonal flowers in large terra-cotta vases. The vases and flowers were long gone. There were no flowers anywhere and the hedges had long since lost their shape.

Elle had received three official notices of "abandonment" in the past six months.

Nick didn't seem to notice, thank God.

Inside the house, though, it was worse than outside.

The house had always been immaculate. Ever since her mother had died, when she was five, the house had been ruled by a benevolent tyrant, Mrs. Gooding, who kept it polished and fragrant with the help of a maid several times a week.

Mrs. Gooding was long gone, as was the maid.

Elle had done her best but the house was big and the last months of her father's life had required round the clock care from her. She napped when she could, exhausted, and did the best she could to keep a bare minimum of cleanliness.

Her father had taken ill during the night and

they'd rushed to the hospital where she'd kept vigil by his side for four days and four nights. Then the funeral.

The house was a mess. A freezing cold mess, because she hadn't turned the heat on, knowing she'd be away all day.

This time Nick noticed.

He stopped inside the foyer and she stopped with him. His neck bent back as he looked up at the ceiling of the two-story atrium. Once there had been a magnificent Murano chandelier with fifty bulbs that had blazed as brightly as the sun. Now there was simply a low-wattage light bulb hanging naked from a cord.

The rest of the foyer was naked too. Watercolors, the huge Chinese rug, the console with the ornate carved mirror atop it, the two Viennese Thonet armchairs on either side of the Art Deco desk with the enormous solid silver bowl full of potpourri—gone.

Nick didn't react in any way. His face was calm and expressionless.

What was he thinking?

Later, after he'd disappeared, one of her high school classmates said that he'd been earning extra money playing poker with lowlifes and he always won because he had the best poker face anyone had ever seen.

She was seeing that now. There was no clue to his thoughts.

Perhaps—perhaps she'd hoped to see some softness or gentleness when he looked at her. But no.

She gestured awkwardly toward the back of the house. "Would you—would you like something to drink?"

He nodded his head briefly without saying anything. She turned and walked into the kitchen, knowing he didn't need her direction. He knew the way.

His showing up had scrambled her brains, but now she forced herself to think, to reason things out. Where had he come from? Had he travelled a long time? Would he stay the night?

Her heart gave a huge thump in her chest at the thought.

"So." In the kitchen, Elle turned to face him, plastering a smile on her face, making a real effort not to wring her hands. "What can I offer you?"

Oh God.

Too late she realized that there was very little to offer. If he wanted alcohol there was none in the house. Her father had had a fine collection of whiskeys but they had gone years ago and she had never bought another bottle. There was no food, either, she suddenly remembered. Only a last frozen pizza in the freezer.

"Coffee would be fine." His voice and eyes were so calm. She tried to cling to that, to calm herself down, but it was hard.

This was *Nick*. Nick was here, right now, in her kitchen, squinting slightly at the last rays of the sun shining through the kitchen window right into his eyes.

"Coffee. Right." There was coffee. Enough for one cup at least.

She turned and tried to keep her hands steady as she opened the cupboard to get the coffee. To her horror, except for the glass canister with an inch of grounds the cupboard was bare.

Exactly like in some horrible fable.

She closed the cupboard making a louder noise than she wanted and set about making coffee with trembling hands for Nick.

Nick.

Who was here.

Preparing the coffee, setting out the pretty Limoges cup and saucer, part of a set that she hadn't sold because there were only four pieces, setting out a silver spoon and the Wedgwood sugar canister calmed her down a little.

He was still standing and that was another blow to the heart.

This had been his kitchen once, too. He had once been completely at home here. She remembered the thousands of evenings Nick had teased her and made her father laugh in here while Mrs. Gooding prepared dinner.

Now he was standing, needing her permission to sit. Tears blurred her eyes but she willed them back. She'd had a lot of experience at that. She could do this.

"Please sit." She pulled out a chair.

He took off his jacket, hung it on the back of the chair, and sat. Underneath the jacket he had on a heavy flannel shirt.

Oh God. She should do the same, of course. Except she was still cold and underneath the jacket she had on a thin sweater. She still had a few thick sweaters. Except her mind had been so befogged by the exhaustion of the last days of her father's life and the funeral arrangements that she'd simply grabbed the first thing that came to hand. As luck would have it, it was a thin cotton sweater.

But she could pretend with the best of them. She hung her own jacket over the chair and sat down across from him.

They looked at each other mutely.

The coffee machine percolated. Elle sprang up and poured him a cup.

Nick hesitated. "What about you? Still don't like coffee? You always liked tea. Can I make you some?"

"No!" Elle cleared her throat. "No, thanks." She'd kill for a cup of tea but it was in the cupboard above the stove and that was bare too. Two bare cupboards—it was too much for Nick to see.

Nick blew on the cup and sipped. As always, the delicate china looked out of place in his large hand but she knew from experience that it was safe. His hands were huge, had always been huge, but he was far from clumsy.

They sat in silence until he finished half the cup, then looked up at her. "How long had he been ill?"

Elle didn't sigh, but she wanted to. "Several years. But his doctor thinks, with hindsight, that the illness started five years ago, only he managed to hide it."

Something—some faint expression crossed his face.

Oh God. He'd left them five years ago. It sounded

like she was accusing him of precipitating her father's decline.

"Must have been hard. For you."

Elle simply dipped her head. Yes, hard. Very hard.

"So—what will you do now? Go back to college?"

"I wasn't enrolled in college."

That surprised him. It took a lot to surprise Nick but she'd done it. "What do you mean you're not in college? You were a straight A student, always had been. Or have you already finished college?"

She had to smile at that. She'd had anything but straight As while she struggled to deal with her father's eccentricities. It would be another year before she understood he was ill. She'd missed almost every other day her sophomore year.

"No, I ah—it's complicated."

Nick was frowning. Ok. That was easier to deal with than that look of pity he'd had. "Well, now there's nothing holding you back, is there?"

Well, if you didn't count no money and medical debts, and put like that . . ."No, there isn't."

The answer seemed to relax him. He looked around again then back at her, dark gaze penetrating.

"You're too thin. And too pale. You need to eat more and get outside more."

That *hurt*. Nick had been in her heart always, since he had first come into their lives. She'd only been seven but she loved him the moment she laid eyes on him. She'd been a girl then but she was a woman now and everything womanly in her was concentrated on him, his handsome face, those broad shoulders, the outsized hands.

Every female cell in her body was quivering. And he spoke to her like an elderly aunt would.

Eat more, get out more. Don't be so pasty-faced and thin.

Yeah.

Next thing, he'd be telling her to bundle up warmly.

"And Christ—what's the matter with you, going out in this weather dressed like that?"

There you go.

How she'd *dreamed* of this moment! For years. And now here he was, sitting across from her so closely she could touch him if she simply reached out, and they were talking about her wardrobe.

"Don't," she said softly. "I had to get dressed in a hurry. But I don't want to talk about this. I want to hear how you've been doing. Where you've been."

And why you disappeared without a word.

But she couldn't say that. He was here. Right now she wanted to fill the empty years with images. She could only do that if she could imagine where he'd been, what he'd been doing.

Once upon a time, he'd told her everything.

Nick settled more deeply in the chair, frowning. "I can't really talk about that."

"Because you're in the military?"

He straightened, shocked. "How did you know that? Who told you?"

Nick sounded actually angry. It had slipped out of her mouth without her thinking about it, which went to show how tired she was. She never let slip things she shouldn't know, but did. She'd learned that the hard way.

She'd seen him. In her dreams. Not normal dreams—that floating phantasmagoria of disconnected images most people had during the night. She had those, too, like everyone else. But she also had Dreams. She went places in her Dreams and it was like being there. Frighteningly, *exactly* like being there.

She'd visited Nick, without a clue as to where he was, but so real she felt she could touch him. He was exercising with a hundred other men, doing jumping jacks and climbing ropes and crawling under barbed wire. Shooting. Shooting a lot. Jumping out of planes.

And with women. That had been the worst of

all. She'd watched, helplessly, as he made love to a series of women, rarely the same one two nights in a row. Elle would be looking down from the ceiling, watching the muscles of his broad back stretch and flex, his buttocks tightening and releasing as he moved in and out of the woman. Usually, he held himself above the woman *du nuit* on stiff arms, touching her only with his sex.

Those nights, as she watched from the ceiling, she would wake up with tears on her face.

A part of her thought she was crazy. And another part of her thought she could somehow travel outside her body.

Whichever it was—and maybe it was both— she'd said the wrong thing to Nick.

He reached across to clamp his big hand over her wrist.

"Did someone tell you something?" he demanded. "Someone spying on me?"

His grip was tight. Not painful, but definitely unbreakable. Nick had always been strong, even as a boy. Now he was a powerfully-built man.

Slowly, unsure if her touch would be welcome, Elle laid her hand over his.

"No one told me, Nick," she said gently. It wasn't the first time she had to answer how she knew something she shouldn't. And it wouldn't be the last. When he lived with them, Nick had never known. Her father hadn't known. *She* hadn't known. "You have the bearing of a soldier, and your hair is cut military-short. There is a pale patch on your jacket. Where there would have been an insignia. You look like you're doing well but you're not in a suit. You've got combat boots on. They're sold in stores, too, but taking all these things together—" she shrugged.

Nick relaxed, smiled. Oh, how she'd missed that smile! It had taken him almost two years to smile when he first came to live with them. She'd been only a child, but she understood instinctively that he'd come from pain and cruelty and she'd made it her personal challenge to make him smile.

Once he started, he smiled often. He was breathtaking when he smiled.

Like now.

He shook his head. "I forgot how smart you are. How perceptive. So you put all that together and came up with military, hm?"

It hurt that he forgot anything about her. She hadn't forgotten anything about him.

"Yes, but I wouldn't want to guess which branch of the service and how far you've climbed." She tilted her head, studying him. "So . . . was I right?"

"Bingo."

Elle relaxed. She'd reasoned her way out of the trap. "Which branch are you in?"

A cloud moved across his face but he answered calmly enough. "Army."

A word flashed across her mind. She didn't even know she'd had it in her head but the information she gleaned in her Dreams had its own agenda. The word came out of her mouth before she could censor it. "Rangers?"

Nick straightened, frowning. "Now how the hell would you know that?" His look was keen, penetrating, impersonal.

There was no sense now that she had a special place in his heart, none. For all her late childhood and early teens, ever since Nick had arrived in their lives, she knew he had a soft spot for her. That she could take risks with him. Like a puppy that could pull a wolf's tail with impunity.

Not now. She had no feeling at all that she was allowed liberties with Nick. His frown was deep and serious and a little scary.

She swallowed, and started on the lies. When she'd never had to lie to him. "Sorry. That was stupid of me. I have no idea what's going on with you. There was a movie on TV the other night and the main protagonist was an Army Ranger. That's what they called him, in fact. Ranger. That's all. I don't even really understand what it means."

Even if she hadn't Dreamed that he was a Ranger, she'd have wagered money that if there was a special place in the army, Nick would have achieved it.

He relaxed slightly. "A movie hero? That's not me."

Oh, but it was. Nick was much more handsome than most of the actors she saw on TV. Most actors had a softness about them that was reflected in their faces. They might spend eight hours a day at the gym, but their faces were puppyish.

Not Nick. Nick had known real tragedy. Wherever he'd spent the first eleven years of his life before he came to them—and he never spoke a word about it—they had been hard, tough years. He'd had the bearing of a man even when young. As a teenager, he'd been wise and tough beyond his years. The other kids in high school either worshipped him or steered clear of him. No one *ever* tried to bully him. They wouldn't dare.

There was no actor on earth who could look as tough as Nick at twenty-three.

He'd had a rough life which had made him hard. The military had taken him and made him harder.

He frowned at her. "How come no one was at the graveside? The Judge was well known and respected, I'd have thought there would be thousands of people."

Elle didn't want to talk about that, about the past. She wanted to talk about the here and now. But he wanted to know and she was hardwired to give Nick what he wanted.

"There were people at the funeral. Some. Not many. They couldn't stay for the interment." She swallowed. "Daddy . . . was sick for a long time."

Nick narrowed his eyes. "Yeah, you said that. So?"

"He also hasn't been a judge for a long time. I think . . . I think people sort of forgot about him."

Nick was really frowning now and Elle understood completely. When he'd left—wait, use the right term. When Nick *abandoned* them, her father, the judge, had been one of the most important men in the county. Nick had felt her father's natural authority firsthand. When she and her father had found him behind a Dumpster, starving and with a broken wrist, the judge had taken care of everything. Within a month, he'd become a ward of the judge and was regularly enrolled in school.

Nick had often said his real life began the day

the Judge found him. He seemed to forget that Elle had been there too. A tiny girl, only seven, but it seemed her real life began that day too.

Nick had lived under the Judge's protective aura. So Elle could understand that he found it hard to understand his last years.

"Daddy . . . declined. Mentally. He was forcibly removed from the bench via an injunction." She swallowed. Her father had been beyond understanding exactly *what* had happened, but he had understood very well that something important had been taken away from him. He'd been agitated for an entire year.

"Alzheimer's?" Nick asked.

She hung her head.

"Tough," he said.

You have no idea. She lifted her head, nodded.

They sat in silence, looking at each other. Finally, he gave a sigh and shifted in his chair. Elle panicked.

He was leaving already! He'd just arrived! She hadn't seen him in five years. She was still gulping up details about him every time she dared look at him. The hard cut of his jaw, the two wiry white hairs mixed in the thick black hair of his temples. His hands, bigger than she remembered.

Clean but callused, with a strip of thick yellow callus on the edges. Judo calluses, or some kind of martial art. She'd read about that.

The shoulders that stretched beyond the shirt seams. He was unshaven. His stubble was thicker than she remembered. He was one of those men who should shave twice a day.

That was new. So many things about him were new.

Including the fact that he was sexy as hell.

That was new, for her. As a child, as a young girl, Nick was : . . Nick. The person she loved most in the world after her father. Always there, always dependable, always fun. With a natural authority that made her feel safe and protected. The two men in her life, looking after her. Her father, with his understanding of the law, his status as a well-respected judge—nothing in society could harm her while he was around. And Nick—always strong and tough, with quick reflexes, always alert for trouble. Nothing in life could hurt her while he was around.

It was only now, alone, that Elle understood what a privileged childhood she'd had. And Nick had been a big part of that.

Nick wasn't her brother. She had no idea what feelings you could have for a brother because

she'd never had one, but she instinctively understood she never thought of Nick as one. Nick was
her friend, her protector.

And, foolish girl, she thought he'd always be
there.

It hadn't even occurred to her that someday
he'd fall in love and leave. She didn't know if he'd
fallen in love, but he'd definitely left.

He'd definitely had women. Tons of them. She'd
never seen male genitalia in person but in her
Dreams . . . Nick was the epitome of maleness.
She'd seen him with women, she'd seen him in
bed pleasuring himself . . .

She swallowed, hoping she wasn't turning red.
She'd always been an open book to him. Please
God let him not understand that she was remembering the violently arousing image of him having
sex with other women and with himself.

Sitting across from him, she totally understood
why women fell for him. As a girl, her feelings
had been starting to turn. But now she was a
woman and what he evoked in her was sexual
desire, of a scale and intensity she didn't know
how to handle.

Nick shifted in his chair, huffed out a breath.
"Well," he began. "I guess I'd better be—"

"Where did you come from?" she blurted.

"What?"

"Where were you today? Or yesterday? When you decided to come?"

"Are you asking why I came?"

"No." And she wasn't. Why he came was clear, to her at least. They were linked by a thread that had become thin and stretched over time but still held. She'd needed him desperately and he came. That was bedrock for her. She didn't even question it.

He wasn't answering her question. She tried another tack. "I can't let you leave without feeding you. Dad would—Dad would have been appalled."

His hard look softened. "Honey, it doesn't look like you have much food in the house."

Elle swallowed, lifted her head. "Dad was very, very ill the last couple of weeks. I didn't have time to do any food shopping." She pulled her cell out of her pocket. "I can call Foodwise, though. Jenny would gladly send us a meal. Promise you'll stay at least to eat."

There were still a couple hundred dollars left on the checking account. The undertaker's bill would come later and plunge her into the red but for the moment, she more than had enough to cover a meal. Two meals, even. She didn't even think of ordering a pizza or a burger and fries. Nick deserved better than that.

He dipped his head. "Okay."

Elle beamed at him. He wasn't leaving right this minute. She still had time with him. There was so much to memorize. The lines beside his mouth, brand new, that disappeared when he smiled. How the tendons in his neck stood out when he turned his head. How she could see his pectorals through his shirt.

How utterly handsome he was.

How he heated her blood.

She had to memorize this effect he had on her, because it wasn't coming back, not without Nick. She knew herself that well, at least. This was her one shot at feeling sexual desire and it would leave when he left.

Everything about her was aroused. Her skin. It was super sensitive, the small hairs on her forearms and on the nape of her neck prickled against her sweater. Even the lightest touch against her clothes seemed to burn her skin. It was hard to breathe, as if oxygen had suddenly mutated into a liquid. She had to concentrate to keep her lungs filled.

The biggies. Her breasts, never large, now felt immense and heavy. Her nipples brushed against the cotton of her bra. Between her thighs—that unmistakable feeling of heaviness and heat and emptiness she had when she woke up from ordinary dreams of Nick.

The changes in her body excited her and scared her. Excited her because, well, heat and pleasure were novelties. She'd been cold and hollow for a long time. These tingling sensations, as if her body were waking up after a long sleep—they were wonderful. They also scared her because as far as she knew, only Nick could make her feel this way.

But he was staying for dinner, or as much dinner as she could muster.

Take this second by second, she told herself. Enjoy every second.

She watched him as she dialed the number. Jenny herself answered. She had a soft spot for them. Once, when she was a young girl, long before Elle had been born, the Judge had kept her out of trouble. Jenny herself had told her, the Judge had never said a word.

"Hey hon." Jenny's smoky voice, as always, was warm. Elle could imagine her leaning against a wall on a cigarette break, short gray hair brushed back, long, lean, elegant frame slightly slouched. "I'm so sorry I couldn't make the funeral. We had to cater two luncheons. I'm really sorry, honey. If I'd had advance notice . . . but that's not the nature of funerals, is it?"

"No, it's not." Elle smiled. Trust Jenny to say the exact right thing. No doubt in the days to come she'd have thousands of people apologizing for not coming, though in most cases it was simply that the Judge had fallen off their radar. He wasn't off Jenny's radar. If she'd been free, she would have come. "That's okay, Jenny. Dad knows you loved him."

"I surely did, hon. So what can I do for you? Can I send you a dinner over?"

Oh, bless her. "Yes, thank you. Today's special." She hesitated. "For two people."

Jenny didn't pry. "Two specials, you got it. I'll send them over around seven, with a nice bottle of wine. All on the house."

"Thank—" Elle stopped. It was an incredibly generous offer. Dinner would be at least $70, plus the wine and tips. But . . . that was the beginning of a long slippery slope straight to hell.

So far, Elle had kept up appearances. No one came to the house anymore so they wouldn't notice that almost everything that could be sold had been sold. But Jenny knew, or suspected. If Elle started accepting charity now, it would snowball. The wives of former friends of her father would start sending over used clothes—*just wore it a few times, Elle sweetie, you're welcome to it.* Maids would start leaving casseroles on her front door-step.

It didn't bear thinking about.

Not to mention the fact that Jenny's smoker's voice came over loud and clear and Nick had undoubtedly heard every word.

She injected confidence in her voice. "That's kind of you, Jenny, but not necessary. I'll give the delivery boy my credit card. But thanks for the offer."

She could barely look away from Nick's dark eyes. It took her a moment to realize Jenny was taking a long time to answer.

Finally—"Okay, hon. That's fine then. But the wine will be on the house."

Yes. That was acceptable. A gesture of solidarity, not charity. "Thanks, Jenny."

"I loved that old man," Jenny replied and Elle nearly broke down.

That was what her father had been. The kind of man other people loved because he'd done such good in the world.

"Yeah," she whispered, forcing the word out, and broke the connection before she broke down.

She raised her eyes to Nick.

"I loved him, too," he said quietly.

And that broke her. It was like a sharp punch straight to the heart. Reaching past skin and bone in a nearly fatal blow.

"Then why did you leave us?" she whispered as tears began rolling down her face.